The Kiss

Neil Bradshaw

Copyright © 2025 Neil Bradshaw

All rights reserved.

The moral right of the author has been asserted under the Copyright, Designs and Patents Act 1988.

No part of this publication may be copied, reproduced, stored in a retrieval system, or transmitted in any form or by any means—electronic, mechanical, digital, photocopying, recording, or otherwise—without the prior written permission of the publisher or author, except where permitted by law for the purposes of review, research, or private study.

This applies equally to printed editions and digital formats (such as eBooks). Distribution via file-sharing platforms, unauthorized uploading, or any use beyond the intended purchase is strictly prohibited.

This is a work of fiction. All characters, names, organizations, locations, and events depicted are either products of the author's imagination or are used fictitiously. Any resemblance to real persons, living or dead, actual businesses, institutions, or events is purely coincidental.

For licensing, permissions, or bulk purchases, please contact the publisher directly.

Introduction

"The Kiss" is Neil Bradshaw's second novel. It continues the story of George Miller, his twin brother Graham and most of the other characters from the first instalment "The Switch".

Set twelve years after the events in Barcelona, George has retired from playing and has become a manager. He is happily married to Debbie and they have two children.

This story can be read as a stand-alone, although there are numerous references to people and events that happened in the previous novel.

"The Switch" is still available in both paperback and E book from Amazon. I highly recommend you read the "The Switch" (ISBN 978-1-80313-729-2) before embarking on "The Kiss". I think it will enhance and enrich your enjoyment of this story.

With thanks to.

Dimitri Dimopoulous.
Yvonne Bradshaw.
Gabrielle Bradshaw.
Rebecca Rouse.
Ian Williams.

And to everyone who encouraged me to write a sequel to
"The Switch"

This book is dedicated to everyone who has suffered, or is still suffering, any form of domestic abuse.

Chapter 1

A gargoyle of a man

The rat's beady little eyes flitted about as he feasted on the soggy morsel of chicken nugget that had spewed from the split in the bin liner. He sat imperiously atop a mountain of rubbish bags, piled high, next to the overflowing, red Biffa bin. The rain fell like steel rods, bombarding the black and yellow plastic refuse sacks. The percussive drum roll of the rain's impact, together with the howling wind whistling down the narrow alleyway, made for a desolate and foreboding scene. Apart from the cacophony of noise created by Mother Nature's fury, the narrow passage was still, dark and deserted. Tucked behind the rows of shops facing onto the main street, the lane was no more than ten feet wide. At night, an intimidating and daunting short cut used by only the stout hearted and a dumping ground for the constant stream of garbage churned out by the traders on Rye Lane.

The rat was unmoved by his bleak surroundings. It was a regular haunt of his. The banquet supplied every night by the local takeaways, fast food outlets and restaurants, always attracted the local rodents and scavengers, but that night he was dining alone. He literally had "the pick of the litter".

The weather was atrocious. Bad enough to keep anyone who didn't have to be out in it, at home, or at least, undercover. Lakes had formed in the numerous and sizeable potholes dotted along the lane. Rivers were flowing in the cambers of the road and spilling over onto the narrow pavements. The drains and sewers were failing to cope with the deluge. It was the foulest of foul nights in South London.

The rat's ear's pricked and his snout began sniffing the air suspiciously. He had heard a new noise and detected movement beneath him. He sensed danger. From deep inside the bowels of the festering mountain of garbage, came a haunting groan. The mound of rubbish reverberated and vibrated, slowly coming to life. The rat hastily finished his meal and scuttled away to safety.

The bag from which the chicken nugget had emanated gently wobbled, then plummeted from the summit to the base, somersaulting on its way down and splashing to its rest in the middle of the ever-swelling lagoon; the split in the bag gaping larger with the impact and disgorging more of its putrid contents into the street. The other rubbish bags began to oscillate and the guttural groan from within became louder. As another bag toppled down into the lake of rainwater, an arm punched its way to freedom. Bursting out of its stinking mausoleum, it began to feverishly clear an escape route. Then a head emerged. The hideously disfigured features of a man's face rose out of the refuse; blinking and unsure. He violently batted away the remaining sacks that had created his tomb and tentatively and warily, staggered to his feet. His face was deformed almost beyond recognition. A gargoyle of a man. His left eye socket and cheek bone had been smashed and crushed like an eggshell, whilst his left eye sat loosely and precariously in its ruined housing. His nose had been flattened in almost comic cartoon fashion; the bone and gristle protruding through what was left of the original structure. The flesh around his mouth and lips, shredded by the razor-sharp edges of his remaining, splintered teeth. The congealed blood that covered his face, being constantly re-hydrated by the heavy rainfall, began to drip from his chin into the puddles at his feet. He smelt of piss, whiskey and cabbage.

He gently touched the battered remains of his face and instantly winced at the pain. In his semi-conscious state, he began to recall the events that had played out earlier that evening. He steadied himself against the large Biffa bin. The memories of what had happened were slowly returning. His face contorted into an angry scowl as he replayed in his scrambled mind, the savage beating and the brutality of the blows he had endured. The scowl intensified as the vision of his tormentor came into view. A tormentor whose face was full of hate and whose fists were full of pain. He needed to get back to his flat and fix himself up. He had some urgent business to take care of. Fumbling around in his jacket pockets, he tried to locate his phone. He would call his son. He would come and help him. But his pockets were empty. The mobile was not there. He had neither the patience, nor the stamina to try and recall what he had done with it or where it might be. He knew he had to get home before his body and mind succumbed to the barbarism he had suffered. He realised he was on his own and didn't have much time. Lurching towards the lights in the main street at the end of the alleyway, he staggered and stumbled, bouncing and ricocheting off the walls, his feet splashing wildly in the ankle-deep rainwater. He was completely blind in his left eye and the vision he had from his right was blurred and hazy. He reached out aimlessly, frantically trying to grab hold of anything that would steady him, his staccato journey punctuated with numerous falls into the cold precipitation. He was soaked to the skin and could sense himself drifting in and out of consciousness with every precarious and uncertain step.

Finally, he emerged into the main street. The neon lights in the shops' windows flashed and flickered, advertising what each establishment had to offer. But there was no one there to see them. The streets were empty, save for him and the hungry vermin. He squinted his right eye against the glare of his new and brighter surroundings and felt the sting from the rain as it stabbed relentlessly into his wounds. He clung desperately to the walls of the buildings, trying to keep himself upright. Turning left onto Rye Lane, he headed straight into the full force of the storm. He had very little strength left in him. The wind pushed him backwards, nearly blowing him off his feet. Bracing himself, he leant his head into the maelstrom and fought his way towards the sanctuary of his flat. He should be there in less than fifteen minutes.

Derek Donnelly was fifty-three years old. Relatively new to his job, he had started driving for London Transport only a few weeks ago. He was taking his number 63 bus towards the Elephant and Castle, where he would turn it around and finish off back at Peckham Bus Garage. If everything went smoothly, he should be done in just over an hour.

It was the first time he had taken the bus out on a late shift unaccompanied. He had been warned by his colleagues to be wary of the increased number of drunks and undesirables that frequented the streets late at night. It wasn't unusual for some to become aggressive and awkward. He had of course, been trained to deal with all situations that might occur on a bus, from childbirth to heart attacks. But what he dreaded most was confrontation. He was a quiet, gentle man, who wanted to lead a quiet, gentle life. He had started his shift hoping for an incident-free evening. So far, his prayers had been answered; the only highlight being a lady who had banged her knee when she tripped on the step, getting onto the bus.

The rain was lashing down and the wipers on the bus were working at full speed, in an attempt to clear the windscreen of the almost biblical deluge. The wind was powerful enough to bully and jostle the large double decker as it made its way along the deserted Peckham streets. Derek shuffled forward in his seat, staring into the empty and flooded world ahead of him, using every ounce of his concentration.

It was as Derek approached the request stop by the station that he saw him. A man reeling from side to side as he entered the street from the dark passageway that led off the main road. He was unsteady on his feet, rebounding off the lamp posts and the street bins that lined the pavement; clutching onto anything that came to hand to steady himself. He could see the man was not only soaked, but covered in blood. Derek's concentration on the road ahead was temporarily diverted. The grotesque and pathetic example of humanity he saw, made him feel both sympathy and fear. The poor man looked like he was in an awful state. Probably pissed, but still alarmingly fragile and vulnerable. Derek couldn't help but feel a mild panic take hold of him, at the thought of the man waving down his bus and getting on. This was what his new mates at the depot had been warning him about. This would be the test he was hoping never to face.

Derek managed to break his hypnotic stare and return his eyes back to the road. He wanted to give the man as wide a berth as possible and not shower him in the torrent of water the bus' wake would create. Although he could see the man was already drenched, he didn't want to compound his misery. He slowed down and felt a huge sense of relief as the bus approached the man. No attempt had been made by the poor fellow to flag him down and Derek knew he would be able to sail past him without having to stop. But as he drew level, the man suddenly lurched to his right. He stumbled on the submerged curb stone and his body buckled. With a look of horror, Derek watched as the man's body collapsed and disappeared under his bus. He slammed on the brakes, bringing the huge, red juggernaut to a violent halt and causing some of the passengers waiting by the door to fall to the floor. There was a dull thud and a slight bump as the big double-decker came to rest. A split second of silence was immediately broken by a loud and piercing scream from one of the passengers on the upper deck. The realisation of what had just happened made Derek shiver. He sat in his seat, frozen to the spot. He stared out of the windscreen, willing the man to reappear, dust himself down, probably hurl a load of abuse at him and disappear into the night. But there was no sign of him. A number of people came tearing down the stairs and demanded to be let off the bus. Derek went numb. He knew he had to get out and see first-hand what had happened; but he already knew, and knowing what kind of gruesome image awaited him, suddenly felt very queasy.

The doors of the bus hissed open and Derek stepped tentatively into the storm. The first thing he noticed was the colour of the rainwater flowing down Rye Lane. It was a muddy red. The flashing neon signs from the shops and the intense beam from the bus' headlights accentuating the vivid crimson hues of the gushing stream. Protruding from under the bus, he could see what was left of a pair of legs. Next to them an arm, animated by the constant flow of the deluge, twitching in a macabre regal like wave. The ghoulish spectacle demanding the onlooker's interest. It was attached to what was left of the man by a few, stringy strands of muscle and tendon. Seconds later, the power of the fast-moving floodwater separated the limb from the remaining torso and it began to float away, bobbing up and down like a canoe on rapids. Derek immediately chased after it and retrieved it. He held it in his hands and looked at the severed limb. He could see some tattoos on the hand and a gold half sovereign ring on the index finger. It was a surreal moment; one he had never imagined. He looked back towards the front of the bus, squinting his eyes in the glare of the bright headlights. A few of the passengers were braving the wind and rain to get a good look at the ghastly view on offer. He saw one young girl actually recording the scene on her mobile phone, bending down to get a close-up view of the grisly carnage. Derek walked back towards the bus and tried to usher the spectators away. The front wheel had passed over the man, crushing bones, muscles and organs. It had continued its journey over the man's head, bursting it like a balloon and splattering the contents onto the pavement and up the side of one of the street bins. The man was now no more than a streak of bloody paté. There was nothing left of him. Nothing that could be recognised as a human being. Derek looked down on the poor wretch. Standing there, holding the man's severed arm and getting soaked to the skin, he bent over and threw up the contents of his stomach onto the ghoulish remains before him.

Chapter 2

Eleven weeks earlier

George had been here before. He paused at the top of the staircase and took a good look around. He was back in the wide-open space of the bright and airy lounge outside the manager's office. In many ways, the lounge hadn't changed much in the ten years since he had last set foot there. The old furniture had gone, but the newer, more fashionable replacements, occupied the same spaces. The smoked glass table at which he had sat on many occasions, waiting for a reprimand, had been swapped for a much larger, white vinyl coffee table. It was simpler and more understated than its predecessor, but looked classier and cleaner. The leather sofas and chairs that once provided the comfort had been superseded by four, three-seater, fabric covered settees which surrounded the table. They were liberally dotted with both cream and blue scatter cushions. A massive vase of lilies sat in the middle of the table, trumpeting their stamens and scent in every direction. There were numerous other vases of mixed bouquets dotted around the room. Gerberas, roses, alliums and carnations, all competing for their audience's attention. The carpet too had changed. The cream-coloured shagpile had been replaced by a soft, pastel blue, wool twisted lawn. The room actually looked bigger than he remembered. The two TV screens on opposing walls were now enormous, almost cinematic in size, both throwing out images in ultra-high definition. Sky Sports News was beaming out of both, but neither had the sound turned up.

As he took in all the familiar, and some of the unfamiliar, sights, he wondered where the past ten years had gone. It felt like only last week he had been bidding a sad farewell to the club he had given seven years-service to as a player. Those years were a patchwork of ups and downs. Good times and not such good times. He had experienced some of his lowest ebbs during that period, but also some of the most enjoyable years of his career. As a player, George had courted both success and disaster in equal measures. On several occasions he had been summoned to the manager's office to receive a scolding for making the wrong sort of headlines. Headlines that had nothing to do with football. Headlines and photographs that were more at home on the front pages than the back. He had been warned, fined and given last chances so many times. Like a schoolboy perpetually breaking the rules, he had taken his punishment and apologised for his misdemeanours, but he had certainly not learned from them, or mended his ways. His return to the "footballing naughty step" was a regular occurrence.

Considering his many brushes with authority, the last couple of years of his career had been both happy and successful. After winning the Champions League final, George had continued to play on for a further two seasons. He was fitter and stronger than he had been at any time in his career. He felt he could go on forever. Sadly, an unfortunate injury to his troublesome right knee at the age of thirty-two had proved to be "the straw that broke the camel's back". He was told that another operation would be needed, rendering him side lined for at least six months. His knee had been a problem to him from the age of sixteen and the numerous injuries he had endured since then had taken their toll on the joint. He had spoken to Debbie his fiancé, his parents and of course, his two dear friends who made up the management team, Doug Fenner and Bernie Rosewell. They discussed the pros and cons of continuing his playing career, but after George had been told that both Bernie and Doug were going to announce their retirement from the game at the end of that season, he thought it apt to bow out with the two men who had helped him so much throughout his time in football. He had accomplished almost everything he had set out to achieve. Apart from the thrill of an international call up, he had ticked just about every box. He had a Champions League Winners' medal from Barcelona and a place in the club's history books. He was loved, revered and respected by the management and the fans alike. His standing in the game could go no higher. He made his decision to announce the end of his playing days while he was still at the top of his game, walking away with his dignity and the bright glow of success still fresh in everyone's memory. Shortly after the announcement of his retirement, came the announcement of his wedding. He and Debbie had decided to tie the knot sometime earlier, but there had never seemed to be the time to make all the arrangements. Now, with the summertime free from sporting commitments, pre-season training and warm-up tours, they had named the date and the place and set the wheels in motion for what later proved to be a fantastic and emotional day. They married in the June and enjoyed a wonderful honeymoon in Europe. During the month they were travelling, Debbie managed to tick off a few more of her must-see places. A year later, they were blessed with a son, Matthew and two years after that, Emily arrived. George remembered thinking at the time, looking at his gorgeous wife, his two-year-old son and his beautiful new-born daughter, that life had never been better. Everything his wealth and fame had bought him over the years paled into insignificance compared to the happiness and joy his family was giving him. In the seven years since Emily had arrived, the contentment and satisfaction had blossomed.

George was now forty-two years old. He and his family lived in the Buckinghamshire house he had owned for fifteen years. He still owned his riverside penthouse flat overlooking the Thames. It was convenient for when he and Debbie travelled up to London, or occasionally, if George had any meetings in town. The flat was a constant reminder of his hedonistic bachelor days, when his life revolved around beautiful women, champagne and late nights out on the town. It was perfect for him in those days and he had enjoyed every minute of his time there. But now he had settled down. He had no need for glamorous young women; he had married the most glamorous and gorgeous of them all. The woman of his dreams. He was a husband and a father and the house in Buckinghamshire was as much a reflection of his life now, as the flat had been all those years before.

After his playing days had come to an end, George was still keen to retain some link with the game. He took his coaching badges and discovered a new drive within himself. He enjoyed the new challenges the courses presented, understanding the game and seeing it in a different way. A game of chess; a game of subtleties and deep thinking. Before, as a player, he was one of the soldiers, sent out with instructions and tactics to follow. Although he acted on instinct and his own intuition, he had to operate within a framework and stratagem, given to him by the manager. Now, as the Head Coach, *he* was the General, giving out his orders for others to follow. *He* was now the deep thinker and planner who would rely on *his* men to carry out *his* instructions. He liked to think of himself as an actor who had taken up directing. Stepping back out of the limelight, but still pulling the strings. He was amazed to discover he gained as much pleasure out of coaching as he did playing.

At the age of thirty-three he had been offered the job as manager of a League Two side. He was keen to test himself. Starting at the bottom, he felt there was only one way to go. He was still well known to the football-loving public as the roguish playboy who would regularly turn up on the front pages, having done something to upset the establishment. That was what so many people loved about him. He was one of them. A rebel who didn't conform to the rules.

The fans of the League Two side were intrigued and excited to have a celebrity manager.

If nothing else, a famous and highly recognisable man like George Miller would be good for the club's profile. If he could weave some magic and bring some long overdue success to the west country outfit, then all the better.

He proved to be a success and took the club from the depths of League Two, to The Championship in just four seasons. During the next five years he managed two other clubs, gaining promotion to the Premiership with one and then consolidating his reputation as a popular and successful coach in the Midlands with the other. His stock was on the rise. At the age of forty-two, his name was being quietly mentioned when it came to the question of future England managers. He was young, bright, successful and English. His time would surely come. All the talk and rumours made George smile. He remembered vividly the days when the experts and the pundits thought he was certain to make it on the international scene as a player. But that never happened. An incident involving an older woman, an unflattering time spent on the front pages of the national press, a divorce case and possible criminal prosecution, had put an end to his chances. It hadn't taken him long to fall from grace in the eyes of the footballing world. From hero to zero in the blink of an eye. He knew how fickle the press and the public could be. Today's shining light could so easily become tomorrow's punch bag.

As the season was getting back to normal after the Christmas fixture mayhem, George was sitting in his office, making plans for the up-coming Black Country Derby, when he received a phone call from a man called Chris Ewens. Chris was the Chief Executive at George's old club in south London. He had taken on the role vacated by George's old nemesis David Blackstone. He was an altogether different kettle of fish to Blackstone. Ewens was charming, charismatic, jovial and ebullient. He gave you the impression that he was actually enjoying life and all its challenges. He was far more likeable and amenable than his predecessor. George wondered if some of his more testing times as a player would have been easier if someone like Chris Ewens had been present at those "last chance meetings", instead of the rather unforgiving and righteous David Blackstone. Chris had asked for and been given permission by George's employers to speak to him about the recent vacancy that had arisen in S.E.16. Chris was keen to know if George was prepared to come back to his "home club" and take over as manager. George had always kept an eye on what was happening there and to his dismay, the club had failed to push on after he had left. Since the departures of both Doug and

Bernie, they had employed six different managers, none of them lasting very long. Bernie Roswell was a hard act to follow. But now George was being offered the hot seat. A job that had gained a reputation as a "poisoned chalice". Again, he spoke to Debbie and his dad about making the move. He even called his old mentor Doug Fenner, to see what his thoughts were. All were in agreement that it was an offer he couldn't and shouldn't refuse. George was a little uncomfortable walking away from his current employers. He had always disliked the way in which both players and management would cut and run, regardless of their contracts, to pursue a better deal. He had always bemoaned the lack of loyalty in the game, but he knew his young assistant would be offered the job in his place and hopefully begin a successful career for himself. The two clubs came to an amicable agreement. His Midland bosses knew the lure of managing the club with which his name would always be associated, would be too much of a temptation for him. Handshakes were shared, compensation agreed and paid and George made his way south yet again.

It was the last week in January and the season was over half way through. George had been tasked with pushing the club into the top four places and qualifying once again for the lucrative and prestigious Champions League.

He stood at the top of the stairs and cast his eyes around the lounge again. It felt like he had come home. All the clubs he had been involved with as either a player or manager, meant a lot to him; but none more than this one. This club was in his blood. This was where he felt he belonged.

Chapter 3

You're the Headmaster now

The happy, comfortable feeling George felt looking around the spacious lounge was momentarily jolted out of him. At the far end of the room his eyes fixed on what he had always referred to as the "Hall of Fame". Framed and illuminated photographs that told the story of the club's rich and varied history. Since its creation, back in 1885, the club had experienced good times and bad. From its humble beginnings, it had progressed and survived two world wars, near financial ruin and had changed grounds five times. The framed pictures told that story. From the grainy black and white images of moustachioed, pipe smoking players in their flat caps and knee length shorts of the late 19th century, all the way up to the digitally perfect photographs of the modern day. The ever-changing kit design, from the original stripes, the all-white and onto the varying shades of blue. The constant shift in trends and fashions of hairstyles; from the short back and sides, long flowing locks and ponytails, dreadful perms and more recently, closely shaved heads. While he was a player, he had yearned to be up there amongst the greats of the game. To secure his place in the history books and take his position in the row of heroes and icons for all to see. That had been his dream. Twelve years earlier that dream had come true; but not in the way he had hoped.

Gazing at the many pictures hanging on the wall, he could see there had been a number of additions since he last looked. Success over the past ten years had been thin on the ground, but a few high points had managed to make it onto the wall. His eyes were immediately drawn to a cluster of three, now nestled into the pack. They were the three photos that celebrated the club's last major trophy, twelve years earlier. They had beaten the mighty Madrid in the Champions' League final, much against the odds. He had seen them all many times before. Two of them brought a smile to his face and memories of his team-mates celebrating, but the third of the three he didn't enjoy looking at. It scared him. It was a "smoking gun". Only three people knew about the damning evidence on show. Evidence that, if discovered, even now, twelve years on, would have catastrophic consequences for both him and his brother

Graham. The picture was calling him. He didn't want to look at it, but the frame had an eerie, hypnotic pull over him. He slowly made his way from the top of the stairs towards the gallery. As he approached it, from an angle, he could see the goalkeeper diving the wrong way. The same look of horror still etched on his face, as it had been for the past twelve years, as he realised in that split second, he had been beaten. He could see the ball suspended in mid-air, still tantalisingly on its journey to glory and he could see the penalty taker, full of concentration. The plaque below proudly announcing, "George Miller strikes the winning penalty". He was now standing right in front of the image. It had summoned him and he had dutifully obeyed. He tried desperately to focus only on the two-dimensional picture and not be drawn into the dark recesses of the photo's sleeping menace. The last time he stared at the frame he had noticed a pair of accusing, sinister eyes looking back at him. A pair of eyes that knew the secret hidden within. He couldn't help himself. He felt his focus slipping beneath the print and sinking below the surface into the murky depths. For a moment he could see nothing, but within a couple of seconds, they appeared. Just as menacing as they had been the last time and just as menacing as they would be every time. No one else could see them. They were visible only to him. They were there to remind him of a time in his life that had been both exhilarating and terrifying. An incident that had not only saved his career, but allowed him to carry on working in the game he held so dear. He owed everything he had to the crime he and his brother had committed. But those eyes, staring back at him, were a constant reminder of the felony they had perpetrated. The evidence was there for all to see, but none to understand. It was hiding in plain sight. Having spent years dreaming of a place in the "Hall of Fame", he would gladly have taken that picture frame down and put it through the shredder. He wouldn't care if he never had to look at the image again. Now he was the boss, maybe he could do something about it.

George's fixation with the ghostly eyes was broken by a very familiar and friendly voice.

'Have you been a naughty boy again, George Miller?'

He turned around and was greeted by the lovely, welcoming face of Brenda. She instantly put the smile back on his face and made him feel at ease again. He hadn't seen her for ten years. Since he had retired, he hadn't set foot back at his old club until that day. He had always meant to call in and say hello to some of his old mates and especially Brenda, but he just never got around to doing it. As the years passed, there were fewer people he would have known. Brenda had now been there seventeen years and had always hoped

George would come back one day and say hello. Seeing her smiling face beaming at him, George felt a wave of guilt wash over him. He should have made the effort, if only for Brenda's sake.

Brenda had started work there when Bernie Roswell was the manager. They had developed more of a father-daughter relationship. Brenda not only respected Bernie, but was very fond of him as well. Those feelings were mutual. She had always regarded those years as the best of times. Bernie retired the same time as George and with the two of them, plus Doug Fenner leaving, she had wondered whether she should start to look for some other job elsewhere. She had stuck it out though and during the next ten years, had worked for six different managers. They had all come into the job with high hopes and grand ambitions, but one by one, had either found the going too tough, had failed to rise to expectations, or in one case, been lured away by a better deal in Italy. Although new managers would sometimes insist on bringing in their own staff, Brenda had survived them all. She had charmed them with her smile and personality and impressed them with her ability. Her seventeen years at the club were only bettered by the Chairman and the ageing kit man Billy Gray, who had been there, rumour had it, since 1885.

'Except now you are the Headmaster, not the naughty schoolboy,' Brenda laughed.

'Hello George. Or should I say Mr. Miller? Maybe you would prefer Sir?' she said somewhat obsequiously and performed a little curtsy.

'Thank you, Brenda. George will do nicely, unless you want me to start calling you Miss Cousins all the time.'

Brenda raised her eyebrows and thrust her left hand towards George's face, wriggling her fingers and showing off her wedding ring.

'Oh yes, I heard you'd met Mr. Right. Congratulations.'

'Well, I don't know about Mr. Right,' she said, as some of the joy drained from her face. For a moment she appeared lost in her own thoughts, just staring into space. She raised her eyes again and looked at George.

'It's not Miss Cousins anymore. It's Mrs Higgins,' she announced. George took hold of her hand and gave her fingers a kiss.

'Well, I'd prefer to stick with Brenda, if it's all the same to you Miss Cousins… Mrs Higgins… Brenda.'

She smiled and the warmth that had momentarily disappeared flowed back into her cheeks. George had always been able to make her smile and she had always had the same effect on him. When they first met seventeen years ago, she had instantly fallen in love with him, and George, being a serial flirt, had done nothing to dampen her ardour. There had been many opportunities for them to have started a relationship together. An idea that George had regularly fantasised about, but in the end, it was just a little too close to home for George's comfort. Brenda on the other hand, had always hoped and dreamed that they would end up together. She had always harboured secret thoughts that maybe one day she would be his. She would be Mrs Brenda Miller. She had adored him from the moment she set eyes on him and if she were to be honest with herself, she knew she still did. But as soon as George had met Debbie, Brenda knew that any chance she had of experiencing the love and tenderness, the passion and the excitement, that always seemed to be associated with his name, had gone. The day she realised that George had finally met the girl of *his* dreams was still a day of great sadness for her. She felt guilty about her emotions. She knew they were selfish and she should be pleased for him, but in her heart, she knew that it was a crushing blow to her dreams and fantasies. She had met Debbie a couple of times during George's final two years at the club. She was lovely. Brenda could see why George loved her so much. Brenda liked her too. It was difficult not to, but at the same time, she cursed her very existence. She knew George had found someone who would make him happy but was still convinced *she too* could have made him happy, if only she had been given the chance. That sadly, was all "water under the bridge". In the past ten years they had not seen, or even talked to each other. Any thoughts or dreams she had had regarding George Miller were buried under a decade of history, presumably gone forever. Worryingly, Brenda instantly knew that was not the case. As soon as she had seen him and he had kissed her hand, she felt the old, suppressed and dormant feelings begin to smoulder again inside her. She did her best to ignore them, but it was impossible. She had no control over them. Ten years down the line, they were about to commence on a working relationship. A *close* working relationship. Brenda didn't know if she felt excited or terrified. A lot had happened in those years. For a start, they were both married. But only one of them happily.

Chapter 4

Spare Parts

Five years earlier, Brenda had received an invitation to go to a friend's dinner party. She had unintentionally secured a little niché for herself. She was everyone's favourite "make-up-the-numbers girl". She was thirty years old, extremely pretty, great company, but most important of all, single. If any of her numerous friends wanted to keep the numbers "even" at their dinner parties and had an old acquaintance, a long-lost cousin, or a work colleague they wanted to invite, who was also unattached, Brenda would get the call. She was the girl they relied on, to entertain the other spare parts that turned up to these evenings. Over the years she had been introduced to numerous men of all ages, shapes and sizes and from all walks of life. Some seemed quite excited at their first meeting, assuming the deal had already been done. She was there as their partner for the evening and if they liked her, she was available to them. The problem was everybody liked her. She was so easy to get on with and definitely "easy on the eye". Unfortunately for most of the male spare parts, Brenda's excitement and romantic urges rarely matched up to theirs. Of course, she was pleasant, polite, even interested in what they had to say, but on most occasions, it had taken her only a few minutes to decide that there would be no second date and certainly no romance. She had been out with a couple of men from these arranged rendezvous, but never with any great success. They did all they could to please and impress, but she found it hard to invest the emotion needed, to develop a friendship into a relationship. Deep down in her heart she knew the reason. She had never really recovered from the realisation that George Miller would never be hers. She didn't really want to admit that to herself, but she remembered the day she knew he was gone forever. The day he met Debbie in Barcelona after all those years apart was, without doubt, the happiest day in his life, but by far the most crushing and disappointing one in Brenda's. She really had believed that one day her fairy tale life would have its happy ending and she would be with George forever.

At this particular dinner party, she had been introduced to and sat opposite, a man called

Jeremy Higgins. Once again, she knew she had been offered up for his perusal, as much as he had for hers. As usual, the gathered diners consisted of three happily married and stable couples and two spare parts. Brenda was keen to settle down, maybe even have children if there was time, but as the years had passed by and she was now thirty, her expectations had lowered somewhat. She had almost given up hope of meeting the perfect man. He had gone. So, she had to lower the bar, but however low she dropped it, there didn't seem to be anyone who could attain even the basic requirements she needed in a prospective husband. Jeremy was pleasant enough. He was tall and slender. He looked athletic and was reasonably good looking, without being devilishly handsome. He was courteous and polite and a good conversationalist. It did occur to Brenda, halfway through the evening, that as good a speaker as he was, his favourite subject of conversation was *himself*. Brenda listened intently to stories about his work, his mother and his sporting prowess (he told her, with no modesty whatsoever, that he was rather good at rugby). He seemed to have an opinion on just about everything and was very eager to share his great knowledge and wisdom with anyone who would listen. Every now and again Brenda would shoot a glance up the table, only to see the other couples intently listening to the progress the two of them were making, all eager to see if their alchemy had worked. After the party Brenda did give Jeremy her mobile number and they agreed to meet again. Jeremy was a million miles away from the 'Prince Charming' she always yearned for, but he was okay and at that time, okay was as good as she could hope for.

After they had been on a couple of dates, Jeremy became very enthusiastic about their relationship. He wanted to spend more and more time with Brenda. He would make arrangements for just about every day of the week, telling her with great excitement and enthusiasm, that he had booked 'this' for Monday night, 'that' for Tuesday evening, something else for Wednesday and Thursday and so on. Brenda began to find it all a little claustrophobic, but she contented herself that he was only doing it because he was so keen on her. It had been a while since she'd "gone out" with someone and if she was honest, she quite enjoyed the attention. Jeremy, however, became increasingly upset and disappointed if she wasn't available some evenings. He would sulk like a petulant schoolboy after being told off by his teachers or parents.

Jeremy still lived at home with his mother Marjorie. She doted on him and treated him more like an eight-year-old, than a man approaching his thirties. She fussed over him, continually rearranging his hair and straightening his clothes, as if she was sending him off to school, or church. She cooked all his meals and bought all his clothes. She spoke to him as if he was a child and he responded as one. In the beginning Brenda thought it was cute as it showed the special bond between mother and son, but after a while, it began to feel a little weird and slightly un-nerving. It struck her as odd that a grown man should still refer to his mother as "Mummy", especially in the annoyingly squeaky, helium inspired voice of a six-year-old.

Brenda's relationship with Marjorie was a strained one. She always felt that Marjorie thought she was there to steal her son away and to break up her idyllic life with her little boy. Although nothing was ever said, Brenda had the distinct impression that Marjorie didn't like her. As their relationship became more serious, Brenda did everything she could to please Marjorie, but it seemed whatever she said or did to ingratiate herself, Marjorie never had a kind word, or a friendly smile for her.

It was never a good idea to go back to Jeremy's house after they had been out. He only had a single bed and Brenda was always shepherded into the spare room, where there was yet another single bed. On the one occasion Brenda had dared to venture from her single bed towards Jeremy's room, she bumped into Marjorie on the landing. It was 3am. Marjorie explained that she was a very light sleeper and was regularly up during the night. As if it were her original intention, Brenda went into the toilet. When she eventually came out, Marjorie was still there on the landing waiting for her. She bid her goodnight and then ushered Brenda back into her own room. It was a manoeuvre Brendan never repeated.

Jeremy worked for a bank and had an office in the city. He kept regular hours and was a stickler for time keeping and neatness. His mother had raised him to be both punctual and tidy. These were qualities he expected from everyone else. He became irritated, sometimes cross, when Brenda would phone him and tell him she had to work late. Especially on match days. Saturdays in particular were always a sensitive time. Brenda's Saturdays were invariably hectic and she was occasionally required to work into the early evening. This infuriated Jeremy most. He played rugby on Saturdays. It was *his* time to shine. He considered it extremely selfish and churlish if she didn't accompany him to the match. But what pissed him off most was not the lack of company, but the fact he would have to get a cab both ways or forgo the after-match revelry and drinking. Jeremy considered this the height of bad manners and disrespect. After everything he had done for her during the week, surely it wasn't too much to ask for her to be there on Saturday afternoons to pick him up, watch him play, then drive him back to hers after he had had his fill of beer. He did, however, enjoy it when she *was* able go with him. He would wallow in what he knew was the admiration and the envy of his mates. He knew they were jealous of his good fortune at having such a lovely and sexy girlfriend. They all told him he was "punching well above his weight", but he always laughed at the thought. *He* was the prize. *He* could have any girl he wanted. As if to accentuate this, he always paid her little attention in the bar after the game. There were no signs of intimacy or affection. He would speak openly about her failings and inadequacies, mocking her in front of his mates and their partners. His supercilious and patronising manner making it appear that it was Brenda who was the lucky one to be with him and not vice-versa. Either way, Brenda rarely enjoyed, or looked forward to her Saturday evenings.

Brenda always assumed his possessive nature was a reflection of the love and affection he felt for her, although his temper would sometimes boil over. He would demand to know where she had been and who she had been with, wanting names, places and times. If she went out with any girlfriends, he would insist she send him a photo of herself and her companions. He would ask her how her evening had been and what she had done, but it was always more interrogation than courteous interest. He would make her go over her story numerous times, almost willing her to get some detail wrong and pounce on any little discrepancy. She sometimes felt she was being questioned by the police, but Jeremy always apologised and told her it was just because he was concerned about her safety. After some of his more explosive tantrums, he would send her flowers with a message of his undying love and devotion.

Brenda often considered talking to him about his mood swings, but she never found the right time. It was only later, after they had married, that she realised her failure to speak up was born out of fear. The fear of making him even angrier. She would generally let it pass without comment and just put it down to the highs and lows of a modern-day relationship. Everyone went through the same thing. She decided it was best to do, and say, nothing. Things were always better the next day.

Brenda had tried on many occasions to persuade Jeremy to come to the club and watch a game of football. She was keen to show him where she worked and what she did. She was proud of herself and the position she had attained. Her job and the people she worked with were a huge part of her life and she wanted to share that with Jeremy, show him the world she inhabited whilst letting him see first-hand that she was an important, if small, cog in a well-run machine. But Jeremy was reluctant. He always had a reason, or an excuse why he couldn't, or wouldn't, attend. He saw no point. He was convinced that once they were married, Brenda would give up work and be the doting little housewife he had always imagined. All the washing, ironing, cleaning, shopping and cooking and eventually, looking after Jeremy Jnr, would leave no time for another job. He would go to work and leave "the little woman" at home to deal with the running of the house. When he got home, his dinner would be ready and he would relax and watch the TV with his devoted wife sitting next to him. That was what he had become accustomed to, living at home with his mother all his life and that's what he would expect in future. He didn't know Brenda at all.

Chapter 5

We all have our little crosses to bare

'Can I get you a cup of tea Mr. Miller? .... Sorry, I will rephrase that. Can I get you a cup of tea George?' Brenda asked him, with a cheeky grin on her face. They both laughed.

'That would be lovely, thank you. Then come into the office, I want to catch up on what's been going on here since I left.'

Brenda brought in two mugs of tea and sat down next to George on one of the sofas. George looked around his office.

'I remember being in here a few times. Mostly to get my knuckles rapped. Mind you, Bernie and Doug were always very good to me. I think any other management team, at any other club, would have given up on me years before and sold me on. David Blackstone was always trying to get rid of me. I know that for sure. He never liked me. Whatever happened to him?'

'He left a few years after you did.' Brenda replied. 'He had a few differences of opinion with the chairman, regarding what he thought he was worth salary wise. He told Mr Morton that he could command much more money elsewhere and would consider his options if necessary. Between you and me, I don't think for one moment David Blackstone thought he wouldn't be paid the extra. He assumed Mr Morton valued him so much, not only as a friend and trusted ally, but also in a business sense, that he would back down and pay him what he wanted. But Mr M,' she glanced up towards the chairman's office, 'just said, *"Fine. Good luck in the future"*. There was no evidence of the friendship or close relationship they had enjoyed with each other through all those years. In the end it just came down to a point of principle. Mr Morton wasn't going to be held to ransom by anyone. There was only ever going to be one winner. Crazy when you think about it. David had a job for life here, or certainly as long as he wanted it. He was on a massive salary, but just got greedy. David packed his things and left, without any fanfares or whistles. There was no farewell party, or any kind of ceremony. No "Gold watch" or presentation, so to speak. He just came in a couple of days later, picked up a few things, said goodbye and well....just disappeared from our lives. As far as I know he hasn't had another job since. To be honest, I don't think there were too many people here that were sorry to see him go. He was quickly replaced by Chris Ewens. You've obviously met him already.'

'Yes,' said George. 'He seems like a really nice bloke. Totally different to Blackstone.'

George thought for a moment about what Brenda had just said. Mr Morton was a ruthless and hard-nosed businessman who was prepared to crush any rebellion or mutinous behaviour without a second thought. In Mr Morton's world, there was clearly no room for any sentimentality or emotion. Business was business and nothing, or nobody, would be allowed to rock Mr Morton's boat, whoever they were, or whatever their history. It made George realise just how strong Bernie must have been when arguing *his* case all those years ago. He had always admired Bernie's principles, strength and ethos, now he admired them just a little bit more. By standing up to the Chairman and sticking to his guns, regarding George's future, he was putting his own neck on the line, even more than George had imagined.

'And what about you Miss Cous... Mrs Higg.... Brenda? What's been happening in your life since I last saw you?'

Brenda then proceeded to tell George what had been happening at the club for the past ten years.

'It was like the changing of the guard' she said, with a reflective sadness in her voice. 'You, Doug and Bernie all leaving at the same time. All my favourite people gone in one fell swoop. It felt like the whole place had been tipped upside down. There were so many comings and goings, it was difficult to know who was who sometimes. The new managers were normally accompanied by a cast of backroom staff who came as a package. Six managers in ten years! You can imagine how many new faces there were. Most of them for a single season. Some even less. The turnover in players was incredible too, with each new regime wanting their own style of footballer. Igor, Pascal, even the lovely, although slightly terrifying Terry Bridges all left, not long after you. I think the only face you will remember from your time here is Barry Allder. He stayed. Every manager seemed to admire him. I like him a lot. He always has a smile on his face and is always so lovely. He reminds me of you in some ways. He always kept his feet on the ground, even after all those Caps he won for England.'

Brenda told him about Bernie. He had gone to live on the south coast of Cornwall with his wife. The last she heard, they were happy and healthy and enjoying the late autumn years of their lives.

She began to tell him what she knew about Doug, but George stopped her. George had kept in touch with his old friend and spoken to him regularly on the phone. Doug still lived in the same house in Sevenoaks, Kent that had been his home for the past twenty years. He and his wife had moved down from Lancashire and settled in the beautiful 'Garden of England'. George had popped in to see them a few times since his retirement. They were a lovely couple. They always made him very welcome and treated him like a son. Doug and Mavis had been married for forty-eight years and were devoted to each another. It was heart breaking when George heard the news, two years ago, that his beloved wife had passed away. It hit Doug very hard and he never seemed to be the same man after that. Since her death, he had become a bit of a recluse. Apart from his daughter Lisa and the occasional visit from George, he rarely saw anyone. The last time George had seen him, he remembered thinking how much older he looked. He seemed smaller and more hunched; quieter and tired. His smile was still there and the warmth in his eyes still glowed whenever he saw George, but the furnace within him, which had burnt bright ever since George first met him twenty-four years earlier had gone out. He had lost half of himself and most of his reason to live. It was desperately sad to see, but George understood. He had always looked at the relationship between Doug and Mavis and imagined that was how he and Debbie would be when they reached that age. He couldn't imagine life without Debbie.

Doug had always enjoyed telling George how many times he had 'dined out' on the story that 'HE' *Doug Fenner,* had been the one to uncover and discover the footballing talent that was George Miller, when he was just a teenager.

George hadn't seen his old friend for a few months. He made a mental note. He would give him a call and go down to visit him, as soon as possible.

'That's all well and good' George said 'but what I really want to hear about is you. Tell me all about the man who finally swept you off your feet. The lucky fella that hit the jackpot when he married you.'

George picked up Brenda's left hand and looked at the engagement and wedding rings. Brenda lowered her eyes and took a deep breath. It wasn't a conversation into which she could put much enthusiasm or excitement. She explained how she and Jeremy had met and a few details about their wedding day.

'There were so many people I wanted to invite. People I had known for years, including you and Debbie, Doug, Mavis and Bernie, but Jeremy said he thought it best if we looked to the future, not the past. One by one, my suggestions for the guest list were crossed off. It was only when my Dad led me down the aisle and I saw so many faces looking at me, faces I didn't recognise, that I wished I had been more assertive. Apart from my immediate family, there was no one else I really knew. It was all his work mates and rugby friends.' She paused, took in a deep breath, then let out a rueful sigh. 'It just seemed to be easier and less hassle to go along with what he and his mother wanted. What with the two of them in total agreement on everything, I began to feel more and more distant from every aspect of the day. If I expressed any doubt or misgivings, about something they were arranging, the two of them would tell me "*not to be so silly"*, then carry on with their plans as if I wasn't there. After a while, I just gave up interfering and let them get on with it. I realised I was never going to get my way, so pretty much agreed with everything they suggested. His mother more or less picked my dress. He chose the music, the food, the venues and the honeymoon. Even my bridesmaids were daughters of *his* friends. When I think back on it now, my only contribution to the day was to turn up!'

As she spoke, George noticed that she had disappeared into an almost trance like state, as if speaking to herself, staring blankly into the distance with a glazed look in her eyes. After a moment's silence, she snapped out of her hypnosis, smiling straight into George's eyes.

'Of course, I would have married you like a shot, if you had asked me' she said.

George was a little taken aback by the announcement. He could feel his cheeks start to blush and was unsure how to react. Brenda's smile quickly faded and she carried on with her story. She explained how possessive Jeremy had become and how he quizzed her on all of her previous boyfriends and relationships. He demanded to know everything about who she had been with, what they had done, (disturbingly, in graphic detail sometimes) and when was the last time she had seen them. The more she told him, the more angry he became.

'It was as if he didn't want me to have had a life before I met him. He appeared to be threatened by my past and wanted me to have nothing to do with anyone I had known previous to him. Any evidence of my life, especially my love life, was discarded. Letters, photographs and mementos were systematically thrown out. I saw less and less of my friends and lost touch with just about everyone, apart from the people I worked with. Even then Jeremy was keen I spend as little time at work as possible and certainly have minimal contact with the people there. Especially the men! The one thing Jeremy had no power over and couldn't throw away were my memories, but as time passed, they began to fade. The care-free, enjoyable and exciting life I used to lead was slowly, but irrevocably dissolving away.'

Brenda told George that Jeremy sometimes made her feel insecure and tentative about anything she said and did. How he always explained that it was because he loved her so much, wanted her to be safe and be with him. While she was talking, George noticed her demeanour had changed. The smiling bubbly girl he knew years ago and the happy and giggly woman he had been talking to about old times, had vanished. She looked sad, blank and haunted.

George frowned. This was not the happy story he had been expecting. She looked dead inside. Just a husk of the woman he had been speaking to half an hour earlier. He continued to hold her hand and stroked her fingers. After a short pause, she snapped out of her trance. A smile of sorts spread across her face and she pulled her hand away from George's.

'Oh well, none of us are perfect I suppose. We all have our little crosses to bear, don't we?' Brenda stood up and wandered over towards the door. 'I do have a lot of work to do and as lovely as it is to see you again, I do have to get on. I don't want to be making the wrong impression on my new boss, do I? I've heard he is a bit of a tyrant.' She laughed. 'Can I get you anything else George?'

'No, thank you Brenda. Listen, if there is anything you ever want to talk about, you know you can come to me. We've known each other for a long time and I have always cherished our friendship. Please let me know if there is anything troubling you.'

'Thank you, George. I will.'

She nodded her head and shut the door behind her. George sat back on the sofa and thought about what Brenda had told him. They were all older and maybe a little less lively and energetic than they used to be, but Brenda seemed to have had the spirit and the sparkle she once had in abundance, kicked out of her. He wondered if he was jumping to conclusions. Was there something more sinister going on in Brenda's life? He hadn't met Jeremy yet, but already he was finding the man difficult to like. He knew he would only find out what was happening if and when Brenda decided to tell him. He would get nowhere if he tried to pry the information out of her. He tried to convince himself that it was really none of his business and that she was a grown woman who could handle whatever was troubling her. Everyone experienced ups and downs in a marriage (apart from him of course), but Brenda wasn't just anyone. He knew his feelings for her ran deeper than that. She had occupied a special place in his heart years ago and she still did. He would keep an eye on her. Hopefully he would see the return of the sparky, fun, exuberant, young lady he had learned to love, in a brotherly way of course.

Chapter 6

I know how easily your head turns, George Miller

For the next few weeks George was very busy settling into his new job, meeting all the staff and players and trying to come to terms with being the 'Headmaster' at his old school. Taking on the job at the end of January, meant he was unable to buy or sell any players. The transfer window had closed and he would have to make do with what he had. He enjoyed re-acquainting himself with some of the people who had been at the club back when he was still playing. Billy Gray, the kit man, had been there for as long as anyone could remember and hadn't changed a bit as far as George could see. Some of the young girls who had worked in the canteen were still there; now a little older and hopefully, a little wiser. He remembered flirting with some of them, all those years ago. From the look in some of their eyes, they remembered those days too. One or two of the security men from the past still wandered around looking menacing, some carrying a few extra pounds around their waists. And on the playing side, Barry Allder was still there. Allder had been an eighteen-year-old youngster the night they had beaten Madrid in the Champions' League Cup final in Barcelona twelve years earlier. Bernie and Doug always had him marked down as a prodigious talent. They were good judges. That eighteen-year-old left winger went on to blossom and get better and better. Numerous caps for England and a hatful of international goals had assured Allder of a place, not only in the "Hall of Fame", but in the hearts of all the supporters. It was great to see him again.

George's relationship with Brenda settled into a friendly, but business-like, partnership. She continued to call him George when they were alone, but always addressed him as Mr. Miller if anyone else was there. Sometimes they would swap a secretive grin when that happened. It always sounded a little odd to both of them.

With January gone and February heading relentlessly towards March, George started to recognise subtle changes in Brenda's moods. Some days she was a very happy, bubbly, young woman, whose company and conversation he loved. She would flit about the office like a teenager, sometimes even singing to herself. But on other days she looked sullen and dowdy. She would speak only when she was spoken to and even then, she was pretty monosyllabic. Her eyes were heavier and darker. She gave the impression she had had very little sleep. She was listless and lifeless. It felt to George like he was employing two completely separate and wildly different people. He was never sure which one of them was going to turn up for work.

He had asked her on a number of occasions, when the dowdy Brenda had turned up, if everything was okay. He asked her if she needed to take time off, but her answers were always the same. "She was fine, just a little tired. She had a lot going on at home, but nothing she couldn't handle". If George persisted in his questioning, she would tell him it was "just the time of the month". That always shut him up. Although it was only something she relied on as a last resort, she knew that no man wanted to have an extended chat on *that* subject. George would look slightly embarrassed, understanding, even apologetic, as if he had just intruded into a particularly private and personal part of her world. It worked every time.

Each time he asked and got the same reply, he just nodded and decided not to pursue it any further, but he wasn't convinced. It wasn't a field in which he could claim to be an expert, but, *"the time of the month",* in his experience, happened on a reasonably regular basis. If Brenda's excuses were truthful, her cycles were erratic to say the least. He began to worry about her. That gorgeous, effervescent, young girl he knew was still in there, somewhere. She was just making fewer and fewer appearances.

The season was heading into its last quarter and the games were coming thick and fast. George's first weeks had been successful ones. The team was unbeaten under him so far and both his main strikers, Wood and Jones, had rediscovered their scoring talents. Barry Allder was also playing as well as ever and the club appeared to be on the way up again.

There were times when George's workload took him deep into the night. With some meetings scheduled for early morning, he had been spending more time at his riverside flat. He hated calling Debbie and telling her he wouldn't be home, but she understood and was happy that he was so content in his work. She did miss him. Every night without him, was a night lost. George had spent the previous two nights at the flat but was determined not to make it three in a row. He phoned Debbie and assured her he would be back around 8:30.

'I've missed you so much' she said as he walked through the front door. She flung her arms around his neck and kissed him. It never ceased to amaze him that every time their lips touched, he felt a charge of electricity shoot through his entire body, just like he had when they first kissed at the bottom of the hill, outside their school, on their first date.

'Are the kids asleep?' he asked.

'Yes, they have been for about an hour,' she said, with a glint in her eye. 'Why don't we go up and check on them?… And then Mr. Miller, maybe we can get those clothes off you and see if we can de-stress that lovely body of yours.' However tired or exhausted he felt, it only ever took a kiss, a touch, or a suggestion from Debbie to fire him up. She had a unique ability to arouse him, with just a look or a word.

The kids were both fast asleep. Debbie and George decided to take advantage of the time by slipping into the huge, deep, sunken bath they had in their bedroom. They were accompanied by a chilled bottle of Laurent Perrier Rosé champagne. Debbie brushed the bubbles off George's chest and snuggled into him.

'I really do miss you when you don't come home you know. I don't know how I'm going to cope when we go away for three weeks at Easter.'

'I know. I'm sorry. Hopefully it will get easier once this season has finished and I have settled in properly,' he said, gently stroking her forehead. They both sipped their champagne in silence. George was staring into space. He was deep in thought.

'What's wrong?' Debbie asked, 'You look like something's bothering you.'

'Oh, just general stuff. You know.'

She lifted her head off his chest and looked at him, her eyebrows raised.

'And. What else?' She could read him like a book. George sighed.

'I'm worried about Brenda. She doesn't seem herself these days. She is moody and quiet a lot of the time. It is so unlike her. I have asked her numerous times if there is anything wrong, but she always tells me everything is fine. She has never said it in so many words, but her inference is, *mind your own business*. I don't want to pry or interfere, but I am certain something is wrong.'

'You do know she still holds a torch for you, don't you?' Debbie sat up and looked at George in the eyes. 'She has always fancied you. You do know that? Maybe she is just struggling, having to work with the man she has always fantasised about. Maybe still fantasises about.'

'Don't be so silly. She is married. Anyway, that was a long time ago.' George said dismissively.

'Well, it sounds to me like she is still madly in love with you. And let's face it, she is probably still a head turner. And I know how easily your head turns, George Miller.' She gently pinched his cheek and eased his head around until he was facing her. 'You haven't been encouraging the poor girl, have you?' Debbie said, with a cheeky humour. George frowned and glared at his wife.

'TURNED' he said bluntly, 'TURNED. Past tense. No more. Never. Not since I met you again. Those days are over. You know that.' George looked at her, slightly hurt by her inference. Debbie laughed at his indignation.

'I know baby. I was just kidding' she said, stroking the same cheek, 'but it must be hard for her, working alongside a man like you.'

She stopped stroking his cheek, lowered her hand below the waterline and began to stroke between his legs, with immediate effect.

'I don't think I would be able to concentrate on my job, if I were constantly near you.' She looked at him. His eyes were closed. His head leant back, resting on the cushioned edge of the bath. He was enjoying her touch. The tension and worry that had been etched into his brow was gone. She kissed him on his neck and nibbled his ear lobe. Between the kisses, licks and nibbles, she whispered,

'Speaking of concentration' …

She slid her left leg over him and straddled her husband. George's eyes opened. He saw his beautiful wife sitting across him and watched as the bubbles covering her silky, shining body, slowly slid away, revealing her beautifully rounded breasts. She clasped her hand around the pulsing evidence of his anticipation and guided him between her legs. She smiled and gently began to lower herself onto him. He felt himself glide effortlessly into the heavenly depths of her soft, moist flesh. He felt her buttocks contract and relax as she moved back and forth, with him deep inside her. She took his glass and put it on the side of the bath. George placed his hands on her hips and stared lovingly into Debbie's eyes. He really was the luckiest man in the world. She leant forward and kissed him.

'You see. Just like I said. My concentration has all gone to Hell.'

Chapter 7

Panda eyes

After a lovely family breakfast with Debbie and the kids, George left for work. His drive into London on the A40, then over Vauxhall Bridge into South London, could take anything up to two hours. It certainly gave him time to think. That morning his mind continually jumped from the warmth and love of his family, to the worrying concerns he had about Brenda's situation. He tried not to let his imagination run away with itself. He was convinced she was not happy in her marriage but knew he could do very little to help, unless she confided in him. Knowing her as he did, George had already laid the blame for any marital difficulties squarely on Jeremy's shoulders. As he parked his car, he wondered which one of the "Brenda's" would be at work that day. Walking past her office, George waved at her. She was on the phone. She flicked her head in his direction but kept her concentration on the job in hand. Moments later she called out to him,

'Tea?'

'Yes, please Brenda,' he shouted back.

She placed the mug of steaming tea onto the coaster next to his laptop. Without making eye contact and without a word, she turned to leave.

'Hang on a minute Brenda. Everything okay with you this morning?'

Still with her back towards him she replied.

'Yes, thank you,' and started to walk away again.

'Brenda. Come over here a minute will you please?'

She stopped again and let out a huge sigh, as if to demonstrate just how inconvenient this interruption to her schedule was. She turned and slowly walked back to George's desk. There was no hint of a smile on her face and no evidence of happiness in her expression.

'Yes,' she barked, almost demanding a reason for his intrusion into her day's agenda. George stared deeply into her eyes and looked at her pretty face. He hadn't been mistaken with his first glance at her, when she delivered his tea. There was a dark shade to her skin around her left cheek and under her eye. As he looked closer, he could see the unmistakable signs of bruising. She stood there while he looked at her.

'What is it George? What can I do for you?'

It was a curt question, said in a tone that betrayed her desire to extricate herself from what was clearly, an inspection. George sat back in his chair but kept his eyes firmly fixed on Brenda's glare.

'I remember when we first met. Must be seventeen years ago now. You were a fresh faced eighteen-year-old, straight out of school and I was a cocky *'Jack the lad'*, who thought he knew it all. I remember the first time I set eyes on you. You nearly blew my socks off. You were so pretty. I remember thinking to myself at the time that you shouldn't have worn so much makeup, as it hid your natural beauty.'

He smiled at her, hoping his compliments and the short trip down memory lane would remove the stern look she was giving him, but he was looking at a face that showed no sign of softening. 'Brenda, you're still just as beautiful, even more so, but I can't help noticing today, you are layering on the makeup, thicker than ever. Especially there.' George leant forward in his chair and pointed at her left cheek. Brenda broke the eye contact and bowed her head. She thought for a moment, then resumed her stare into his eyes, this time with even more fiery irritation. In a tone George had never heard her use before she said,

'Is that all?!! Surely my makeup is no concern of yours. I will do my job to the best of my ability and I can assure you, *Mr Miller*, that my makeup will have no bearing on my performance. Now if that *is* all, I really do have more important things to deal with.' Brenda spun around and marched purposely towards the door. George was visibly shaken by the tone and ferocity of her reply.

'Wait. Brenda. I'm sorry. I didn't mean to be so rude. I...I..'

Brenda had stopped walking and stood still in the doorway. George wondered if he was about to receive another angry reprimand from his secretary.

'I'm just worried about you. Please forgive me.'

He watched and waited anxiously for her reaction. Her shoulders began to twitch and her head bowed. She slowly turned to look at him. Tears were rolling down her cheeks, leaving tracks in the thick foundation and making her mascara run. The angry woman who had just admonished him, turned her back on him and stormed off, had been replaced by a pitiful, sobbing, child. George wasn't sure what he was expecting Brenda to do or say, but he certainly wasn't expecting the sight before him.

'No. I'm sorry' she said, stuttering through her tears. 'I didn't mean to snap. It's me that should be begging forgiveness.'

George jumped up from his desk and rushed over to her. He took her in his arms, cradling the back of her head gently. For a brief moment she allowed her limp body to wallow in his embrace. It felt nice; it felt comfortable; it felt safe. But after a couple of seconds, Brenda reluctantly broke away. She dabbed her eyes with a tissue.

'There are a few things I've got on my mind at the moment, but I promise they won't affect my work.'

'To hell with the work,' George shouted, 'I don't care about the work. I care about you.' He held her by the shoulders and looked into her watery eyes. He could feel her body trembling. 'Is there anything I can do to help? Do you need some time off? Take as long as you need. You know all you have to do is ask.'

'Thank you, George' she said, trying desperately to regain some control over her tearful outpourings. 'Everything will be fine, I promise. I'm just being silly. You know', she glanced down at her waist and silently mouthed the words, "*that time*".' She finally managed to smile.

'I really do have a lot to do, so unless you want anything else, I think I should get on.' He knew, *"that time",* was a smoke screen, but he also knew it wasn't the time to force the issue.

'What about a quick drink after work? We can have a little chat then, if you like.' Brenda's eyes looked distant.

'Sorry, can't make tonight. I have to get home. I told Jeremy I wouldn't be late. Thanks anyway.' She smiled at him, with as much reassurance as she could manage. 'Everything will be okay, I promise you. Please don't worry. Maybe we can have that drink another time.'

The following morning George walked into the lounge on the second floor and saw Brenda's office door was shut. Her door was *never* shut! He was about to knock, when he heard the unmistakable sound of crying. He opened the door and walked in. Brenda was a little shocked by the unannounced intrusion and momentarily tried to look busy, shuffling papers and randomly tapping at her computer, but she had no strength left in her to continue the charade. George shut the door. Brenda buried her face in her hands and wept openly. She couldn't hide her emotions anymore.

'What on Earth is the matter?'

George gently placed his fingers under her chin and tried to raise her face. There was a moment of resistance, but then she relented and stared up at him. Her mascara had run and blurred again, giving her "panda eyes". At any other time, she would have looked rather comical, but there was no humour in evidence that morning. George became even more aware of the bruising to her cheek. He softly cradled her face in his hands, as he had done, so many times with his kids when they were upset.

'What's going on Brenda? Please tell me. As a friend. I care about you very much and I hate to see you like this.' He softly stroked her cheek, gently running his thumb over the bruising. 'Is it Jeremy? Did he do this to you?' Brenda's eyes released another wave of tears.

'Don't think too harshly of him. It is as much my fault as his. We got into an argument. Sometimes he loses control. He has a bit of a temper and occasionally I seemed to goad him into lashing out. I should know better. He doesn't mean it and he's ever so sorry afterwards.' She grasped his hands in hers and squeezed them tightly. With a look of desperation in her eyes she pleaded with him. 'Please don't mention this to anyone else. It only happens once in a blue moon and I know it is just as much my fault as his. Please George, just forget about it. I'm sure it won't happen again. He loves me very much and I know he doesn't mean to hurt me.'

The sympathy and concern George had been feeling towards Brenda had now changed to a burning sense of fury and outrage. His urge to go straight over to Jeremy's workplace and give him a bloody good hiding was almost unbearable, but he knew he had to bite his lip and do whatever Brenda wanted. He had to respect her wishes, even though they went against the grain. He felt helpless and angry, but most of all, he felt sadness.

Sadness for this lovely young girl, who deserved so much better.

Every day after that, George checked Brenda's face for any further evidence of brutality. To his great relief, he saw none. The bruising on her cheek quietly dissolved beneath her ever-decreasing amounts of makeup and after a while, the smile came back to her face. The bubbly, happy, Brenda, came back to work. Chatty, humorous, and occasionally a little suggestive, Brenda's mood made the office a much nicer place to work. Every morning she bought George in a cup of tea, put it on his desk and beamed at him with her gorgeous smile and every morning, George regularly made his daily and clandestine inspection of her features, searching for any tell-tale signs that her mood might be about to change.

Chapter 8

The lovely Doug Fenner

Brenda was back to her old self. The bruising on her cheek had faded, as had the memories of all the tears. The incident hadn't been mentioned again and Brenda carried on as if nothing had ever happened. On the odd occasion Jeremy's name came up in conversation, she always spoke of him in an affectionate and loving way, as if she were trying to impress on George what a warm-hearted, considerate and tender man he really was. Stories about his heroics on the rugby pitch, or any romantic gesture he might have made towards her, were described with glowing adoration. George was convinced that all the accounts of Jeremy's lion-hearted and passionate deeds had been enhanced and exaggerated for his benefit. An attempt by Brenda to persuade him, (or was it herself?) that her husband was in fact *a "Prince among men"*. George did his best to smile and nod while she revealed what a fine man her spouse was, but he didn't believe a word of it. He suspected, neither did she. It was now completely clear to him that Brenda's mood swings were totally dependent on Jeremy's state of mind. All the while Jeremy was being "Mr Wonderful", Brenda was a joy to be around, but when "Jeremy the Magnificent" became "Jeremy the Bastard" he knew he would be confronted with the sad, sobbing and probably bruised Brenda that so upset him. He despised Jeremy more and more each day. To think that a man could command so much control and induce so much fear over another person, especially his wife, made George sick to his stomach.

Along with the smile and sparkling eyes, George noticed something else about Brenda. She had started to wear less makeup. A lot less makeup. Her natural beauty and cheerful personality lit up the entire office. She looked more radiant than he could ever remember. There was a freshness about her; she looked younger. He flattered himself it had been something to do with what he'd said to her, when pointing out her bruising. He had told her how much prettier he thought she was with less paint on her face. Maybe she was doing it for his benefit. Although she looked great, that was a worrying notion. What if Debbie was right after all and she did still harbour feelings for him. The same feelings she had had for the last seventeen years. He tried to dismiss the idea. Brenda's home life was obviously not the Utopian dream *he* was accustomed to, but she was married and so was he. Surely, she didn't think anything would, or could, happen between them.

Brenda came skipping into his office with a beaming smile.

'Guess who I've got on the phone!' she said excitedly. Without even waiting for a reply, she carried on. 'It's Doug. The lovely Doug Fenner. I've been having a chat with him for the last ten minutes, but he really wanted to speak to you. Shall I put him through?'

George had kept in touch with his dear old friend, but he hadn't seen him for a few months.

'Hi George. I'm sorry to disturb you at work. I know a manager's job is a hectic one,' he laughed. 'Sometimes anyway! Do you think you could spare me an hour of your time? I think it might be worth your while.'

'Of course, Doug. I have been meaning to pop in and say hello for a while. Are you free tonight? I could drive down once I've finished here.'

George left the office a little earlier than usual. The journey to Sevenoaks took him just over an hour. Close enough for him to visit more regularly. He felt a twinge of guilt as he pulled up outside, realising it had actually been nearly six months since their last meeting.

On entering Doug's house, he was shocked by how untidy the place was. Local newspapers and pizza menus littered the hallway. There was a pile of junk mail six inches high, forced up against the skirting board by the opening of the front door. The air was stale and musty. He doubted whether any windows had been opened for a while. In the kitchen there were plates, glasses, cups and cutlery all waiting patiently to be washed up, in and around the sink. Some of them had been waiting *very patiently* by the look of them.

'Come on in and sit down, George.' Doug picked up a tray, which contained what looked like the remnants of his dinner, from the sofa and put it on the floor. He moved a jumper and a couple of books from the seat of the armchair, before brushing off any crumbs from the cushions. George sat down and watched the elderly man fuss about, clearing more space on the sofa so as he could sit down himself.

'Sorry about the mess George. I never seem to get around to properly putting it all away. Lisa normally tidies up when she comes, but she hasn't been round for a couple of weeks. She is on holiday with some friends.' He looked at the clutter, shaking his head. 'I suppose I should make an effort and clean the place up a bit before she gets back, otherwise she will tell me off again. She's a good girl, but she does fuss over me.'

George made himself comfortable. There were a number of photographs dotted around the room, the largest of them hanging over the fireplace. A beautifully framed picture of Doug and Mavis, arm in arm, taken only weeks before she died. That was two years ago. George looked at the picture and glanced around the room. He knew the slovenly disorder and disarray would never have been tolerated when Mavis was alive. Back then, their house was always spotlessly clean and Doug would be constantly nagged if anything was out of place.

'I miss her.' Doug said sadly, noticing George looking at the picture above the fireplace. 'Life is not really the same without her. It would have been our Golden wedding anniversary in a couple of weeks' he said, with equal amounts of pride and heartache.

'I know,' said George, but he could think of nothing else to say.

On the table was a photograph of Doug and George. It had been taken when George first signed for Doug and his Championship team up in Lancashire twenty-four years earlier. George picked it up and took a closer look. Doug was a sprightly sixty-year-old enjoying his time as a manager. George was a fresh-faced eighteen-year-old, full of expectation and ambition.

'Happy days, eh George.' George smiled and nodded.

'We've had some good times along the way, you and me. You were a bit of a scallywag to say the least. Bit of a lady's man, liked a drink, always pushing your luck with authority. Reminded me of myself when I was that age.' The old man chuckled to himself, wallowing in the memories. 'It was a full-time job just sticking up for you and making excuses for your errant behaviour.' George laughed.

'Yes, I know. I'm sorry.'

'Don't be silly. It was worth all the effort.' He leant forward and patted George on the knee. 'You were always my favourite, you know that don't you? The son I never had.' He smiled. A wonderfully warm and loving smile. 'I felt close to a lot of players during my years in the game, but I always knew you were special.' He glanced up at the photograph above the fireplace. 'Mavis knew you were special too.'

George could hear the emotion in Doug's voice. He could sense the sadness and the loneliness in the old man's heart.

'I know Doug. She was a very special lady.'

For a few seconds Doug gazed lovingly at the picture above the fireplace. George remained silent.

'You know, after all those ups and downs, it all came good that night in Barcelona. Twelve years ago! Can you believe it? I can remember it as if it were yesterday. When Bernie told you to go on, I remember you looking unusually nervous. Normally you would have been champing at the bit to get on. I recall you looking like you were going to throw up. Anyway, it all worked out in the end. *Cometh the hour and all that.*'

Doug sat back in the sofa and raised his eyes to the ceiling. He clasped his hands together and rested them on his chest.

'I think that was the happiest moment I ever had in football. Seeing you come back from all that negative publicity. I always knew you had it in you.'

George watched and listened, as Doug recalled some of the memories he had from that night and many others. He spoke as if narrating the story of his life, laughing and smiling at some of the memories. George was happy to let the old man lose himself in the past. For his part, George just listened and nodded, content to hear the ramblings and reminiscences of his dear old friend.

Eventually he got around to telling George why he wanted to see him. A teenage boy had been brought to his notice. Some of Doug's old scouting acquaintances had been talking about a lad who had started to grab the attention of those "in the know". The footballing grapevine had begun to twitch with the name *Jayden Saunders*, a precocious young talent currently playing non-league football.

'He's not yet seventeen, but I thought you might want to go and have a look at him before some of the other clubs start sniffing around. He is playing tomorrow night for Woking. Apparently, he's a bit feisty and thinks rather a lot of himself, but he does have talent. That *is* for sure.'

George stayed most of the evening. The two of them wandered down memory lane again and again, remembering old names and faces. George was always keen to get back home to Debbie and the kids, but knew the time spent with his old friend and mentor was just as important and equally enjoyable. Since Mavis had died, Doug had become a bit of a hermit. He had little enthusiasm for any social events. His enjoyment and happiness at a night out would never be the same without his wife by his side. He was happier staying at home with his memories. He was regularly visited by Lisa his daughter, but apart from her and her family, George was the only other contact he had with the outside world. George made a mental note to make the effort to get down and visit him more often.

The following evening, George, accompanied by his chief scout, made his way to Woking and watched the young Jayden Saunders perform. George had done a little research into the boy's history. It was a sorry story so far. He had spent most of his life in care homes or foster homes. His father had been behind bars for most of the boy's life and his mother had died from a drug overdose when he was only four. George also discovered that Jayden's father was due for release from prison in a few days. From what he had been told, it appeared the plan was to reunite father and son and house them in a council flat in Peckham. The hope was, they would both have a positive and uplifting effect on each other. Maybe, George thought, their sad lives were about to experience happier times.

Doug's contacts had been right. The boy did have talent. He shone out amongst the other players on show. He was small and slight in build, but he was fearless and willing to take on opponents twice his size. He was fiery and aggressive, not only to the other team, but to the officials and occasionally to his own team-mates; but he was quick, sharp and looked like he had a good footballing brain.

Shortly after his trip to Woking, George, along with Chris Ewins, met with the boy. He had with him a lawyer and was also accompanied by Howard Church the Woking manager. They talked about his future and agreed a deal. George would take him on for a trial period until the end of the season. After that they would sit down and discuss a long-term deal, assuming everyone was happy.

George was excited to be able to bring in a new player. The transfer window had shut in January, so getting players from other professional clubs was impossible, but thanks to Doug, he had made, what he hoped would be, the first of many great signings to strengthen his team.

During his first few days at the club the young boy showed no sign of nerves or uncertainty. He swaggered about the place like he owned it. George was shocked by his cocky attitude. It was as if Jayden was doing them a favour by signing, not the other way around. Jayden told George what he expected from the club and from him as a manager. He told George what he would do and where he would play. He also suggested how the other players in the team would be best employed to maximise his effectiveness. George listened and smiled. He put the brashness down to over-excitement, but he knew he would have to keep an eye on the lad.

He hoped that once Jayden had met with the other members of the squad and staff at the club he would calm down and put all his efforts and energy into proving himself in front of the established players, realise the chance he had been given and do his best to make the most of it. Unfortunately for George, Jayden's sense of superiority and bravado only increased with his larger audience. Within the first week he had managed to either upset or enrage most of the people there. George had received complaints from the Catering staff and the ground staff. Even some of his senior players were a little disgruntled by what he had said to them. Criticising them, telling them where they were going wrong and offering to show them how to better themselves. At first, it was all taken with a pinch of salt. A young boy full of confidence, looking to make his way in the game, but it quickly became apparent that there was more to it than that. A need to undermine everyone else and barge his way to the front of the queue. To be the top dog straight away. He showed little respect to anyone, including George.

George wondered if he had bitten off more than he could chew. He remembered how he was when he had been given his first chance as a teenager. Yes, he was cocky and brash, but he was never rude and always had great respect for the management and the other players. He hoped that once the boy had settled in with his father, it might bring a bit more stability and structure to his life. His father had been released earlier that week and the experiment of them living together was just a few days old. He decided that he should meet with Jayden's father as soon as possible. If he could make him understand what a golden opportunity his son had been given and impress on him the need for hard work and humility, he was sure that between them they could turn Jayden into not only a valuable asset, but also a decent human being. By the sound of it, they had both had a pretty rough time up until then. Maybe this was a chance for them both to turn their lives around.

Chapter 9

Sawn-off shotguns and balaclavas

Coming into the world at an eye watering 10lbs 8oz, Barry Saunders was a big baby. From newborn, through childhood, adolescence and as a fully grown adult, he had always towered over most of his contemporaries. He was broad shouldered, thick set, muscular and stood well over six feet tall. Weighing in at seventeen stones and without an ounce of fat on him, he was a formidable looking man, with the stature of a heavyweight boxer.

From an early age he exuded an arrogance and a swagger. He felt superior to all around him and wallowed in the fear and anxiety his presence inspired.

He was forty-two years old, although he looked more like sixty-two. The craggy lines on his face reflecting the struggles and stresses he had endured. From deep within his weather-worn, leathery expression a pair of piercing, sapphire blue eyes radiated out. His forehead seemed permanently set with a sinister and threatening frown. With a square jaw and short cropped blonde, but rapidly greying hair, he could easily have played the part of an SS officer in any second world war film.

But the most striking feature on Barry Saunders was a blemish that weaved its way from just above his left eyebrow, around his eye socket and down onto his cheekbone. Slightly lighter in colour than the rest of his skin, the scar tissue, standing proud like a mountain range in a desert, was what drew everyone's immediate attention.

It was a duelling scar "Ernst Kaltenbrunner" would have been proud of. But Barry Saunders didn't see it like that. To him it wasn't a badge of honour or a "Mensur scar". It was a constant reminder of events that had taken place during his school days; an outstanding invoice that would one day have to be paid.

The day of release had finally arrived. Prisoner 'Saunders. B. 6931008' had been incarcerated for the last sixteen years. At last, he was going to be thrown back into society, having been deemed no longer a threat to the public.

After leaving school, or rather having been expelled from school, at the age of sixteen,

Saunders had been arrested and convicted for a number of shoplifting offences. He had also been charged with numerous counts of breaking and entering. He had spent most of the next eight years, in and out of young offender's institutions and prison. At the age of twenty-four he had been released after serving eighteen months for burglary. He was back on the streets. Shortly after gaining his freedom, he met a girl called Gina and moved in with her. It was a relationship built on mutual need. Unfortunately, neither of them had anything to give. They lived, (or took shelter) in a disused office block in Deptford, with half a dozen other homeless waifs. She was unemployed and relied on begging and hand-outs. She also performed sexual favours for anyone who would part with their cash. A blow job, a hand job, or a quick shag, normally in a dingy back alley or a pub toilet, if it was raining; *anything for a quick buck!* He had no trade, experience or qualifications and with his criminal record hanging like a millstone around his neck, found it impossible to find a job. So, it didn't take him long to revert to a life of crime. It was all he knew. Once again, he began visiting people's houses in the middle of the night, without an invitation. The small pickings he managed to purloin were never going to make them rich. The money he made from the stolen items put food on their table and ensured Gina didn't have to sell herself to the local drunks. It also just about kept him in whiskey and cigarettes and helped sustain Gina's increasing addiction to hard drugs. Their lives were going nowhere and Saunders was ready to cut and run and start afresh somewhere new. Then Gina announced she was pregnant. They couldn't afford another mouth to feed and neither of them wanted the responsibility of a child. They tried everything to get a termination, but it was too late. Gina went full term and Saunders stayed with her; probably the most noble thing he would do in his entire life. Their son was born the following year. With an ever-increasing need for money, Saunders was forced to become more active. He became involved in bigger crimes, yielding bigger pay days. He was mixing with serious villains. Along with three other hardened criminals, a plan was hatched to rob a security van. It was hoped the four participants would each net a six-figure sum. They were all armed with sawn off shotguns and all wore balaclavas. Their plans had been meticulous and precise. Rehearsed over and over again, down to the last detail; with split second timing. They were confident everything would go off without a hitch. But someone had informed on them. There had been a tipoff. The Police and the Flying Squad were there waiting for them. In the heat of the moment, amidst all the shouting, screaming and confusion, one of the shotguns had been discharged and a man fell to the floor, dead. Within seconds, one of Saunders' accomplices, the man who had fired the shotgun, lay dead as well; dispatched by a police sharpshooter. The scheme that had been months in the planning, was all over in less than a minute. Saunders and his two remaining companions dropped their weapons and lay face down on the tarmac. They were all sentenced to twenty years. Parole for Saunders had come after sixteen of the twenty years. It was felt he had paid his debt to society, (a view not shared by the wife of the dead security guard) and he now posed no threat to the general public.

Saunders had played the game. He had pretended to be remorseful about his past and repentant for all his wrong and evil actions. He was a changed man and wanted to prove to society that he was fit to be part of it; but it was just an act. He was a bitter man. Furious that someone had informed on them and denied him his big payday. Whoever it was, had taken away sixteen years of his life. He was entering back into society, but not to embrace or enrich it. He was going to make it pay, for everything he had suffered over those years.

Saunders had been genuinely heartbroken when he was told, three years into his stretch, that Gina had died. Up until then she had been the only person to whom he felt, what he supposed, was love. Now he was looking forward to spending some time with his son. He had barely seen him at all, apart from the odd supervised visit.

They had spoken on the phone, when the idea had been mooted that they might live together. It was an idea both were keen to try. Neither of them had any real family apart from each other. There was a lot of catching up to do. Jayden was now nearly seventeen-years-old. He had told his father of his plans to be a footballer. He had great ambitions and even greater confidence he would be a huge success in the professional game.

At 7:30 am that morning the double-locked cell doors clicked open. The wing officer stood in the doorway. He was a huge man, blocking out most of the light from outside. The massive, silhouetted figure spoke.

'Collect your things Saunders and follow me.'

Saunders dutifully did as he was told and with no back chat or intimidation, which was a rarity for him. It had been one of the few daily pleasures available to him during his time inside. Throwing abuse at the screws or anyone else in authority was what had kept him going through all those long years. In the early days he would take a swing at them, if he got close enough, but today wasn't the time. He marched between the two officers and was taken to the reception area. After filling in numerous forms and signing for his belongings he was led away and strip searched. The final indignity he would have to suffer. He knew the screws were taking great delight in this last opportunity to demean him. They were far from gentle. He bit his lip, determined not to show any pain or weakness. One last debasement at the hands of these *officers* and he would be free. The officers smirked at him as they removed their blue latex gloves. He stood before them naked, but defiant.

'Put your clothes on Saunders.' He put on the civilian clothes he had been given.

'Maybe I will bump into you two clowns on the outside. Then we might have even more fun,' he said with a sinister growl.

The officers ignored him and marched him to a holding cell. He waited there for what seemed like hours, convinced they were keeping him there for no other reason than being bloody minded. Finally, the doors opened and he knew his sixteen year wait was about to end. He was led to the main gate. With no fanfares, handshakes, or fond farewells, he was ushered through the doorway. He stepped into the real world. As he gazed up into the cloudless, blue sky, he heard the door slam behind him. He didn't even look round. He had stepped into a different dimension. The sky looked bluer, the breeze felt more refreshing on his face and the sun was warmer; there was colour all around. Cars, buses, buildings, advertising hoardings, everywhere he looked he could see an abundance of reds, blues, greens, and yellows. For the previous sixteen years, all he had known was grey and black. He could hear the birds singing in the trees. He looked up and down the busy main road and saw life carrying on as usual. The world hadn't noticed his absence and it was blissfully unaware of his return. As he took in the wonderful scenery, he raised his left hand and gently stroked the raised scar tissue that weaved its way around the outside of his left eye. Even after twenty-seven years it was still tender to the touch.

'Dad! Dad!' He heard a voice calling from the other side of the road. It was Jayden, his son. Jayden jogged over to his estranged father and they shook hands. After a couple of seconds, they embraced.

'Hello son. It's good to see you.'

They stared into one another's eyes with a mixture of hope, expectation and curiosity. They knew almost nothing about each other but were about to embark on an adventure together. An adventure that demanded trust and understanding, tolerance and sensitivity; all attributes that, until then, were alien to them both.

The first thing on the wish list was a pint of beer and a whiskey. Saunders had been given a little money from the 'Prison Discharge Grant' and he knew what he was going to spend it on first. They walked to the bus stop.

'By the time we get back to Peckham, they will be open. We can get a drink then.'

Jayden sat and watched his father down four pints and four large whiskeys in less than an hour. Between the gulps and the slurps of alcohol, Jayden told his father about the deal he had signed and the riches he would earn as a professional footballer. He explained he was on trial until the end of the season, but after that, the world would be his. Money, fame, everything he had ever dreamt of. On the wages he expected to be earning in the next couple of years, they would both be sitting pretty. Jayden told his Dad he wanted him to share in it all. Together they would be fine. They would both start afresh. Saunders sat and listened as the young boy excitedly described his vision of *their future*. It was a future Saunders would be very happy to be a part of. The boy was a cocky little bastard. But he was *his* cocky little bastard. He could see a lot of himself in Jayden. He listened to all of his great plans, nodding in agreement, while all the time gently stroking the scar around his left eye with his index finger.

Chapter 10

Two bottles of McCallan's whiskey

'Hi Doug. It's me, George. I just wanted to thank you for putting me in touch with the Saunders boy. I watched him play as you suggested, a couple of weeks ago and we have signed him up on a short-term contract until the end of the season. Hopefully, after that, we will secure his talents for the long term. You were right about his attitude though. Fiery little thing. A real rough diamond. He has already ruffled a few feathers at the club. His father was recently released from prison and they have moved in together, so I'm hoping that will calm him down a bit. How are you feeling?'

Doug answered in a frail and croaky voice. He was okay. Every day was much the same as the day before and probably the same as the day to come.

'Doug I'm pretty snowed under for the next couple of days, but what would you say to me coming over one night later this week with a bottle of that McCallan's whiskey you like? We could have a good old chat. Compare notes. You can tell me where I'm going wrong in the managerial world.'

'You seem to be doing pretty well at the moment my boy,' he chuckled. It was good to hear some humour in his voice. 'That would be lovely George, but only if you've got the time. I know you're a very busy man.'

On the Thursday morning, George arrived at work carrying two bottles of whiskey in his hand.

'Oh dear, has the stress got that bad?' said Brenda, watching him walk from the top of the stairs over to his office. 'Does this mean you won't want a cup of tea this morning?' She smiled at him. "Bubbly Brenda" had been turning up to work for the last couple of weeks. The subject of Jeremy and her bruised face hadn't been mentioned again. George was relieved to see she had been right, when she told him these incidents happened once in a blue moon, but even so, he still berated himself for being satisfied that Jeremy had only lashed out once. Once was still one time too many, but he didn't want to disturb the status quo. As long as his perky, happy PA showed up each morning, that was fine.

'I bought them for Doug. I'm going over to see him tonight. Today would have been his and Mavis' Golden wedding anniversary. I've spoken to Lisa and she is going to see him this morning, but he will be on his own after that. I thought these,' he waved the whiskey bottles about, 'mixed with a few old memories, would make him feel a little more cheerful. I'm going to leave my car here and probably end up staying at the flat. We will demolish the first bottle and then he can drink the second one at his leisure. I spoke to him earlier in the week. He sounded a bit down.'

'Ahh that's nice. I wish I could come with you, but I suspect you boys will be talking nothing but football.'

'You're very welcome to come.' George said enthusiastically. 'I'm sure Doug would love to see you again. Probably prefer to see your lovely face than my ugly mug. I can drop you back home on the way to the flat later. You can……'

Brenda cut him off, suddenly worried that George was being serious.

'It would be nice, but I do have to get home tonight. I promised Jeremy. Maybe some other time. Give him my love though, won't you?'

Brenda was never available to have a drink, or a chat, after work. She always had to get home. But, if she was that eager to get back to Jeremy, presumably things at home couldn't be that bad. If it meant the happy, smiling Brenda he had once again become accustomed to, kept turning up for work, he could forgo the odd drink after work.

Just after midday, all the smiles and happiness, that had been in abundance first thing in the morning, disappeared. Brenda came into George's office, almost staggering, unsteady on her feet and using the door for support. Tears were streaming from her eyes. Her panda face was back. She looked like she was going to collapse at any moment. George frowned and stood up.

'Whatever is it matter Brenda?' She tried to compose herself as best she could. George walked around his desk and stood before her holding her by the shoulders. She managed to splutter out only a few words.

'I've just had a phone call from Lisa Fenner, Doug's daughter. Doug passed away during the night.'

A tidal wave of emotion poured down her cheeks again and she fell into George's arms. He held her tightly, but felt his body go weak under the impact of the news. Instantly, George felt his own tears slide down his face. Without saying a word, they both gave in to their grief and unashamedly cried their eyes out on each other's shoulders. After a few minutes they sat down on the sofa and tried to come to terms with the devastating news.

'Apparently, he passed away quietly and peacefully,' Brenda said. 'He had spoken to Lisa last night. He told her how excited he was that you were coming over to see him. She said he sounded happier than she had heard him for a long time. Lisa went to see him this morning, as she usually did, but he was still in bed. She said he had a calm look on his face. The doctor said he had almost certainly slipped away while he'd been sleeping.' Brenda unleashed another wave of tears. 'Oh George. He was such a lovely man. I'm going to miss him so much.'

'We're all going to miss him,' George stammered as he too, released another flood of emotion.

Chapter 11

The Funeral

It was the last week in March and mercifully, on that Monday morning, the sun was shining. It was the day George had been dreading, ever since Brenda had taken that phone call from Lisa. Doug's funeral.

As they waited patiently outside the church, George watched as the number of mourners steadily grew. There were so many faces he recognised, from both the past and the present. Debbie was with him. His brother Graham and Kerry his husband were there, having delayed their departure to the Maldives to be in attendance. Their mum and dad, John and Paula, were there as well. Doug really had been part of their family. There were so many famous faces from Doug's past. Players, managers, backroom staff, officials and friends he had worked with over the last sixty- five years or so. All around him old acquaintances were being renewed. He saw Barry Allder in deep conversation with Pascal, Igor, Terry and Casey. They had all made the journey, to say farewell to a dearly beloved friend. Pascal had flown in from Nice and Casey had come all the way from LA. Doug had meant so much to so many people and had been an inspiration to them all.

As they began to walk inside, George saw a car speed into the car park. The violent, ear-splitting sound of screeching rubber cut through the tranquil and peaceful atmosphere created by the birdsong and the warming spring sunshine. It was Brenda and Jeremy. They had only just made it in time.

During the service, George couldn't help looking over at Brenda and Jeremy. He was intrigued to see what he looked like. Each time, George saw them sitting close to one another holding hands. They looked like any other loving couple. On the odd occasion, he noticed Brenda glance over at him. They exchanged sad, but reassuring smiles with each other. He sat there wondering if he had made a mountain out of a molehill in Jeremy's case. Had he condemned the poor man, in his own mind, without really knowing all of the facts. He took a close look at Jeremy. He was tall and athletically built, but he looked innocent and harmless. Brenda had told George that he was two years younger than her, which would make him 33 years old. George thought he looked younger. He could almost have passed for her teenage son. Maybe Jeremy wasn't as evil as he had first thought. Maybe he should give him another chance. But he could still vividly remember the bruising to Brenda's cheek and how she had sobbed uncontrollably in his arms. Accident or not, provoked or otherwise, no one should do that to someone they love. Another glare and George found himself disliking Jeremy even more than he had to begin with.

From the lectern at the front, George read an emotional eulogy. There were many stories that brought laughter and happiness to the congregation, briefly easing the sadness away and there were other stories that produced tears. George struggled to read out some of the passages he had written and had to pause on numerous occasions to gather himself. He had always thought of Doug as a surrogate father. He now knew he wasn't the only one to think of him in that way. That dear old man had touched so many lives and meant so much, to so many people.

Scanning the sea of faces watching him, he saw Brenda and Jeremy. She was openly weeping, clutching a white handkerchief to her face and holding tightly on to her husband's arm. George was slightly angered by Jeremy's manner. He should have been comforting his wife, holding her and reassuring her, but he sat there like a granite statue. Cold and unmoving and looking like he just didn't want to be there. He stared straight at George, without any expression on his face, showing no sympathy for his wife and no empathy for the occasion. George held his gaze for a second before moving on with his speech. He really didn't like him.

A local rugby club had been hired for the wake. Security was very tight. With all of the 'A' listers on show, there was a concern about gatecrashers and unwanted press men. The burly band of doormen had been instructed to let no one in, unless their name was on the list and they had an order of service.

George did his best to speak with as many old friends as he could. A small reunion of the 'Barcelona boys' drifted together. Terry, Casey, Barry, Pascal, Igor, George and Graham all reminisced about Doug and what that famous night in Spain had meant to him. George repeated the conversation he had had with Doug when he visited him for the last time.

'He said, "I think that was the happiest moment I ever had in football".' The rest of them chipped in with some of their recollection of that famous night. Terry recalling how he almost had to order George to take the defining penalty. Graham suddenly blurted out, 'I remember you taking your teeth out and putting them in your locker, then waggling your tongue through the gap like a Maori warrior doing the Hakka,' looking directly at Terry. There was a moment of deafening silence as five pairs of eyes all looked at him beneath puzzled frowns. George's eyes were wide and desperate.

'*You* remember that?' Terry said, now looking totally baffled. 'You weren't even there!' 'Unless it was you playing that night, instead of your brother'

Casey added with a smile. There was a collective laugh, but Graham felt his face start to burn and his heart start to pound. That unique feeling of nausea he had experienced, on numerous occasions, while pretending to be his brother, in Barcelona twelve years earlier, immediately engulfed him.

'Well,' he stuttered, 'I remember George telling me about it when he got home.' He turned to look at George hoping for some backup. 'You said it was the only splash of humour, in an otherwise tense dressing room. Don't you remember George?' Amazingly that explanation seemed to satisfy everyone, but it was a very awkward moment for both of the brothers. More stories about Doug came to the rescue and diverted attention away from Graham's slip up.

George spent some time talking with Doug's family. Lisa told him that Doug had always considered George "the son he never had". She told him how much her father had loved him and how he always referred to him as *"My Boy George"*. He loved listening to those stories, but they did manage to force more tears from his already overworked eyes.

Glancing over to his right, George saw Debbie talking to Brenda and Jeremy. He excused himself and wandered over.

'George,' said Brenda, 'this is Jeremy.' Jeremy held out his hand and George shook it. His grip was firm, but it was cold, almost clammy. It felt like

George was holding a wet fish. As soon as the handshake was over, George instantly felt the need to wipe his hand on his trousers, or his jacket, anything, but he resisted the urge. Debbie threaded her arm around George's waist.

'Jeremy was just saying that he is more of a rugby man.' Jeremy jumped straight in.

'Oh yes. Proper game, for proper men. None of this rolling around, pretending to be injured. Lying there like you have broken every bone in your body and screaming for your Mamma, only to jump up seconds later as if nothing has happened. Seems to me that all these overpaid footballers are better at playacting than actually kicking a ball. Give me rugby any day,' he said pushing back his shoulders and sticking out his chest. George smiled. There really was nothing to like about this man.

'Maybe you could come along and watch a game at our place,' George suggested. 'We would make you very welcome and you would have the best seats in the house. You never know, we might even be able to change your lowly opinion of us all.' Jeremy let out a condescending sneer.

'I don't think so. Watching a bunch of mummies' boys, spending most of their efforts on cheating and trying to con the referee. No thanks. I think I'll stick with rugby.'

There was an awkwardness that hung in the air. Uncomfortable looks shot between Debbie, George and Brenda. Jeremy appeared oblivious to the atmosphere his rambunctious comments had created. The conversation was taken up again by Jeremy. He blustered on, mostly talking about himself. He had an opinion on just about everything, which he was glad to share with anyone who wanted to listen. George, Debbie and Brenda seemed content to let him waffle on. George suspected that any interruption, from any of them, would be talked over and dismissed straight away. Speaking about how he had met Brenda, and their life together, George couldn't help but feel he was putting her down at every opportunity, even belittling her. On more than one occasion, George looked at Debbie, whose face was betraying a growing anger and dislike. George squeezed her hand to signal agreement, but they stayed silent, for Brenda's sake. Jeremy continued to refer to Brenda as "the little woman" and patted her repeatedly on the head, like she was a pet dog. George hated him more with every second. The way he spoke, suggested everything Brenda did, needed his approval or permission. He seemed eager to impress on them, that he was the one who made all the decisions. He was in charge.

'I keep telling her to give up her little job. It's not like we need the money. I suppose it keeps her amused though and gives her something to do.' He looked at her in the most patronising way and pinched her cheek. George squeezed Debbie's hand again.

'I will let her carry on for a while, but I think the time is coming when she will need to concentrate all her efforts into becoming a proper little housewife,' he said looking down at her and again patting her on the head. George had never heard such condescending, supercilious crap. He looked at Brenda amazed. She timidly smiled back at him, with nervous eyes that begged him not to say anything.

'Well, don't become a housewife too soon,' said George, trying to lighten the mood. 'I don't know what I would do without you Brenda.' She looked like she wanted to say something, but she kept quiet and just smiled at him.

On the drive home, George and Debbie talked about the day's events. The sadness and the celebration. Seeing so many old friends and realising just how special Doug had been to so many people. George told her about Graham's "Barcelona blunder" and how his blood had run cold in his veins. But mostly they spoke about Jeremy. He hadn't made a very good impression on either of them.

'He has got to be the most stuck up, rude, arrogant, nasty arsehole, I have ever met,' said Debbie. 'I think Brenda has got her work cut out with that prick. It's such a shame. She is such a sweet girl and he is such a twat.' George nodded in agreement.

As soon as they arrived home, Debbie started to pack the last few items into their suitcases. The following morning, she and the kids would be going away on holiday for three weeks, visiting her parents in Mallorca. They would be away for the Easter holidays. Every moment they were apart was tough, but it would be the ideal opportunity for Matthew and Emily to see their grandparents. It would also give George the time and space he needed, to concentrate on what was, one of the busiest periods of the season. They had also decided to use that time to have their entire house redecorated and a new bathroom fitted. The work was due to start at 8.30am the following morning. The decorators and builders who would be doing the work had assured them it would all be finished by the time Debbie and the kids returned, but for nearly three weeks the place was going to resemble a building site. George had already packed what he needed for the next three weeks. He would be living in his riverside apartment on the South bank of the Thames, giving Mr Bell and his lads a free reign.

Chapter 12

The return of Mr Hyde

The journey home from the funeral, in Jeremy's car, was frosty to say the least. He had a face like thunder. His eyes were fixed on the road ahead, beneath a stern frown. The hour drive had been completed largely in silence. Brenda already knew what the problem was. She had tried to throw in a couple of comments about the lovely food at the wake, even the hymns at the service, just to disturb the stillness and tension in the air, but Jeremy didn't respond. He remained tight lipped, staring intensely through the windscreen and showing no emotion or desire to communicate. She didn't want to say anything that might start him off, or fan the flames of his brooding fury, while he was driving, but as soon as they got home, it started in earnest. He immediately flew into a rage, slamming the front door shut and hurling the car keys to the floor. He questioned her about every man she had spoken to that day. He demanded to know who each of them were and what sort of relationship she had had with them. How many of them had she slept with and what had they done? He wanted to know every sordid detail and continually berated her for being so friendly with them all.

'Can't you see that all you were doing was flirting with them, like some cheap whore?' he shouted directly into her face. 'And in front of me. How do you think that made me feel?'

She tried to remain calm, breathing in deep breaths and letting them out slowly and rhythmically, but she was scared. She could feel the fear rising in her. He was going through the gears and soon he would lose all control. That's what she dreaded most. She had learned to absorb all of the verbal abuse and deal with it in her own way, but it was the physical abuse she was finding harder and harder to cope with. She tried to explain to him that she hadn't had any sort of relationship with any of them, apart from friendship. All she had been doing, was catching up with some old friends.

'Just as you would have done in the same situation,' she told him. But Jeremy wasn't listening.

'And what about that George Miller? He's the one you work for, isn't he? He should buy himself some new cologne. That shit he was wearing smelt cheap and nasty. It suited him. I could see the way he looked at you. Even in the Chapel, while he was reading that Godawful eulogy. He couldn't take his eyes off of you. I saw him smiling at you *and* you smiling back. So, what's going on between you two?' he asked accusingly, again shouting directly into her face.

'Nothing I swear. He is my boss and an old friend. That's all. Anyway, you met Debbie, his wife. She is lovely. What would he want with me, or any other woman for that matter, when he has such an adorable wife?' Brenda was desperately trying to diffuse the situation, but already feared it was now too late to stop the inevitable explosion of his wrath. Even her soft, self-deprecating words of reason, appeared to drive him even deeper into his rage.

'Men like that will take exactly what they want, when they want. I know his type. Arrogant and superior. They think all they have to do is click their fingers and every woman will come running. And you! You are so simple and gullible, I bet you'd be running the fastest. I wouldn't be surprised if he is having numerous affairs, as well as the one he's having with you. *The bastard.*'

Brenda's tolerance suddenly snapped. Her desperate attempts to steer the conversation away from anything that might enrage Jeremy even more were forgotten. She could listen to his tirade no longer. She punched him on the arm with all of her strength.

'No, he isn't!' she screamed back at him, her anger fuelling her bravery. 'George Miller is a good, decent, honest and charming man who ...'

Before she could finish, Jeremy spun around and grabbed her by the throat, pushing her up against the kitchen wall. Her valiant counterattack was over. She could hardly breath, let alone talk. It had started.

'Don't you ever hit me like that again, you fucking bitch,' he growled. 'And how do you know so much about him then?'

His grip around her throat was getting tighter, as his anger increased. Her face had gone bright red. She could feel the spray of his spital on her face. She was standing on her tip toes, as he forced her higher and higher up the wall.

'So, you think your Mr Wonderful is perfect. Well, maybe we'll see what his wife thinks about it when I tell her that you and he are at it, all day, every day, in the office.' Brenda had started to feel faint and was turning blue. Jeremy released his grip on her and watched as she slid slowly down the wall and crumbled into a heap on the kitchen floor, coughing and spluttering. She sucked in as much air as she could and softly massage her bruised neck.

'You haven't heard the last of this, I can tell you that,' he shouted. He glared down at her, waiting for any response, but all he heard was the pathetic sound of his wife whimpering at his feet, still gasping for breath. Petulantly, he kicked her leg, just for good measure, then stormed out of the house, again slamming the front door behind him. The noise echoed around the house like a gunshot. She heard his car start up and drive away. It had been the first explosion for a few weeks, but it all seemed horribly familiar. She sat on the kitchen floor, put her head in her hands and wept.

After sitting on the floor for what seemed a lifetime, she tentatively got to her feet. She shakily opened a bottle of red wine and tried to calm herself down. Sitting at the kitchen table, with a blank look on her face, she tried to make some sense of her life. Raising the glass to her mouth she realised how much she was trembling. She had to hold onto it with both hands to stop it spilling. She sipped her wine, but it was painful to swallow. An hour later, she was still shivering and quaking from the shock. By 10 o'clock, Jeremy still hadn't returned. She wasn't worried or concerned for him. She wouldn't have minded if he hadn't come home at all. *EVER AGAIN!* She briefly considered double locking and chaining the front door, but she knew that would only start the process up all over again when he did return. She took herself off to bed and hoped that would be the last of it. When he did eventually get home, hopefully he would have calmed down and started to feel remorse for what he had said and done. It was always the same. A contrast in his character and emotions that never ceased to amaze her. She really was living with both Doctor Jekyll and Mr Hyde. She crawled into bed and turned off the light.

She was awoken by the sound of his key in the front door. A shiver went down her spine. She wondered if she had done the right thing, leaving the door unbolted. She looked at her watch. It was just after midnight. He had been out for several hours and had almost certainly been drinking. There were a few noises from downstairs. The clink of glasses and the opening and shutting of cupboard doors. Then she heard the sound of footsteps on the stairs. She closed her eyes again and pretended to be asleep. She lay as still as her beating heart would allow. She didn't want to endure anymore of his accusations and certainly didn't want to listen to any of his apologies. She just wanted to sleep.

She heard the sound of the bedroom door opening, sliding across the carpet with a swoosh. She felt a bump on the bed as he sat down and removed his shoes. She heard the unbuckling of his belt and imagined the process of his undressing. He brushed his teeth in the en-suite. The light clicked off and darkness returned. Brenda lay as still and as quiet as she could, straining her ears to give her a clue as to his whereabouts and what he was doing. His footsteps sounded on the carpet. He was walking around the room. She could feel her breathing becoming heavier and her heart beating fast and loud. She had been through this so many times. Sometimes he would just get into bed and fall asleep, but other times he felt the need to carry on the argument, or worse still try and apologise. She despised his contrition knowing how temporary and how meaningless it was.

Again, the soft sound of his feet on the carpet filled the room. A creak from one of the floorboards screeched out, like an early warning siren. He had walked around the bed and was now on her side of the room. She could sense his presence. She could even hear him breathing. She was frozen in the moment, like a small mouse, waiting to be pounced on by a predator. She felt her eyebrows begin to involuntarily furrow and her eyes twitch. She had no control over her tics and spasms. She desperately wanted to open her eyes and see where he was and what he was doing, but sheer panic kept them shut tight. Everything was still and quiet again. There was no sound or movement. She could feel her body shivering. She suddenly needed a pee. The soft touch of his hand on her cheek made her jump and she felt herself gasp, but she continued to feign sleep.

'Wake up baby. It's me.' She heard him whisper. She concentrated with all her might, trying to lie as still as she could. She prayed he would leave her alone and go to sleep, but the soft hand became a little rougher. He pinched the flesh on her cheek and pulled at it. No one would be able to sleep through that. It hurt. Brenda slowly opened her eyes. The ambient light creeping around the curtains from the full moon, was just enough for her to see what was in front of her. To her horror, the first thing she saw was his erection, pointing straight at her, only inches from her face. Jeremy was gently playing with himself.

'Wake up baby. It's time to wake up and make up. Look what I've got for you.' He shuffled forwards, pushing his penis nearer to her face. She tried to pull away, but his hand was holding her head still.

'Not now Jeremy. I'm tired,' she pleaded, but he wasn't listening to her. Her feelings meant nothing to him. He moved his hand from behind her head down onto her jaw, pulling her mouth open. As the look of horror once again pervaded Brenda's face, he forced himself between her lips. She lay there, still and emotionless, as he repeatedly slipped himself in and out.

'Oh yeah. Oh, that's nice baby. Come on, join in. Don't let me have all the fun.' He peeled the duvet off of her, exposing her trembling body. He picked up her right hand and placed it on his shaft, helping her move it, up and down. 'Join in my love. It's no fun with just one.' Brenda did as she was told. She knew the consequences of disobedience. He forced himself deeper and deeper into her mouth, making her gag.

'Come on my darling, you can do better than that, I know you can. Open wide.'

Brenda had started to shut herself down. That magical ability she had perfected. Her body was there, being abused, but her mind and soul were slowly drifting away to some far-off place. She knew through experience, the best thing to do was just give in to him. Let him do what he wanted. If she were to put up a fight, or show any sort of struggle, the horror would just last even longer and she would have a few more bruises to explain the next day. Her body went limp. Soon it would be over. She felt the first of many tears fill her eyes, then trickle down her face.

'It's always good to make up before we go to sleep, don't you think? And you are so good at this.'

Brenda glanced up at her husband, towering over her with what looked like a snarl on his face, as he continued to pleasure himself in her mouth. Brenda did everything she could to hurry things along. The sooner he finished, the sooner she would be able to escape, back to the haven of sleep. Finally, he withdrew himself from her face, clambered on top of her and forced her himself inside her. There was no love, no passion, nothing erotic or thrilling. Just a selfish, domineering brutality. He pumped and pumped until she felt his body tense and his ejaculation squirt into her. She felt his hands, squeezing her buttocks until they hurt. Gripping and pulling her apart. Once he had finished, he rolled off of her and laid on his side of the bed.

'There now, wasn't that nice? Remember what my mum always says, *"never go to sleep on an argument".*'

Brenda said nothing. She couldn't even bring herself to look at him. She just lay there staring blankly at the ceiling. Her throat was throbbing, from both the strangulation and the penetration. She felt the damp evidence of Jeremy's pleasure slowly seep out from between her legs.

'Goodnight my darling. See you in the morning. Sleep tight.' Brenda closed her eyes, and rolled over, turning her back towards him. Surely it wasn't meant to be like this.

Chapter 13

The calm after the storm

The morning after Doug's funeral George said a sad goodbye to Debbie and the kids. They would be gone for nearly three weeks. It would be the longest they had been apart since they were reunited twelve years ago. They both knew it would be tough, but they both knew it was for the best. Once he had waved them all goodbye, he jumped into his car and headed into London. He was looking forward to getting back to normality and the task of running the football club, with the smiley, happy Brenda by his side.

He left James Bell and his team of decorators and builders laying dust sheets over floors and furniture alike. The skips had turned up and the business at hand had started in earnest. George would be staying at the flat until the work had been completed. Although he would miss his family, there was a part of him that was looking forward to spending some time back in his old "bachelor pad". He had so many great memories of his time there *and* it was only a twenty-minute drive to the club from the Embankment. It would save him the two-hour journey, there and back, he endured every day on the A40.

George took the stairs to the second floor, almost running up them two at a time and bounded into the lounge. It was a bright, sunny and uplifting morning. The arrival of spring and the warm breeze, wafting through the open windows, had given the day some colour and a freshness that made it feel good to be alive.

His first appointment of the day was with Jayden Saunders. George wanted to talk to him about his attitude and his behaviour. He needed to explain to him that having made the leap from non-league football, where he was outstanding, to the professional game, he would have to prove himself all over again. The step up in quality and the need to constantly push yourself to become better every day, was a whole new world to the one he had been used to. The speech he had listened to from his father and Doug on so many occasions, about talent not being enough, came to mind. He had heard that speech when he was a young tearaway who thought everything was going to come easy. Two older and wiser heads had tried to steer him onto the path of hard work, dedication and respect. It had worked with him, but now *he* was the old, wise head. He hoped he would be as successful with Jayden as they had been with him.

George was also keen to talk to the boy about his father. To see how they were getting on with each other and how they were settling into their new home together. He was eager to meet his father. Just out of prison, Jayden's dad was about to start a whole new chapter in his life. A fresh start. Jayden had been given a similar chance by George, to prove himself in the top league and hopefully begin a career that would blossom and develop into a huge success that would benefit both of them. Both Saunders Snr and Jnr would hopefully grasp their new-found opportunities and find that both of their lives would be heading in the right direction. George wanted to do as much as he could to help them both.

George noticed that Brenda's office door was once again closed. He shouted out,

'Good morning Brenda. It certainly is a lovely day.' He skipped into his office and put his bag and his laptop on the desk. He had heard no reply from the other office. Maybe she was on the phone. He decided to make some tea. He would see if Brenda wanted one. He knocked on her door and opened it slowly. She was on the phone. He listened for a few seconds to her beautifully clipped, but slightly croaky, voice. Sometimes she even sounded posh. She glanced up at him.

'Tea?' he mouthed. She nodded her head. George made the tea.

'In here!' he shouted as he walked past Brenda's office.

Two minutes later Brenda came in to get her drink. Immediately, George could sense her mood had changed. Her increasingly chirpy and flirty demeanour had vanished. She looked tired again. Her shoulders were slumped and her back was a little stooped. He wondered if it was a hangover from Doug's funeral. It had been a very emotional and somewhat draining day.

Brenda was wearing a thick, white, woollen polo neck sweater. It looked far too heavy and hot for the day's weather.

'Thank you, George' she said picking up the mug. 'You've got Jayden Saunders coming in to see you first thing. He should be here any moment. I will send him in as soon as he arrives.' Her voice was flat and husky, devoid of any sparkle. It was information not conversation.

'Okay thank you.' Brenda turned and began to walk towards the door.

'Brenda are you okay? You seem a little down again today. Is everything alright?' Brenda stood still, with her back towards him. He waited for her to turn around and answer him, but she remained stationary and silent. She began to tremble and her head bowed. He saw her shoulders twitch and heard the sound of sobbing. His heart sank; he knew what was coming next. George stood up and walked towards her.

'Brenda, what's the matter?' He turned her around to face him. Yet again he saw the moisture in her eyes. He took her mug of tea and placed it on his desk. Without saying a word, she turned her head into his chest and threw her arms around him. He pulled her into him and held her tight.

'What is it? Is it Jeremy again?' Brenda's head was nuzzled deep into George's chest. She had never felt so comfortable, or safe, in her life.

'I just don't know what to do for the best' she sobbed. 'It's like living in a nightmare. I never know when he will explode. I knew something was wrong when we were driving home yesterday after the funeral. He was silent and moody; a sure-fire indication that things are about to get a lot worse. When we arrived home, he flew into a rage, accusing me of flirting with all the men, like some cheap whore. I tried to explain to him that they were all just good friends, but he wouldn't listen to reason.' She shook her head in dismay and disbelief. 'Before we got married, he had always been a bit inquisitive about my past, but I thought he was just showing an interest. Since we have been married, he questions me about everyone I know and everyone I have ever known. My past boyfriends and people I work with. He is suspicious of them all. He even told me to stop flirting with the paperboy and he is only fourteen for God's sake! He assumes I'm having it off with all and sundry. It's just never ending. The more I try to explain to him that he has nothing to worry about, the more he thinks I am keeping stuff from him. And it feels like it's getting worse. He checks my mobile phone to see if there are any messages, to or from other men. If I get any post, he always opens it, in case it's a love letter from one of my many admirers. *As if!* In company he is charming and polite.' George's eyes widened. He hadn't noticed! 'I know he seems to derive a certain pleasure in putting me down in front of people, but I think that's mostly because he is a little shy and nervous around strangers.' Again, George looked baffled. Were they really talking about the same cocky, brash, arrogant, arsehole he had met at Doug's funeral? 'He tells me I'm not the brightest when it comes to intelligence and he regularly makes fun of both my height and my weight. It feels like I have everything wrong with me. If ever I dare engage another man in conversation, he thinks we are having an affair, or at least planning one. He is paranoid that I am mocking him all the time, laughing at him behind his back with my numerous lovers. I have to constantly think twice about what I tell him, where I have been, who I have seen and what I have done. Every evening he asks me about my day, but it's not because he is interested in what I might have achieved or accomplished. It's to find out what I have been getting up to with you or the many other suspects he thinks I am shagging. It's like permanently being on trial; under constant cross examination. Probing for any anomalies in my stories and pouncing on them triumphantly, as if he has just uncovered a vital piece of evidence that proves his warped mind right.' She let out a big sigh. 'It's so unfair. I see happiness in so many people's lives; but there is none in mine. What am I going to do? What am I doing wrong?'

George held on to her stroking the back of her head. He felt the sympathy and the fury rising again, in equal amounts.

'Nothing. You are doing nothing wrong. It's him. It's that bastard you are married to.' George found it impossible to hold back, or water down his thoughts on Jeremy. He didn't want to upset Brenda, or make her situation anymore awkward, but he knew he could no longer pretend to like, or even tolerate the man.

'Why don't I go and talk to him? This can't go on Brenda.' She pulled her head away from his chest and looked at him square in the eye. There was even the beginnings of a smile on her lips.

'Talk to him?' she asked. She squeezed his bicep. 'I don't think you mean talk, do you? Anyway, no thank you. I think that would be the worst thing you could do. He already has you down as lover number one. He has convinced himself that we have been at it for years.' Again,

she smiled. Just as her mouth was about to release the words, "I wish we had", she managed to stop herself. 'I'm going to sort it out. I don't quite know how, but I will think of something over the next couple of days. I have decided this nightmare has to stop. And it will.'

George was trying to calm himself down. As she looked up at him, George slowly placed his fingers on the polo neck of Brenda's winter jumper and began to ease it down over her neck. Instinctively, she grabbed his hand, in an effort to stop him, but after a second she relented and let him expose the purple and blue markings around her throat. The rage poured back into George's face again. He felt his eyes begin to fill with water as he looked at the brutality that had been inflicted on her. He could see the broken skin where Jeremy's fingernails had cut into her flesh. He moved his hand softly between the white wool jumper and the vibrant ghastly hues on her flesh, uncovering the full horror of what she had been trying to conceal. He looked at Brenda who had tears in her eyes. For reasons he could not explain, he bent his head and softly kissed the discoloured flesh at the base of her neck. He kissed her three times, quietly and slowly moving along the line of the carnage. Brenda's head fell to the side, revealing as much of herself as she could. She let out a whimper. 'Oh God' she whispered. It was the most tender, caring and sensuous contact she could ever remember. For a brief moment, her legs felt weak and her head felt dizzy. George pulled his head away and gently eased the jumper back into place. Again, their eyes locked together. There was a warmth and a love in George's eyes. A warmth and love she had never seen in Jeremy's. She pushed herself up on her tip toes, wrapped her arms around his neck and kissed him. It was but a brush of the lips to begin with. Then she pushed herself onto George's lips with a little more force. He was momentarily spellbound. He knew he should break away, but he couldn't. The kiss increased in intensity and vigour. It was the first time she had tasted George's lips on hers and it felt wonderful. Pushing her luck, she began to open her mouth and ready her tongue for a foray into George's mouth. His lips slowly started to part. He could feel the tip of Brenda's tongue as it gently brushed against his. He pulled her closer to him, almost lifting her off the floor and eased himself deeper into her mouth. He felt excitement and passion rampage through him, making every cell in his body tingle. He knew it was wrong, but he couldn't break away and Brenda was certainly not going to be the one to bring the embrace to an end. As their tongues danced a frenzied waltz with one another, he felt the euphoria give way to fear and guilt. *WHAT THE HELL WAS HE DOING?!!*

A loud coughing noise bought the passionate mouth play to an instant halt. Both Brenda and George snapped their heads towards the unexpected sound. Jayden was standing just inside the doorway with a huge smile on his face. He was pointing his mobile phone in their direction, presumably recording the amorous exchange. George wondered how long he had been standing there watching. What had he been witness to? George had been so lost in the moment with Brenda, he probably wouldn't have noticed if the entire squad had walked through the door.

'I'm sorry,' Jayden said, staring back at the horrified couple in front of him. 'It looks like I have interrupted something. Would you like me to come back another time George?' George and Brenda realised they were still in each other's arms. They relinquished their hold on one another and took a step backwards.

'I'm sure you two would rather carry on with whatever you were doing, than have to talk to me,' he said, with a widening smirk on his face. 'It all looked very cosy.' He patted his mobile phone and replaced it in his pocket. George was momentarily dazed and confused.

'Didn't anyone ever tell you to knock before entering a room?' George shouted, trying to stamp some kind of authority on the situation.

'The door was wide open,' Jayden said, almost apologetically. He turned his head and looked at the open door, as if to justify his intrusion. 'So, I just came in. I didn't want to disturb you as you looked like you were having such a lovely time. Anyway, I didn't think you would mind. I mean it's not like you have anything to hide is it? It all looked very innocent to me,' he said, patting the phone in his pocket again.

There was an uneasy feeling in the room. The three of them stood looking at each other; two frowning and one smiling. Brenda was the first to move.

'I will be in my office if you need anything else Mr. Miller,' she said, wiping the remaining tears from her face. She made her way out of the office, glaring at Jayden as she passed him.

'Sit down Jayden. I want to talk to you,' George ordered, pointing to one of the chairs in front of his desk. Before the boy had arrived, George had decided to go easy on him. Give him the benefit of the doubt and treat him with kid gloves. The arm around the shoulder approach that had worked so well with him when he was a teenager. But now George was furious. Any good will or leniency he felt earlier had vanished. He was angry with Jeremy for what he had done to his wife, cross with himself for kissing Brenda like that and livid with the boy, whose unnoticed presence had suddenly made him feel vulnerable and threatened in his own office.

'Okay George. What's on your mind?'

He sat down, leant back, crossed his legs and clasped his hands behind his head. George had never really been one for formality, but there was an unwritten rule that the manager, no matter how young or familiar with his players, had to be shown some respect. Even Barry Allder didn't call him George anymore.

'I would rather you not call me George. Mr. Miller, Boss, or even Gaffer, if you have to, just like the other players and staff.

'Okey-dokey George,' he replied. 'Sorry'…. 'Boss.'

George explained to him how he would have to learn to show everyone at the club a little more respect than he had managed up until that point.

'No one is above good manners and everyone deserves politeness and courtesy. I won't tolerate rudeness or impertinence from anyone do you understand? Remember you are here on trial. You can be moved on at any time. I will put you in the youth team if you don't buck your ideas up.'

'I'm too good for that and you know it George. I'm sure I will fit in, if everyone else makes the effort to fit in with me. I've got more talent in my little toe than most of the has-beens you've got here. A lot of them are old and well past their best. I am the future. You are lucky to have me.'

George was astounded by the boy's arrogance. He was rather lost for words.

'Anyway, I'm sure I will fit in. I mean it all seems very friendly around here.' Jayden looked over his shoulder in the direction of Brenda's office. She seems to be very accommodating, from what I've seen.' The smirk on Jayden's face got even bigger and he winked at George. 'How is your wife? She's gone away for a while, hasn't she?' He raised his eyebrows in a suggestive manner. 'Very nice too. How long is she away for? Does she know about...' Again, he glanced over his shoulder, in Brenda's direction. George was on the verge of losing his temper completely.

'Now look here. Firstly, my wife is no concern of yours. Secondly, I have got you here and given you a chance on the advice of an old friend, but I can put you right back where I found you and make sure that no one in their right mind will want to sign you into this league for a considerable time.' George leant forward and stared menacingly into the young lad's eyes. 'I will not have any disruptive influence at this club. I don't care how talented you are. If you don't fit in, you will be thrown out. Do you understand? Now get out of my office.'

Jayden showed no sign of fear at the angry threats. If anything, his smile became wider as George grew more venomous. He was the one remaining calm. He was the one in control of his emotions and both of them knew it. He slowly removed himself from the chair. He still had the same mocking smirk on his face as he did when he first arrived, savouring George's loss of composure.

'Okay George. You're the boss.' He saluted him, like a military cadet to an officer, smiled and swaggered towards the door.

'Do you want me to send her back in, or have you finished with her for now?

'Get out.'

As soon as he had gone, Brenda rushed in.

'I'm so sorry George, that was all my fault. I don't know what came over me. Do you think he will say anything to anyone?' George was still fuming at the impudence of the boy. He had already made up his mind that Jayden Saunders had no future at his club. He would spend the remainder of his short contract rotting in the youth team. George would have nothing more to do with him and would hopefully not have to see or talk to him again.

'We were doing nothing wrong, Brenda. Don't worry about it. I'm more worried about you and Jeremy.'

At that precise moment, that was a lie. His mind had already started to worry about the ramifications of what had just happened. If Jayden had recorded the entire incident, what would he do with the footage? Who would he show and where would the images end up? He thought of Debbie and his blood ran cold. How would she feel if she were to be exposed to the sight of her husband with his tongue in his secretary's mouth? The very same secretary she suspected was still in love with him. He took a deep breath and tried to re-focus. Brenda was staring at him with a worried look in her eyes. He managed an unconvincing, reassuring smile. 'Everything will be okay. I promise. Are you sure there is nothing I can do to help with Jeremy?'

'No. I feel better now that I have decided to do something about it. I can see the light at the end of the tunnel. I am certain I will be fine for the next couple of weeks. Once he has exploded, it takes him a few days to stop apologising and buying me gifts to absolve himself from any blame. This is what I always call 'The calm after the storm'.'

Chapter 14

Hot stuff, eh

George hadn't taken part in the training session that day. He had remained in his office doing his best to concentrate on football matters. He was failing. He was finding it impossible to wrestle his thoughts away from the calamity that had happened earlier that morning. The more he dwelt on it, the guiltier he felt; and the guiltier he became, the more panic and uncertainty began to engulf him.

Bob Hunter, George's right-hand man, had overseen the session. Bob had already been on the phone to George telling him what a pain in the arse Saunders had been. He had managed to get under everyone's skin. He had been rude and arrogant. Bob told George, *"something's got to be done about that boy, or you're facing a mutiny, from players and staff alike"*.

'Hopefully it won't come to that Bob,' George reassured him. 'I'm hoping to meet his father very soon. Fingers crossed, we will be able to talk some sense and some manners into the lad. If not, I will get rid of him.'

Jayden returned home after training. He knew he had rubbed the coaching staff and some of the players up the wrong way, but he didn't give a shit. None of them were as good as him. None of them were worthy of even lacing up his boots. They certainly weren't worth making an effort to be nice to.

His father was sitting in the front room, watching the horse racing on the television when he walked through the door. They had started to settle into their new home. A two-bed council flat between New cross and Peckham. It wasn't Buckingham Palace, but it would do for the time being. Father and son had been getting to know each other. There was no mistaking the Saunders' genes. They were definitely built from the same bricks. They hit it off immediately. Their mutual intolerance of authority and the self-belief that they were superior in every way, gave them a feeling of solidarity with each other. They were blood. They were family. Neither of them had ever trusted anyone, but now they had each other. For the first time in either of their lives, they had someone they could rely on.

'How was your day Dad?'

'Not too bad son. I've been trying to contact some old friends. Seeing if there is any work out there. I've decided to give robbing security vans a rest for a while,' he said laughing. 'Trouble is, I've been away for so long, I don't know who's about and who's not. Some of these contacts are dead, some have moved away from the area, some are still inside and worst of all, some of them have become respectable.' He tossed the list of names and telephone numbers onto the table, shaking his head in disbelief. 'I called an old mate from school. He owns a construction company now. *"De Costa Construction"*. We used to hang around together when we were younger. *Big time Charlie Cheesecake* now, by all accounts. A multi-millionaire. Couldn't even get through to talk to him personally. Would seem he doesn't want to know *me* anymore. Wanker. Always was really. How was your day?'

Jayden sat down opposite his dad.

'Well, I had a very interesting day. You know I had to go into the club this morning, before training, to see the manager?'

'George Miller,' Saunders growled, through gritted teeth.

'Yes, George Miller. Well, when I got to the top of the stairs, I noticed his office door was open. I walked up to it and guess what I saw. George, *"happily married"* Miller and his secretary

Brenda, kissing and cuddling. It looked quite intense. God knows what would have happened if I hadn't disturbed them.' Jayden started to laugh. 'You should have seen the look of horror on both of their faces when they realised I had been watching them. It was magic. Miller was furious.' Jayden's laughter became even louder and more raucous. 'Look. I managed to get most of the action on my mobile.'

He handed the phone to his dad and showed him the footage of the amorous encounter, beginning with the neck nibbling, all the way through to the open mouth kissing. 'Hot stuff eh?' he said still chuckling.

But his dad wasn't laughing. He watched the recording closely, several times. A smile of evil intent spread across his face. He softly stroked the scar tissue that snaked its way around his left eye with his fingers.

'So, the squeaky-clean George Miller isn't quite as squeaky clean as he would have us believe.' Jayden had stopped laughing and was looking puzzled at his dad's reaction.

'He said he would like to meet you and have a chat with you. I'm sure he thinks you and he together will be able to put a leash on me and quieten me down.'

'Oh, I bet he would. Well, I've been wanting to talk to him and his brother for years. Yes, I think it's time me and the Miller brothers were re-acquainted,' he said, in a sinister growl.

'Have you met him before then?' Jayden asked, struggling to make sense of his father's melodramatic tone. Baz broke his trancelike stare.

'We were at school together, years ago. It was one of the Miller brothers that gave me this.' He stroked his scar again. 'I've never had the opportunity to repay the favour, but now it seems one has come knocking.' He looked straight at his son. 'Don't say anything to him about me. Let him find out who I am when we meet face to face. I'm sure he will enjoy that more.'

The room fell silent for a few moments while Baz' brain started to plot. Jayden explained to Baz that George had threatened to get rid of him, or let him rot in the youth team, if he didn't buck his ideas up.

'I'm only on a short-term contract. The big deal is going to be sorted out at the end of the season, so he could get rid of me without too much fuss.'

'Don't you worry about that son. I think you're just about to become an integral part of the starting eleven. In fact, I will go so far as to say your name will be the first on the team sheet. Whether Miller likes it or not.'

He began to imagine all of the ways he could make George Miller's life a misery. Baz had always harboured a grudge against the Millers. Everything that had happened between them, when they were at school, was fresh and vivid in his memory, thanks to the tender two-inch blemish that wound its way around his left eye. Along with finding out who had grassed him and his mates up sixteen years earlier and the retribution he would inflict on them, paying back the Miller twins had been one of his main incentives for getting back into society. He was a bitter and a vengeful man. He had read about George's success, his fame and his wealth in the press while he was inside. The adulation and the sumptuous lifestyle George enjoyed just fuelled the hatred and jealousy within him. He was going to make the world pay for what he'd endured and he couldn't think of a better person to start with than *Fucking George Miller*. He wanted Graham Miller just as badly. He was certain one would lead to the other. Jayden had given him the opportunity to meet with Miller. Now his son had provided him with the stick to beat him. Forty seconds of irrefutable proof that George Miller was being less than straight with his wife and family. Forty seconds of mobile phone footage, that the press and the public at large would be very interested to see. The world loved George Miller. His reputation as an honest, straight-talking example of a happily married family man was admired by most. But if there was one thing the public enjoyed more than a perfect role model it was a scandal. One that would see that perfect role model crash and burn in the most humiliating and degrading way possible. He had hatched the plan. It was a plan that would firstly benefit Jayden and fast track him into the spotlight. Secondly, it would give Baz the chance to play with Miller's emotions; keep him guessing as to what was going to happen next. To watch him squirm and worry about what he was going to do with the 'evidence'. And finally, the icing on the cake, the exposure of George Miller as a fraud and a philanderer. The idea of ruining his job, his reputation and most of all, his happy and comfortable family life, was something Baz had been dreaming about for many years. Now, he had the opportunity.

Chapter 15

A moment of unforgivable stupidity

George's first night back at the flat wasn't as restful as he'd hoped. He had a lot on his mind. He had spoken to Debbie, who had landed safely and was settling in with her Mum and Dad. It was good to know she was there and looking forward to her time in the sun, but somehow hearing her voice made him feel lonely. He was missing her and the kids more with every passing second and they had only been apart for twelve hours. He had also received a voicemail from James Bell to tell him that the decoration and building work was underway and with no unforeseen problems they should be finished a couple of days before Debbie was due home. All good news. Information that should have enabled him to kick back, relax and dedicate his full attention to the games he had coming up over the next two and a half weeks. But he had more pressing issues bouncing around in his brain. He was genuinely worried about Brenda. Having noticed the bruising on her face she'd tried to hide under her makeup a few weeks ago and then the marks on her neck she had tried to conceal with her polo neck sweater that morning, he hated the thought of her spending another night in the same house as Jeremy. He felt the muscles in his arms tighten and his toes curl when he pictured him staring back at him in the church as he read his eulogy, with that sanctimonious and supercilious look of contempt and superiority. But Brenda had assured him that the 'calm after the storm' was always the most sedate and trouble-free time in their relationship. The time when Jeremy realised what he had done was wrong and spent the next week or two, trying to make it up to her. But as much as he wanted to believe Brenda was his main concern, he knew what was really vexing him were the events that had taken place in his office earlier that morning. He went over the scene again and again in his mind, desperately trying to sanitise the images that flickered like a horror show in his head. He kept trying to convince himself there was nothing wrong in what had happened between him and Brenda. He had been comforting a friend in distress, that was all. A shoulder to cry on. But he knew in his heart it had been more than just a consoling gesture. The guilt he was feeling was testament to that. Brenda had kissed him in a moment of weakness and confusion. She didn't know what she was doing. But he did and he went along with it, kissing her back in the most intimate of ways. However much he tried to persuade himself it was a "forgivable moment of madness" from Brenda, he knew full well it was a "moment of unforgivable stupidity" on his part. He wondered how the young eyes of Jayden had interpreted what he'd witnessed? The way he had spoken to George after Brenda left his office and the cocky innuendos and suggestive comments he had made, gave George the impression he wasn't going to just forget about it overnight. The fact he kept patting his mobile phone suggested what? What exactly, if anything, had he captured on it? He had no idea. It was that mystery that was the most frightening. If he had nothing, then he was in the clear. He would try and come to terms with what he had done and berate himself for being so weak and so stupid. He would take his own admonishment and move on, wiser and stronger. But, if Jayden had managed to capture any of the sordid imagery of that morning's *kiss*, he knew he could be in deep trouble. If the worse-case scenario was true and the little brat did have video evidence, what did he intend to do with it? Being hard on the boy and relegating him to the youth team might spur the lad on to doing something out of spite. The terrifying thought of anything leaking out and starting the dreaded rumour mill turning was unthinkable. He knew how gossip spread in a close-knit environment like the club. Information and hearsay would pass from person to person, each time becoming more scandalous and shocking. Nods, winks and giggles between people would make their lives almost impossible and the more they denied it, the more people would be convinced it was for real. Everyone knew there was no smoke without fire. If, on the other hand, he was to be soft on Jayden, would the teenager see it as a sign of weakness and take advantage of his contrition. He couldn't afford to relinquish his authority in the boy's eyes. If Jayden's behaviour and attitude were to be ignored, or tolerated, George knew he would have a full-scale mutiny on his hands. He was between a very big rock and a very hard place. The more George battled with the conundrum, the more confused he became. He knew, as well as the damage it could do to his marriage, if word started to spread about him and Brenda, Jeremy would probably go berserk and that couldn't be allowed to happen. He had nearly mentioned it to Debbie earlier but thought better of it. He would wait for a couple of days and try and get things straight in his mind; see how the situation developed. Hopefully things would become clearer and he would be able to make a more rational decision as to what he should say and what he should not.

George felt he was sinking deeper and deeper into despair over the situation. Maybe after he had

had a chat with Jayden's father things would settle down. Jayden had been given a huge opportunity to become successful in the world of professional soccer with all the wealth and fame that went with it. Surely his father would see that and explain to his son how he should *toe the line* and not make waves. He stood to lose so much; it would be crazy to jeopardise his entire future, just to humiliate the man who had given him the chance in the first place. The confidence with which George was trying to convince himself though, was less than solid.

There was one other nagging issue that George was struggling to come to terms with. Something that worried him as much as anything else. Why had he kissed Brenda's neck, in what he knew was a sensuous manner? And why had he let her kiss him on the lips with equal passion? The kiss had been interrupted before it had had a chance to develop into anything more. Again, he tried to convince himself that there was no way the kiss would have blossomed into anything more serious, but he also remembered his mouth slowly beginning to open. He could still feel the sensation of Brenda's tongue on his. Even more worrying, he could remember pulling her towards him and pushing his tongue even deeper into her mouth. He winced with guilt at the memory and bit the offending organ in self-chastisement. He had been furious with Jayden for the unwelcomed and unannounced intrusion and was worried about the ramifications of what he had seen. But he was just as worried about what would have happened if Jayden hadn't burst in. If they hadn't been distracted from their embrace. How long would George have remained in the trance and how much further would they have gone? For the first time in twelve years, he had let himself be led by the appendage in his trousers. He hated himself. He knew he didn't want any other woman but Debbie. Although he didn't want to admit it to himself, he wondered if it had been a blessing that the young boy had stumbled in on them.

George opened the fridge. As always, it was well stocked with beer, wine and of course, his favourite Laurent Perrier Rosé champagne. As he stared into the fridge, he had a flashback to the night, twelve years earlier, when he and Debbie had been reunited for the first time in seven years. The night she had revealed she knew the brothers' Barcelona secret and the night they had promised to stay together forever. That night they had made love and snuggled up in bed for nearly twenty-four hours. They drank three bottles of champagne during that time. The subsequent twelve years had been the happiest of his life. He grabbed a cold bottle of beer. Champagne always tasted nicer when you were sharing it with someone you loved. He would leave the bubbles until Debbie returned.

Chapter 16

She had never liked those bloody lamp shades

On her journey home from the office, Brenda tried to formulate a plan. She had decided to leave Jeremy. The way he treated her the previous evening was the final straw. As her mind wandered back over the previous few years, since they had been married, she remembered the many occasions he had mistreated her. Physical, mental and sexual abuse had been a common theme throughout. She had tried to banish those memories and pretend they had never happened; but they had. As she reluctantly replayed some of the sadistic episodes in her mind, she realised just how horrifying her life had been. One by one the gruesome flashbacks came to haunt her. The sound of Jeremy's voice screaming at her, echoed inside her head. The muscles in her neck tightened and she instinctively gasped for breath at the thought of his hands wrapping themselves around her throat. She swallowed hard and felt a shiver of fear run down her spine. She desperately wanted to find some good memories to "balance the books", but she could think of none. The realisation that she had spent her entire existence as Mrs Higgins either being beaten, shouted at, or raped, made her question why it had taken so long for her to get to this point. She had to get away from him. She knew the beatings were becoming more frequent and the savagery more uncontrollable. She wondered how long it would be before she ended up in hospital; or worse still, the mortuary. She had thought about moving back in with her Mum and Dad, but she knew that would lead to no end of aggravation and harassment from Jeremy and she didn't want to subject her parents to all that anxiety. No, she would start packing a few things over the next couple of weeks, take them into the office and hope to find somewhere to stay, either permanently or temporarily, until the situation with Jeremy had been resolved. He would doubtless take it hard and probably make her life a misery for a few months, but at least she would be able to go to bed at night without worrying about his anger and brutality. She knew the weeks, maybe even months to come, would be difficult and uncomfortable, but they couldn't be as bad as living in permanent fear of "Mr Hyde". She would divorce him, make a clean break and a fresh start. It shouldn't be too complicated. She didn't want anything they had bought together. They would divide the value of the house and she would find somewhere else to start her life all over again. She wanted nothing that would remind her of him, or their time together. Having decided all this, Brenda felt a calmness flow through her body. She had finally come to her senses and could see brighter times ahead. She tried to convince herself that the dark days were behind her. All she had to do now was bide her time for a week or two, find a flat she could rent and then walk away.

The house was empty when she arrived home. She let out a sigh of relief. Any moments without Jeremy were good moments. She looked around the hallway trying to make a mental note of anything she would want to take with her. Any item that had belonged to her in her previous life; anything that reminded her of happier times, but there was nothing. It was all his. It occurred to her that there wasn't a shred of her character or personality visible. He and his mother had chosen the furniture, the carpets, the pictures, even the lamp shades. It was as if she had never existed. Brenda Cousins had put on a wedding ring and disappeared from the human race. She had been replaced by Brenda Higgins, a completely different person. An individual that had had the sparkle, ambition, confidence and vivacity literally knocked out of her. She turned on the hallway light and looked up. She had never liked those bloody lamp shades anyway.

She walked into the kitchen and began to make supper. It was always a good idea to make Jeremy something he liked, to put him in a good mood. He wasn't a great one for experimenting or trying new things, so their diet was limited. She couldn't remember the last time she had eaten a good spicey curry or a Chinese takeaway. That night she was making cottage pie. It was guaranteed to put a smile on his face. It was one of his favourites. He had told her many times that hers was nowhere near as tasty as his mother's cottage pie, but he always ate it up.

Just after 8 o'clock, she heard the key in the front door. Perfect timing. Supper was just about ready. But the sound of *his* key instantly sent another shiver down her spine. She felt her mood change and her heart start to beat a little quicker. She felt the anxiety and the fear creep back and the all-too-familiar nervousness grip her. She tried to reassure herself that she would be safe for the next few days, during "the calm after the storm".

'Hi darling. I'm home. Something smells nice.'

Brenda was constantly amazed by his drastic change of temperament. From a rampaging, statistic bully, to a loving, courteous husband, as if by magic and as if nothing had happened. Very rarely were violent incidents mentioned the day after. All those actions and memories had been washed away by the overnight tide and the clean and pristine sandy beach of their marriage reset, without a shred of any evidence of unhappiness, anger, or strife. There was never any remorse. There were sometimes flowers, occasionally chocolates, but always smiles and good humour in large amounts, to help paper over the strained atmosphere.

'Dinner is just about ready,' she called back. She was relieved to hear the upbeat tone in his voice. Jeremy walked into the kitchen with a big grin on his face and his arms open wide.

'Hello darling. How are you? I've missed you. Did you have a good day?'

As loving and as caring as any husband could ever be. He kissed her on the cheek and then kissed her on the neck, making no reference to her discoloured and bruised flesh. He pulled his head away, frowned and began to sniff like a bloodhound who had found a scent. He sniffed around her head, taking in short, sharp whiffs of air.

'What's that smell?' he asked. Brenda frowned.

'What smell?' She started to sniff the air too. 'It's probably the garlic I used in the cottage pie.'

'No, it's not garlic.'

Jeremy was now sniffing more vigorously, snorting in deep breaths of air around her head and body. It made her feel uncomfortable and uneasy.

'Come on let's have some dinner and stop being so silly.'

She started to walk away, but Jeremy grabbed her by the shoulders and continued his nasal examination.

'That's not your perfume. Who have you been cuddling up to?'

'No one,' she said, trying to laugh it off with a little chuckle. She made another attempt to move away, but Jeremy held her tight and wouldn't let her go.

'I've smelt that scent before. That's what your bloody George Miller wears. I remember it from the funeral. He stank of it.' He looked her square in the eyes and shook her by the shoulders. 'What have you been up to at work today? Tell me. You've been fucking that boss of yours again, haven't you?'

The shaking became more violent. Brenda's head was bouncing back and forth. She had already started to weaken. She could feel herself beginning to shut down. The tears of resignation had already started to well in her eyes.

'Tell me bitch. Tell me the truth.'

He was now shouting maniacally. He slapped his right hand across her cheek, jolting her head to the side, the red glow of his fingers instantly radiating on her face. She felt the burning pain, but her mind was already drifting away, trying to find a better place. He continued to shake her, then struck her again, this time even harder. She had no breath in her body and no stamina to protest her innocence. It would have made no difference anyway. Once he had reached that point, there was no stopping him. Once the mutation had started, it ran its course. He hit her for a third time, this time, with the back of his hand across the other cheek. She felt the warm trickle of blood start to run out of her nose and over her lips. She had tasted her own blood many times before.

'I'm going to teach you a lesson you will never forget.'

He grabbed her by the hair and began dragging her out of the kitchen. She could feel the searing pain on her scalp as he tugged harder and harder. Brenda stumbled and fell but each time was yanked to her feet. He hauled her up the stairs and into the bedroom. He flung her onto the bed, face down. Brenda was now no more than a ragdoll. She lay there, limp and sobbing. She heard him unbuckle his belt and remove his trousers. She felt him lift her blue skirt and force it up over her waist. He then tore off her underwear and dragged her towards him. Her legs were hanging over the side of the bed.

'Jeremy, please don't. I haven't done anything, I swear. Please. I don't deserve this.' She tried to raise herself up with what little strength she could muster but felt Jeremy's hand smash between her shoulder blades forcing her back onto the bed. He pulled her buttocks apart and spat between her cheeks.

'Jeremy, I beg you. Please don't.'

He wasn't listening. He lined himself up and cruelly started to burrow his way into her. Brenda let out a scream, as the pain stabbed its way through her body. Jeremy continued to force himself into her. She let out a few more cries, but they became fainter as he punched his way deeper and deeper inside. He slapped her thigh. Brenda had gone quiet and apart from the recoiling and juddering from Jeremy's evil intrusions, remained motionless. It was all over in a few, horrendous minutes. Once he had finished, he pulled himself out and rasped his hand again across her crimson buttocks. He bent down and stared into Brenda's dead eyes.

'Let that be a lesson to you. Don't go screwing about with other men. You are my wife and you had better remember that.'

He left the room, slamming the door behind him. Brenda lay there, hanging over the side of the bed, with her skirt wrapped up around her waist and her bare arse aching and sore. She felt worthless. She felt dead. She had no dignity or self-esteem. She had no hope. All she was, or ever had been to her husband, was a sex toy and a punch bag. If that was what life had to offer, she no longer wanted any part of it.

Somehow, she must have fallen asleep. She didn't know for how long. When she woke, she tried to understand what she was doing and why she was in such an uncomfortable position, still dangling over the side of the bed with her skirt up around her waist. It only took a few seconds for her memory to remind her of the sodomy that had recently been perpetrated on her. The blood from her nose had congealed on her face and stained the white duvet cover. She pulled herself up and crept towards the shower, removing the rucked-up skirt and the rest of her clothes as she walked. She wanted to wash all evidence of Jeremy off and out of her body. If she could have washed him out of her mind she would have done so too. She stood still, hands down by her side, letting the warm flow of the shower massage her face, wondering why life had chosen to be so cruel to her. She crawled into bed, drained both physically and mentally. She was still in a lot of pain but closed her watery eyes and drifted off into an uncomfortable sleep. When she woke the following morning, Jeremy had already gone to work. She hadn't heard him come back after storming out the night before and she hadn't heard him get up and leave that morning. She hadn't even had to pretend to be sleeping this time. Her first emotion of the day was relief. She gingerly got out of bed. Her body was still hurting and reminding her of the savagery she had endured. She was struggling to get herself ready and focus on the day ahead. Everything she did was at half pace. She looked at her watch. She was going to be late for work. She was never late for work. She packed a holdall with some toiletries, some underwear and a number of outfits. She knew that once she had left the house that morning she would not be going back ever again. At the front door she found a note.

'You looked so peaceful and so happy when I left, I didn't want to wake you up. I'm sorry I was a little bit rough last night. You have to understand that it is only because I love you so much. See you later my love. Jeremy X.

P.S maybe we could have the cottage pie tonight.'

Brenda screwed up the paper and threw it across the hallway.

Chapter 17

I like your cologne

When George arrived at the office on Wednesday morning, he was surprised to find that Brenda was not there. Immediately, he wondered if she had experienced more trouble at home, but eventually contented himself with her explanation that the 'calm after the storm' was always the quietest time. He dropped his bags on his desk and made his way to the kitchen to get himself a cup of tea. It was very unusual for Brenda to be late. In fact, he couldn't ever remember her not being there when he arrived. Even on the odd occasion when he had to be in the office at "stupid o'clock", he had been surprised to see her sitting at her desk. He sometimes wondered if she ever went home at all.

Walking back to his office, sipping his tea, he heard the reassuring clip, clip, clip, of Brenda's heels on the wooden stairs. He waited as she rounded the curve of the staircase and slowly came into view from below the horizon of the top stair. He nearly dropped his mug of tea. He had never seen Brenda look so awful. He was staggered by her appearance. Although she was wearing some of the usual, stylish, designer clothes he had seen before, the frame on which they hung was wretched. The grace and poise Brenda always exuded, had gone. She was a walking catastrophe. Her hair, normally perfect, was all over the place. She looked like she'd been driven to work in a convertible, with the roof down. She was unsteady on her feet. The elegance with which she would glide around the office on her stiletto heels had deserted her. She staggered from one foot to the next, looking for all the world as if she were drunk. Her body was deflated. There was no structure to it. She looked like a crushed human being. She was a pitiful sight to behold. George slammed down his mug on the nearest table and rushed over towards her. She looked at him through eyes that were already half closed and dead inside.

'What the hell has happened?' he yelled, as he reached the stairs.

As soon as Brenda arrived at the top her legs buckled. She stumbled and reached out an arm to steady herself, but she collapsed, straight into George's arms. He caught her and held her up. He swung her legs over his right arm and carried her into his office. He placed her gently on the sofa and sat next to her. George wrapped his arms around her and held her as tightly as he dared. She looked like she might disintegrate at the slightest touch. She was lifeless and bereft of feeling or emotion. She was a zombie. Brenda just stared into space. George noticed that she wasn't wearing any makeup whatsoever. He had told her so many times how she would look even more beautiful without the paint, but today he wasn't so sure. Her pale face looked drained of all colour. Her eyes, sunken and dark. He cradled her gently, holding her head like a father comforting a child. They sat in silence for a few moments, George softly stroking her forehead.

'What the fuck has that bastard done to you now?'

Without the camouflage of the previous day's white polo neck sweater, George could see the full extent of the damage around her throat. There were also signs of new bruising and swelling around both of her eyes. He felt an overwhelming urge to drive over to Jeremy's office and beat the shit out of him, smashing him to a bloody pulp and then, when all of his colleagues wondered why, he would tell them just what sort of a vicious, wife beating cunt they had been working with. George could feel the anger and the violence once again bubble up inside him. He remembered when he had sat astride Frankie De Costa at school, in a worryingly, uncontrollable rage, poised to deliver the crushing punch that had been building up for years, but even that fury paled into insignificance compared to the venom that was coursing through his veins at that moment. He sucked in a deep breath and tried to calm himself down. His first priority was to take care of Brenda. She leant into him and put her arms around his waist. She began sobbing and shaking, as if she were in shock. She just couldn't understand why life had turned out to be so unbearable.

Once the sobbing had slowed and she had stopped shaking, George softly raised her head.

'What happened? Do you want to tell me?'

Brenda shook her head. She couldn't even bring herself to talk about it. To recount it, would be to relive it and she certainly wasn't going to do that.

'All I know is I can't go back there. Not tonight. Not ever. I was hoping to make some plans over the next few weeks, but after last night I never want to see him again.' She buried her face back into George's chest.

'I like your cologne,' she whispered to herself.

'Okay. Okay. You will never have to see him again if you don't want to, I promise.'

George laid her down on the sofa, propping up her head on a couple of cushions. She instinctively curled herself up into the foetal position, with her knees tucked into her chest.

'Stay there and shut your eyes. Everything will be okay.'

'But I have work to do George. I will be alright.' She tried to get up, but George held his hand on her shoulder.

'You have no work to do today Miss Cousins and you will do exactly as I say. Is that clear? This is your boss speaking to you.' He smiled at her as his mock, stern voice, made its point.

'Just for half an hour. Then I will get on.' George left her on the sofa and skipped down the two flights of stairs to the reception area.

'Brenda is not feeling very well. I'm going to take her home in a couple of hours. She probably won't be in for a few days, but don't worry about getting anyone to stand in for her. I'm sure I can manage. If you just transfer all my calls direct, or to my mobile.' Janice on reception nodded and smiled.

'I did wonder when she came in. She looked awful. I do hope she will be okay. Has she been mugged or something?'

'I'm not sure exactly what has happened yet, but I'm sure she will be fine in a few days. She just needs some rest. Thanks Janice.'

George ran back up the stairs. He found a blanket in Brenda's office and laid it over her. In the time it had taken him to go down and up the stairs, she had fallen into a deep sleep. He looked at her and softly stroked her hair. He had been right about the makeup. Peacefully asleep and with no paint on her face, she looked even more beautiful than she normally did, even with her puffy, swollen eyes.

George had a few things that needed his immediate attention, but by 11 o'clock he had sorted everything out. Brenda hadn't moved for two hours and was still fast asleep. He whispered softly into her ear.

'Brenda. Brenda.' She woke up with a start. Her eyes were full of fear and her body had tensed with panic. Her arms raced up to protect her face, whilst her eyes flashed around the room, trying to work out where she was.

'It's okay. It's me. George. You're safe. Everything is going to be alright.'

A few seconds later, George felt the anxiety drain from her body. She relaxed and the fear disappeared from her eyes. She grabbed George around the neck.

'Oh George, what am I going to do?'

'You're going to stay at my flat, with me, for a couple of days, while we work out what to do for the best,' he said. 'Now, if you feel strong enough, I want you to put on your jacket and get your things together. Then come with me.'

Brenda was beyond questioning anything and dutifully, did as she was told. She still looked incredibly fragile. He took her by the arm, the way you would help an elderly lady cross the road. This time they took the lift down to the ground floor. George told Janice he would be back in about an hour. It was a bright, sunny morning and both George and Brenda welcomed the warmth of the sun on their faces and the gentle breeze on their cheeks as they walked across the car park towards George's Range Rover. He helped her into the passenger seat and they drove to his flat. Not much was said on the way. Brenda spent most of the journey with her eyes shut. Asleep or not, George decided it was best to leave her to her own thoughts. She looked peaceful and serene, but he knew there were many demons in her head. Demons that would haunt her for some time to come. He still didn't know what atrocity Jeremy had perpetrated on her, but what he did know was, it would definitely be the last. If Brenda wanted to talk about it, he would listen. If she didn't, he wasn't going to pry. She probably just wanted to forget about the previous night and all of the nights with Jeremy before that.

George opened the front door to his Riverside penthouse.

"You are going to live here for a few days.' Brenda's eyes were now wide open and her abject disposition, transformed. She stood up straight and looked around in wonder, taking in her luxurious new surroundings.

'Come this way.' George took her by the hand and led her down the corridor. He showed her into the second bedroom. 'This is yours. There is an en-suite with a shower and a bathrobe hanging on the back of the door. Down the hallway there is a bathroom and further on down, is the kitchen. The fridge is well stocked with food and drink. Please help yourself to anything that takes your fancy. If there is anything else you need, or want me to pick up, call me on my mobile, or text me and I will get it on my way home. I suggest you run yourself a nice, deep, hot bath and then try and get some rest. Don't let anyone in or answer the intercom. I'm going back to the office for a few hours, but I will be back later. You're safe here Brenda. No one will ever treat you like that again. I promise.'

'Thank you, George. I really don't deserve you. You're too good to me.'

'What you don't deserve is Jeremy, that's for sure. Now relax and I will see you later. Before George left, Brenda gave him her keys and asked him to retrieve the bag she had packed that morning, from the boot of her car.

Driving back to the club, he felt confident that for the first time since Miss Cousins had become Mrs Higgins, Brenda was safe and out of harm's way.

Chapter 18

A schoolgirl crush on a popstar

Even in her disturbed and agitated state Brenda managed to feel a tingle of excitement rush through her bruised and abused body. She had finally made it into George Miller's flat. The very same flat she had been desperate to see twelve years earlier, after watching the Milan game with him from the Directors' box. They had got on so well and enjoyed each other's company so much that evening, she was convinced he was going to ask her back for a "nightcap" or a "coffee". She would have had said yes to anything. She had started to fantasise about spending the night with George as soon as he had asked her if she wanted to sit next to him during the game. She remembered sitting in the players' bar after the match, full of anticipation and excitement. She had prepared herself for the best night of her life. To give herself to George and let him make all of her dreams come true. But George had driven her home instead. It had been such a crushing disappointment. She knew and understood that he was only being a gentleman and doing what he thought was right. Sometimes she admired him even more for his gallantry, but twelve years on, she knew the events of that fateful evening still ranked as the most heart wrenching and saddest moment, in her life.

Things had changed overtime. George was married, as was she. She knew what she had felt for him in those days was more akin to a schoolgirl crush on a pop star. She adored him; she worshipped him. She also knew that now, years later, her feelings for him had changed. She was no longer the schoolgirl and he was no longer the pop star. Of course, she still adored him, but she looked at him through different eyes now. Thirty-five-year-old eyes. Eyes that could see him just as the man he was. A thoroughly decent, generous, lovely, human being. She knew she no longer worshipped the pop star. Now she truly loved the man.

She walked around the large, open plan space of the lounge and looked at some of the ornaments and nick-nacks. They were all lovely. The sort of things she would have liked in her home, instead of the "old tat" that Jeremy had filled their house with. She saw a silver framed photograph hanging on the wall. It was a picture of George, Debbie and the two children. It was one of those professionally posed, black and white photographs that just reeked of happy families. Brenda stared long and hard at the picture and tried to imagine her face on Debbie's body, sitting on the sofa, surrounded by their two young children and the man of her dreams.

She ventured into his bedroom and took a long and loving look at the large bed. The one she had hoped to share with him twelve years earlier. She sat down on the soft mattress and slowly ran her hand over the duvet cover, knowing she was destined never to experience the love, the passion, or the warmth she had longed for; not between those sheets anyway. She laid her head on the pillow, stretched herself out and stared up at her reflection in the huge mirrored ceiling. She rolled onto her side and tried to imagine George lying next to her. Again, she felt both excitement and sadness in her heart.

After smoothing out the duvet and re-plumping the pillow, making sure there were no tell-tale signs of her presence, she wandered back into the lounge. The view from the huge windows, that ran all the way around the room, onto the River Thames were spectacular. It was a clear, sunny day and she could see for miles in every direction. She looked in awe at the vista before her. She had lived in London all her life but had never seen *her city* like this. From her vantage point, nearly 600 feet in the air, she marvelled at the treasures London had to offer, all laid out beneath her. Brenda felt safe and cocooned in the luxury of George's apartment. It was a feeling she could happily have grown used to. A long sigh of resignation escaped from her lungs; she knew all of it was just temporary. It would only be a matter of days before she would have to start her life afresh, away from the five-star opulence, the magnificent views and of course, *her new flat mate*. The next few months were going to be a challenge for her and although she knew she would always be able to count on the support and friendship of George, she also knew that was all it would ever be. As traumatic as the last few days had been, she loved the attention George had paid her. Taking care of her, holding her and reassuring her. She would miss that.

She made herself a cup of tea and filled the bath. She put some music on and slid beneath the mountain of bubbles in the soothing, hot water. She sipped her tea. A feeling she hadn't experienced for a long time wrapped itself around her. It was the feeling of safety.

Chapter 19

Another nail in Miller's coffin

It was just past 11 o'clock on Wednesday morning. Baz pulled up and parked the rust-riddled, fifteen-year-old blue Vauxhall Astra he had bought from a local dealer, adjacent to the football club's main entrance. The car was a piece of shit, but it was all he could afford. He sat outside the football club mulling over his plans. He couldn't wait to see the look on George Miller's face when he introduced himself as Jayden's father. He had been wondering how best to unsettle him and get under his skin. He had with him the unexpected ammunition of his son's rather fortunate recording of "the kiss". It was a good start. George was known as a loyal and loving family man. Since his wild bachelor days, he had quietened down and become a model husband and father. His reputation and image were now spotless. Baz knew if he could somehow tarnish that image, both the press and the public would almost certainly turn against him. With all the gossip that would bring, he was convinced life would start to become intolerable for not only George but Brenda and Debbie too. The rumours would continue and the accusations would increase. It would turn into a soap opera. And he couldn't wait to watch it unfold. He was armed with an A4 print from the footage his son had surreptitiously filmed. The two of them, mouth to mouth, in what looked like a passionate embrace. It was just the appetiser. A tantalising hint of the main course to come. Baz wasn't the smartest man in the world, he knew that, but during his time inside, he had developed a sixth sense. He could read situations and feel when the time was right to either attack, or back off. In prison, your life, or quality of life, depended on it. If you were accepted and respected by the upper echelons of the gangland monarchy that ruled the inmates, you could expect to enjoy a comfortable existence. If you were not, you could expect a miserable life and servitude to the same mob. Knowing the right time to "play your Ace", was crucial. Revealing a winning hand too early, could be disastrous. Moving in for the kill was not only about power, but timing too. He wanted to destroy everything Miller held dear. His family, his job, his entire lifestyle. He knew he had the material to make him uncomfortable, but he wanted more. He wanted to have some fun in the process and watch him squirm and panic. He had had an idea he hoped would not only undermine Miller's authority and confidence, but advance Jayden's career into the bargain. Baz wanted maximum enjoyment out of the next few weeks, squeezing every drop of life out of George Miller's highbrow and happy existence. The evidence that one of the country's most loved and admired sporting heroes was not quite as squeaky clean as everyone thought, would be revealed, by him, for the press and the public to view. They would be the judge and jury in this case and Baz was pretty confident he knew what their verdict would be.

It was ten past eleven. The bright sunshine was gleaming off the glass-fronted façade of the football club's main entrance. Baz was still weighing up all his sinister options when his attention was grabbed by a blinding flash of light. The doors were opening, blasting the sun's reflection right into his eyes. He blinked several times, trying to recover his vision. A woman and a man stepped out gingerly, arm in arm. Baz squinted his eyes to see who they were. The dishevelled and fragile looking woman seemed to be rather unsteady on her feet and totally reliant on the help and support of the man. As Baz looked closer, he realised the woman fitted the description of Brenda, Jayden had given him. He took a quick look at the print in his hand. It wasn't very good quality, but he could make out enough of the facial features to be sure it was her. He concentrated his stare on her male companion. As soon as the man's face looked up into the sunshine, Baz knew it was Miller. He hadn't seen him in the flesh for over twenty-six years. He had been reminded of his ugly mug when reading some of the newspapers and watching the TV whilst in prison, but this was the closest he had come to his old enemy since their school days. Baz frowned as he watched the pair of them walk towards, what he assumed, was George's Range Rover. He tried to make sense of what he was watching. George was almost carrying the woman. Baz wasn't sure what was going on, but anything that tied George and his secretary together would only fan the flames of doubt concerning an affair between them. Any additional footage he could collect, or any other evidence he could find, would all sit nicely alongside "the kiss" and give the rumours he planned to start spreading, credibility. Confused or not, it was an opportunity he couldn't afford to miss. Baz immediately got out his phone and turned on the video camera. He zoomed into the couple, framing a touching closeup. They got into the car. Baz couldn't believe his luck. He stuck his phone onto the dashboard mount and continued to record. He followed the Range

Rover for about half an hour, until it pulled into a gated compound on the South Bank of the Thames, just west of Vauxhall Bridge. It disappeared into an underground car park. Half an hour later, the Range Rover drove out of the car park and headed back. Once again, Baz followed and filmed the journey. On arrival back at the club, he saw only George get out of the car. He watched, as his unknowing victim jogged over to the glass doors and vanished back inside.

Things were happening and he needed time to understand what they were and what they meant. There was no point in rushing in. With the footage of the kiss, plus the recording he had just made of George dropping Brenda back, at what he assumed was his flat, in the middle of the day, he knew there was more to this story than he had originally imagined. Any more evidence he could collect before he confronted Miller, would make his position even stronger. He would wait and see what developed.

Baz sat patiently in his car, his eyes fixed on the doors. At 5 o'clock he saw George leave the club again. He followed him back to the flat on the South Bank. If the secretary was still in there, he might catch them leaving together, maybe in another damning and incriminating embrace. Another nail in Miller's coffin. He would wait there all night if he had to. Baz let an evil smile play on his face. He had George Miller just where he wanted him. It had been as good a day as he could have possibly dreamed of. And the best part was, George was doing all the hard work for him. Miller was shovelling away, unknowingly digging his own grave.

Chapter 20

The best bits are the least worst bits

At 5 o'clock on Wednesday afternoon, George left the club and drove back to his flat; unaware he was being followed and filmed by the rust-riddled blue Astra behind him.

'Hi Brenda. It's me George. Everything okay?'

'Yes, everything is just fine, thank you.' Brenda was in the kitchen making supper.

'I hope you don't mind. I thought I would make myself useful.' George wasn't much of a cook. When Debbie was away, or he was staying at the flat, he largely relied on takeaways, eating out, or at a push, microwave ready meals. He took a deep breath in through his nostrils. From the wonderful aromas emanating from the pots and pans on the hob, he could tell that Brenda was a pretty handy chef. She looked at home, standing at the cooker, stirring the pans and sprinkling in various herbs and spices. She was wearing the dark blue bathrobe she had found hanging on her bedroom door. For a second she looked remarkably like Debbie. On numerous occasions in the past, he had returned to the flat after work, to find Debbie cooking, wearing her blue bathrobe. He would sidle up behind her, wrap his arms around her and kiss her gently on the neck, whilst his hands would fumble with the cord around her waist. He would ease the garment open and run his hands over her delicious flesh, exploring all of the delights within. Sometimes, the hobs would be turned off, while they made love there and then in the kitchen. Other times, he would have a wooden spoon waved at him and be told to "get off". But it was usually the former. They were wonderful memories and watching Brenda standing at the cooker, as Debbie had so many times before, brought them all flooding back. He felt the twinges in his groin start to tingle and the arousal in his body start to mount. He contented himself it was the thought of Debbie that had got his juices flowing and not the sight of Brenda. Either way he would have to behave himself this time. As similar as they were, Debbie was the only girl for him. As lovely and as beguiling as Brenda looked, she was his secretary and his friend and nothing more. He was pleased to see the twinkle and the sparkle had returned to her eyes and the smile to her face. The crouching, hunched, sullen, hangdog frame and expression had vanished. She looked happy.

'What time would you like to eat?' she asked. 'It can be ready anytime. It's only a chicken curry, so it can bubble away for as long as you like. You do still like a curry, don't you? I took your advice and had a wonderful soak in your bath. It was gorgeous. I didn't want to get out. I've been lounging around ever since. As you can see, I have rather made myself at home.' She held her arms open and looked down at the bathrobe.

'Good,' he replied. 'That's what I want you to do. This is your home for the next few days.' Brenda wasn't about to start arguing on that subject. 'Shall we leave supper for an hour? Let's sit down and talk for a bit. Drink? What do you fancy, beer, wine, champagne?' He saw Brenda's eyes widen at the mention of champagne.

'Champagne it is then. Very appropriate. We can celebrate the beginning of your new and happy life. Go and sit down. I will bring the drinks over.' Brenda perched on one of the two sofas. She tucked in her legs, adjusted her bathrobe and nuzzled herself in amongst the cushions. The cork popped out of the bottle and George walked in with the ice bucket and two glasses. He sat on the sofa the other side of the coffee table, facing Brenda.

'Cheers. Here's to you,' he said, raising his glass.

'I really don't know how to thank you George. The thought of sitting back at home now, scares me to death. I know now what a fool I've been, putting up with his mood swings and his temper for all this time. Looking back over the years we've been married, I can't really remember anything nice. The best bits are the least-worst bits, if that makes sense.'

'Well, you're safe now. That's all that matters.'

They talked about Jeremy and all of the pain he had caused her over the last few years. How his character and attitude towards her changed as soon as they had tied the knot. His insistence on putting her down and ridiculing her in front of his friends. How she began to see less and less of *her* friends and how they had slowly vanished from her life. She told George that he had demanded to know about all of her previous relationships. Names, dates, what they did, every minute detail.

'I had a sense of guilt just telling him. He insisted I reveal everything. How many times I had been to bed with them, what I had done and if I'd enjoyed it. The more he forced me to tell him, the more guilt I felt, and the angrier he became. He made me feel grubby and unfaithful, but these were people I'd known before I even met him. It was horrible and it started pretty much from day one. I remember wondering on the first night of our honeymoon, who this man in my bed was. He had totally changed. Every day after that got worse. There had always been, what I like to call, "the calm after the storm" days. The days and weeks after he had exploded. The time it took for him to calm down and apologise for his behaviour. If I heard *"it will never happen again"* once, I must have heard it a hundred times. The big problem was, the explosions were becoming more regular and "the calm after the storm" periods were becoming shorter.' Brenda had started to revert back to the haunted and lost soul he had seen that morning. It was a tough conversation and her face was showing the signs of the emotion she was feeling, with each uncomfortable revelation. George was keen to move the talk away from Jeremy and all the traumas he had been responsible for. Apart from anything else, he could feel himself becoming angry and his blood beginning to boil. But Brenda seemed to want to carry on. She was cleansing her soul. Washing away all of the dreadful memories and letting the stories float out of her mouth and drift away forever. She told him how Jeremy could flare up at the *"drop of a hat"*. How she always had to think twice before she said anything, in case of a cross examination. George sat and mostly listened. He was shocked by what he was hearing. He knew Brenda had had a rough time and that Jeremy had obviously been aggressive with her on a couple of occasions, but after listening to her account of her life as Mrs Higgins, he gradually became aware of just how much abuse she had endured over the years. He couldn't believe his ears. Verbal, mental, and physical abuse, as well as the sexual abuse and the regular rapes.

'Do you know, now I think about it, I'm not sure we ever actually made love, in the true sense of the phrase. He just fucked me and used me for his own pleasure. I don't think it was ever about "us" or "me". Just him,' she said, her eyes glazing over into that lost and distant stare George had seen so many times before.

God Almighty! Did men really treat women like that? He felt sick to his stomach. He knew from the papers and the television that that sort of thing happened. But to be told about it in such gruesome detail, from someone who had not only experienced it firsthand, but someone whom he held very close to his heart, made him feel ashamed of his gender.

'What do you say to another bottle? Come on, let's lift the mood. Let's pop another cork and talk about the future. Let's have some of that delicious smelling curry.'

Brenda's smile instantly flashed back. She nodded and stood up. George served the fizz and Brenda served the food. After dinner they sat back down and resumed their chat. The subject matter was more light-hearted. They spoke of their happy memories, back when Bernie and Doug, Igor, Pascal, Casey and Terry were all part of their lives.

The magical, almost family-like bond they had between them. They recalled the times when the two of them used to flirt with one another; when George had been summoned to Bernie's office. Brenda remembered every detail. Every wonderful second of the time they spent in each other's company.

The second bottle of champagne was nearly empty and it was getting late. It had been an evening full of contrasts. From the dark, cathartic accounts of Jeremy's thuggery BC, (before curry), to the happier and more relaxed meanderings of their lives, back in the good old days, AD (after dinner).

As they reminisced and sipped the last of the champagne, Brenda cast her eyes around the flat.

'I was hoping to have been invited back here about twelve years ago,' she said, with a cheeky grin. 'Do you remember the night we watched the Milan game together? I was convinced you would ask me to come back with you, here, for another drink. I was so hoping you would.' She swung her legs off the sofa and planted her feet on the floor. She leant forward. 'I was ready to give you everything. *Everything!*' She paused for a moment, letting her tantalising admission hang in the air. 'When you offered to drive me back to my parents' house, I felt the bottom fallout of my world. I don't think I have ever been so disappointed in my whole life.' Brenda smiled at him, in an almost forgiving way. 'I know you were only being chivalrous, but I can tell you, that night you dealt the hopes and dreams, let alone the fantasies of a young girl, a devastating blow. When I got back to my parents, I went straight to my room and cried my eyes out, all night.' George looked apologetically at her. He recalled his own mixed feelings that night. How pleased he had been with himself, at the strength of will power he had shown, by taking her home and not giving into his lustful yearnings. And how deflated he had felt when he actually got back to his flat, alone.

'I have to be honest with you Brenda, there was a moment I considered calling you up and driving back to get you,' he laughed. 'I remember that night so clearly. So many mixed emotions.' He paused for thought. 'Who knows what might have been, if things had been different?' George smiled at her, his curiosity almost begging an answer to his own question. Brenda's expression became more serious. She frowned as if in deep thought. The room had fallen eerily silent. She put her glass of champagne down on the table and slowly stood up, keeping her eyes fixed on George. George's eyes followed her up. The light-hearted atmosphere of their conversation had instantly vanished. There was suddenly a spark of electrical intensity in the air. George felt his body tense and his heartbeat increase. His concentration fixed on her every move. For a few seconds they stared at each other, both fully aware of the change of mood in the room. With a slip of her hand on the bathrobe cord and a slight shrug of her shoulders, the dressing gown slid off her body and crumpled onto the floor by her feet. She stood there before him. Wonderfully naked.

Chapter 21

The little sister role

Once again, George found himself transfixed by the vision in front of him, unable to move, or to speak. A paralysis caused by the shock of what had just happened. She was sexier than George had ever allowed himself to imagine. He could feel his mouth open, his eyes widen and the blood start to race into his groin, as he wallowed in the glorious sight before him. He took a sharp intake of breath. After a few electrifying seconds Brenda began to slowly walk across the room towards him; her eyes locked on his. George sat still, frozen to the spot, his eyes frantically scanning every delectable inch of her radiant flesh, until she stood right in front of him. As she stared down at him he tried desperately to keep his gaze fixed on her eyes, but it was impossible. She had a magnificent body. At his eye level were her hips and the beautifully sculptured Brazilian demanding his attention. Raising his eyes, he saw her breasts. They were beautiful. They were perfect. Her skin looked soft and silky. It glistened. He wanted to reach out and touch her. To run his hands gently over her thighs and up onto her waist. He quickly slid his fingers under his legs, in an attempt to stop them exploring. A shiver convulsed through his entire being, making him judder. Now she reminded him of Debbie even more. She really was stunning. As his eyes floated over her beautiful body, he gaped in awe at what he saw. Brenda could tell by the look on his face that he was not only surprised but aroused by her. She lingered for a few seconds, enjoying the sensation. She could almost feel his eyes on her flesh, revelling in her nakedness. She slowly knelt down in front of him and placed her arms on his thighs. She was looking straight at him.

'This is what I dreamt of twelve years ago,' she said. 'This is what I have always dreamt about. Even during those years when we didn't see each other. Even after I got married. I've longed for this moment, from the very second I met you.'

George desperately wanted it to stop. But he couldn't bring himself to end it. This had also been a fantasy of his, twelve years ago. He had pictured this scene in his head so many times, and now it was playing out in front of him, the way he had always imagined it would. Brenda eased her elbows onto his inner thighs and gently moved his knees a little wider apart. She felt no resistance from George. She slowly lowered her hands until they were resting on what had already developed into quite a substantial bulge in his trousers. She ran her fingers over the mound and gave it a little squeeze. George felt his buttocks clench and his entire body tense. He shuddered and shivered at the same time. Brenda then moved her hands up onto George's belt and began to unbuckle it. He watched as her fingers delicately unfastened the button above the zip. She could feel the throbbing flesh beneath her palms, pounding and pulsating as if desperate to be liberated from its confines. Brenda looked intensely into his eyes. She began to slowly lower the zip with her left hand. As the zip opened, the fingers of her right hand gently and softly started to ease their way behind the waistband of his boxer shorts, effortlessly gliding over the soft stubble. She could sense the heat and the power radiating from within. It was now or never. He had to do something. As Brenda's fingers inched tantalisingly closer towards her *"Holy Grail"*, George, keeping his eyes firmly fixed on hers, slid his hands from under his legs and gently took hold of her wrists. He held them softly, halting their erotic progress. For a brief moment, time stood still. Brenda's fingers poised, achingly close to her prize. In the blink of an eye, she felt him ease her hands away. She didn't fight against the interruption or the extraction. She looked at George with her big, beautiful eyes. There was a sad expression of resignation and defeat on her face. She bowed her head. She knew, in that moment, her bold and impudent, albeit, alcohol inspired, attempt to recreate the fantasy that had been smouldering within her for over seventeen years, had failed. She felt two tears fall from her eyes and watched them splash on George's jeans. It was over.

George got to his feet and pulled her up with him. He felt his stare once again start to wander over the delicious landscape of her body. He felt a massive surge of guilt gush through him and he dragged his eyes north, to look into Brenda's eyes. He let go of her wrists and softly rested his hands on her hips. He pulled her close to him, wrapped his arms around her and gave her a hug. He stroked her back, making small circles with his fingertips on her satin like skin and wondered what to say next. He knew he couldn't make love to her. He felt her arms wrap around his waist and she rested her head on his chest.

'I'm sorry,' he whispered into her ear.

She nodded her head. He could still feel the full erection that had developed, ever since the bathrobe had hit the floor, relentlessly pounding. He knew Brenda had felt it when she was undoing his trousers. She could probably still feel the swelling rubbing up against her as they held each other. Her body had gone limp again and he could sense that she had started to sob.

'Come on now. Let's not get upset. We both know this can't happen. We both know that maybe it should have happened twelve years ago, but there is nothing we can do about that now.' He wished the throbbing in his pants would stop and the evidence of his arousal would disappear, but while he was holding onto her, it was going nowhere. He eased her head away from his chest and held her tear streaked face gently in his hands.

'I'm married to Debbie and I wouldn't change or jeopardise that for anything. Brenda, I love you very much, but it is the same love I would have for a little sister. That's all it can be. That's all it can ever be.' He kissed her on the forehead. She looked at him with watery eyes.

'I know,' she said. 'I'm sorry. Please forgive me. I'm not crying because you won't make love to me. I know you can't and I love you even more for that. I'm crying because, for the first time I can remember, I've felt the touch of a man's hand on my body, that I know isn't going to hurt me. A touch that was full of love, kindness and tenderness. A touch I haven't felt for a very long time.' George pulled her back into his embrace and held her tightly. He could feel the tears in his eyes start to well.

They stood there in silence for a few minutes, clinging onto one other and both trying to come to terms with their emotions. Each of them felt a sense of relief and regret. George took her by the hand and walked with her, back across the room, to where the bathrobe still lay. He picked it up. She stood before him naked and exposed, with her arms down by her side. He held the robe open and without a word she slipped her arms in. George wrapped it around her body and tied the cord. He kissed her once again on the forehead.

'Go to bed and get yourself a good night's sleep. You've had a rough ride these last few days. You've had a rough ride these last few years! See how you feel in the morning. If you want to stay here you can, if you want to come into work with me, then that's fine too. It's up to you.' He brushed his hand across her cheek, softly wiping a tear away. 'Good night Brenda.' She smiled back at him. After everything that had happened in the past twenty-four hours, her overriding feeling was one of relief. Relief that she was in no danger of being beaten, abused, or raped. Like the gentle touch of George's hand, softly tracing small, delicate, circles on her naked back, it was a feeling she hadn't experienced for a very long time.

'Thank you, Mr. Miller. I love you very much. I always have and for my sins, I think I always will. I love you because you are decent, lovely, man. Your wife is a very lucky lady. In my opinion, the luckiest lady in the world. I know I will have to settle for the "little sister role". It will be tough, but I think I will manage. Night-night. And thank you.'

By the time George got into bed it had gone midnight. In Mallorca it was gone 1am, too late to call his wife. He would call her tomorrow. He had so much to tell her. And a lot that maybe, he shouldn't tell her.

Brenda lay in her bed. It was now her turn to feel the pang of guilt inside her. She realised she had put George in a very difficult position. But she also felt a sense of relief. She had finally told him how she felt about him and laid herself bare, literally, before him. She replayed the events of the last hour over and over again in her head. She was amazed at how brazen she had been. She put that down to the champagne. She let a wry smile dance across her lips as she remembered the hard mound in his trousers, pulsing beneath her palms and how she felt the same glorious throbbing, rhythmically nudging up against her body, while he held her in his arms. As much as she wished he would have taken her there and then, she was quietly pleased he hadn't. He obviously loved Debbie very much and the last thing she wanted to do was jeopardise that happiness. She admired him for his cursed strength and his confounded will power.

Wrapped up in the duvet of George's spare bed and knowing the man of her dreams was in the room just up the hallway, she gently caressed her breasts and eased her fingers down the Brazilian runway. As her fingers went to work, she shut her eyes and whispered to herself,

'I love you George Miller.' She fell into a deep and contented sleep.

Chapter 22

Hand in hand like two young lovers

George knocked gently on Brenda's door. There was no answer. He slowly pushed it open. Peering in, he could see she was still fast asleep. He quietly ventured into the room. She was tightly cocooned in the duvet, with just her head poking out of the top. He set down the cup of tea on the bedside table and whispered in her ear.

'Brenda. Brenda.' He stroked her forehead gently with the tips of his fingers. She made a soft grunting noise and blinked her eyes open, stretching her arms above her head and letting out a slightly more guttural sound. Immediately her eyes we're fully open, he saw the instantaneous look of fear explode onto her face. Her body lurched away from him and she raised her arms in front of her face to protect herself.

'It's okay. It's okay. You're safe,' George said, smiling down at her. As soon as she saw it was him, she relaxed and the panic dissolved away.

'I've bought you a cup of tea. There is no rush. You can stay here today if you want. Recharge your batteries. Take it easy.' She took a deep breath and slowly sat up in bed. As she pushed herself into a sitting position, sliding herself out from beneath the covers, her beautifully sculptured breasts sprung from under the duvet. Brenda sat there, unmoved and seemingly, unconcerned at their exposure, smiling up at him as if nothing untoward had happened. She gleefully saw George's eyes widen and glance down, as if drawn by a magnet, but only for a brief moment. He looked into her eyes and smiled. She smiled back, almost apologetically.

'Oops. Sorry' she said, giggling and very slowly pulled the duvet up over her chest, tucking it tightly under her arms. She took a sip of her tea.

'It must be wonderful waking up to a smile like that every morning,' she said, grinning at him.

'Brenda,' George said, wagging his finger at her in mock reprimand.

'Oh sorry. Did I say that out loud?' she giggled again. 'I will come in with you, Mr. Miller, if that's okay.' George nodded.

'As long as you feel strong enough.'

'I feel better than I have for a very long time, thank you.'

Over a breakfast of poached eggs on toast and orange juice, the limit of George's culinary skills, she apologised again for her behaviour the previous evening.

'I am sorry George. It must have been the drink. It doesn't take much to get me a little tipsy. You know that from years ago. And I think with all the emotions that had been stored up inside, the champagne just opened the floodgates for all my inhibitions to pour out. I hope you can forgive me. On the bright side, I really am quite a cheap date you know.' George laughed.

'There is nothing to worry about and nothing to be sorry for. You have had a terrible time recently, so it's not surprising that you're a little bit 'mixed up'.' They smiled at each other, in a way that made sense of the previous evening's drama.

George's Range Rover pulled into the street from the depths of the underground car park. Baz jumped to attention. He had spent an uncomfortable and sleepless night waiting for the re-emergence of his victim. It was nine o'clock. The sun was shining brightly and it was easy to see the two occupants clearly. Both George and Brenda sat in the front seats. Baz saw Brenda putting the final touches to her makeup, with the aid of the passenger seat vanity mirror. He followed them back to the club, recording all the time. When they reached the club, the two of them jumped out of the car and walked, hand in hand, towards the main entrance. They looked for all the world like two young lovers, the jaunty skip of their gait a stark contrast to their deportment the previous morning. They were playing right into Baz' hands. He couldn't have scripted the scene any better. They were providing more and more evidence with every passing second. Even Baz was now convinced that something must be going on between them. About twenty feet from the door, they were approached by a man. He was shouting and screaming at them both, waving his arms about and pointing aggressively. For all his hostility and bluster Baz noticed that the man kept a safe distance between himself and George. This was certainly unexpected. Baz frowned and tried to make sense of this unforeseen slice of drama. He got out of his car, his phone still trained on the action. The man's rants were loud enough not only to be heard, but also to register clearly on Baz' recording.

'You, fucking slag. I know where you've been. Don't think you can fool me. You've been shagging this bastard for years. At work and now back at his flat.' Jeremy made a move towards Brenda. 'You're coming home with me now and we will sort this out.' Brenda cowered behind George, peering out from the safety of George's shelter. George took a step towards Jeremy, with a terrifying look on his face. Jeremy stopped in his tracks. He wasn't about to pick a fight with

George. Not only was he easily Jeremy's equal, physically, but Jeremy didn't have the stomach, or the balls, to pick on anyone who might fight back. George marched towards him, with fists clenched and fire in his eyes.

'Back off Jeremy, or so help me God I will fucking kill you, here and now.' Jeremy continued to retreat, away from the smouldering Miller. This time the fear and the panic were in Jeremy's eyes. Brenda grabbed George's jacket and tugged him back.

'Leave him George. Just leave him. He's not worth it,' she pleaded. George grudgingly went back to Brenda's side and put a protective arm around her. He glared at Jeremy and pointed his finger at him.

'If you ever come within a mile of her again, I swear I will tear you apart with my own bare hands. Now fuck off and don't come back.' As they disappeared into the main building, they could hear Jeremy hurling more abuse at them.

'I bet your fucking wife would like to know about this. And she's going to. I've been so stupid and so has she. That poor woman. Well, Debbie Miller is going to hear about this. I will tell her how long this has been going on for. You're a dead man, Miller. I will see to that. A dead man.'

Baz was aghast. The confrontation, the shouted accusations and the abuse, were not cast-iron evidence of an affair, but on top of everything else he had on Miller, it was a pretty damning episode, to add to the already growing amount of footage he had managed to record of the two of them. He watched the angry stranger as he was frogmarched out of the main gates by a couple of security guards who had eventually turned up to see what all the commotion was about. He would have a chat with him. It was clear they were going to be allies. Both were committed to the destruction and the humiliation of George Miller. But Baz was adamant he would be the one to administer the "coup de gras", and he would do it, only when he was good and ready.

Chapter 23

All puff and no wind

Baz' eyes followed the disgruntled stranger, as he furiously stomped his way down the street. Jeremy's face was red with fury and rage. Every few steps, turning his head back towards the club and shouting more vitriolic and threatening abuse.

Baz waited until Jeremy was only a few yards away, then stepped out into the middle of the pavement.

'Excuse me. Can I have a word with you?' Jeremy stopped dead in his tracks.

'What? Who the fuck are you?' The anger and the menace were still evident in his voice, but there was a sudden flash of fear in his eyes.

'I wonder if you could spare me a few moments of your time. I have a proposition to put to you.' Baz smiled at him and tried to put him at ease. Having seen him back away, as soon as George had moved towards him, Baz knew the type of man he was dealing with. All puff and no wind. A coward.

'What sort of proposition could you possibly have, that I would be interested in?' he demanded.

'George Miller,' Baz said bluntly. Jeremy's eyes narrowed under the weight of his frown.

'What about George Miller? What do you know about that arsehole?' Baz slowly stepped towards him, smiling.

'Well, I know he has been fucking your wife for years. It's been common knowledge around here for ages. Everybody knows. And now,' Baz patted Jeremy gently on the cheek, making him instantly flinch, 'even you know.' The fury once again flooded back into Jeremy's face.

'And what's that got to do with you?' His frown deepened and his tone became more intimidatory.

'George Miller has been screwing up my life since he was eleven years old. In fact, I must be the only person in the world, at this very moment, who hates George Miller more than you do.' As Baz' smile grew larger, so did Jeremy's look of confusion. Again, Baz patted Jeremy in a friendly way, this time on the arm and again Jeremy flinched.

'Look, there is a pub about a mile down the road. They do breakfast. Why don't we meet in there and we can discuss our mutual friend in a bit more detail?

Over a coffee and a sausage sandwich, the two men swapped stories. Baz didn't want to give too much away about his past, or his real reasons for wanting to see Miller go down, so he let Jeremy do most of the talking. Every suspicion Jeremy voiced about his wife's indiscretions, Baz confirmed as true, as if her flagrant flirting and sexual activity with her boss and others, had been common knowledge. He fanned the flames of Jeremy's contempt, for both George and Brenda and did nothing to alleviate his growing insecurity. He told him of their school days together and George's relationship with Debbie. Everything he said cemented Jeremy's conviction that what he was saying must be true. With a doleful look on his face, Baz told him that years earlier, Miller had had an affair with his wife and destroyed his family and his happiness; so, binding them as brothers against a common enemy.

'Trust me Jeremy, I know what you are going through right now and I know how tough it is to see the woman you love betray you for a man like Miller. He has shagged so many other people's wives. He just takes what he wants and couldn't care less about who he hurts. Your wife must be a bit special though. I can't imagine what exotic tricks she must perform for him. She has certainly lasted longer than any of the others. They have been at it since his playing days, years ago. I'm surprised you didn't find out earlier! I guess the only person who doesn't know now, is Miller's wife. Poor cow.'

Baz showed Jeremy some of the footage on his phone. The kiss, Brenda getting into George's car and driving to his flat and, after spending the night together, leaving that morning.

'It's all on here,' Baz said, tapping his mobile phone. 'He just thinks he is immune. But I'm going to nail that homewrecking bastard, once and for all. I will need your help though.'

Jeremy leant forward and nodded, eager to ingratiate himself to his newfound friend. All of his suspicions and distrust had evaporated. He was convinced Baz was an ally. A powerful and menacing ally whom he could rely on to not only bring Miller to book, but also to confront him physically; something he had no stomach for.

'Okay. Anything. I'll do anything to see him destroyed.'

'Good. Then this is what I need you to do.' Baz leant forward and paused. 'Nothing. Don't do a thing. Don't put anything on social media. Don't go to the press and definitely don't say anything to his wife. I have a plan that will destroy him, but not before we've had a bit of fun at his expense. I want to watch him suffer for a while first. Trust me. Leave it to me and in a couple of weeks we will be back in here, toasting the utter destruction and humiliation of that adulterous git.'

For the first time since they had met, Jeremy had a huge smile on his face. He knew he had met a man with just as many reasons to hate Miller as he had. He would do as he had been told. Sit tight and do nothing. He would stay out of George's way and any danger and watch as Baz' plan, whatever it might be, played out. Jeremy felt the warm burn of hatred, revenge and satisfaction glow in his body. He would deal with his wife when the time came. He could do that. He was looking forward to it. But he would let Baz take care of George Miller first.

They shook hands as allies. Baz said he would keep in touch. They swapped phone numbers and went their separate ways.

Baz had taken an instant dislike to his new comrade. He was everything he despised in a man. As violent and as cruel as Baz could be, he had never taken out his anger on a woman. In Baz' mind there was nothing more despicable or cowardly. Jeremy was a bully with no balls. He was chicken shit. There was no substance to the man. He was a weasel. But he might prove to be a very valuable weasel. Baz realised that Jeremy hated Miller so much, he would say, or do, anything to incriminate him. Baz could make up any story about Miller or Brenda, tell Jeremy and he would believe it as gospel.

He would keep in touch with his new friend for as long as it suited him. But not a second longer.

Chapter 24

'Thank you, my hero'

The ease with which George had managed to scare Jeremy off gave Brenda an added sense of security. She knew as long as she was near George, she would be safe. She had felt both shock and excitement in her veins when she saw the fear and the panic in Jeremy's eyes, as George went to confront him. There was a little part of her that regretted pulling George back, stopping him from delivering what she assumed would have been a savage and humiliating beating. She may even have had the pleasure of seeing Jeremy turn and runaway. Just the thought of that made her smile. Bloody coward. But it was the look in his eyes that had given her the most pleasure. The very same look of terror he had induced in her for so many years.

During the morning, she constantly checked her phone, expecting some kind of contact from her disgruntled husband. But there were no missed calls, text messages or voicemails. She didn't know whether she was expecting a torrent of abuse, or a pitiful apology. Frankly she couldn't care less what he did or said. She knew, after the scene outside, earlier that morning, there was no going back. That thought made her feel good. As far as she was concerned her new life had just begun. She was relieved, however, to see that he had in fact left her completely alone. She wondered how long that would last for.

Brenda took George in his second cup of tea and tried to behave as if everything was normal. Just another day.

'Thank you, Brenda. Are you okay?'

'You're welcome and yes I am fine, thank you Mr. Miller.' George frowned at her. She laughed.

'Sorry. You are welcome and yes, I am fine, thank you. My hero.' She giggled and wiggled her hips out of his office, with the same exaggerated sassy swing he had been used to seeing years before. It seemed that not only was the "happy smiley" Brenda back, but also the youthful, effervescent and fun-loving girl he'd known when he was a player.

The day to day running of the club was a pleasant distraction after what had happened that week. Doug's funeral on the Monday, Debbie and the kids leaving on the Tuesday and all the shenanigans that had been going on in Brenda's life. It had been a hectic few days. It was Thursday and all George's attention could now be focused on the game coming up on Saturday. Football matters. That's what he was paid to do.

Brenda bounced into his office. It was just after midday. Her smile lit up the room.

'I've just had a call from Mr. Saunders. He is Jayden's father. He asked if he could speak with you, face to face. There are a number of things he wants to discuss with you, about his son. He is interested in what you see as the boy's long term, and short term, future. He said he had a few ideas he would like to share with you. Ideas he thinks might help you get the best out of the boy. Apparently, he has been *away* for some time. He said he thinks it will be beneficial to everyone concerned if he can meet with you. You have a relatively clear afternoon. He suggested four o'clock, so I said okay, if that's good with you?'

'Great. That sounds perfect. I've wanted to talk to him about the little sod's attitude anyway. Four o'clock it is then. Thank you, Brenda.

Chapter 25

Sweet cheeks

At four o'clock precisely Brenda knocked on George's door.

'Mr. Saunders is here to see you Mr. Miller.' George stood up and began to walk around his desk to greet his guest.

'Mr Saunders. It's so nice to meet……. YOU!! As soon as Baz emerged from behind Brenda, George's expression changed. The warm and welcoming smile had disappeared and had been replaced with a look of shock and horror. He recognised him straight away. George stood still, rooted to the spot, his arm still extended for the intended handshake. Baz looked down at his offered hand and shook his head.

'No thanks. Don't think I will. Sort of goes against the grain, shaking one of the Millers by the hand.' He looked at George with menacing and piercing eyes. 'Shaking one by the neck would be more to my liking.'

Brenda frowned as she felt the atmosphere in the room turn instantly frosty.

'Thank you, Brenda, that will be all.' Baz just stood there grinning, bathing in the immediate impact his presence had had. Brenda shut the door, a worried expression on her face.

'Hello Miller. It's been a long time.' George could think of nothing to say. He was dumb struck.

'You look like you've just seen a ghost.' Baz chuckled. 'Well, maybe you have and I think the haunting is just about to begin.' Without being asked, Baz brushed past George and sat down on one of the chairs in front of his desk. 'Sit down Miller,' he ordered. 'Cosy little setup you've got here.' Baz craned his neck towards the door from which Brenda had just left. 'Plenty of perks on offer for the man in charge I suspect.'

'What do you want Baz? I've got no time to waste on you. If you think you can come waltzing in here after all these years and start throwing your weight around, you've got another think coming.'

'Oh, I don't know about that George. I wouldn't be quite so aggressive if I were you. I think, for your own good, you should listen to what I've got to say. So many things have changed since we last met.'

'The last time we met? Oh yes, I remember that occasion very well. I don't think I have ever seen someone bleed so much. It was a wonderful sight….and of course, a treasured memory. Looks like you kept a reminder of the incident as well.' George gestured towards the scar that snaked around his left eye. 'I would be happy to give you a matching pair.' Baz rubbed the scar softly with his fingers.

'Yes, it's been a constant reminder to me of unfinished business. And here we are. Maybe it's time to settle our affairs.'

'Anytime you want Baz.' George stood up and glared at him. Baz remained seated.

'As much as I would love to beat you physically, I have the means to hurt you even more severely and permanently than just a few blows to your angelic face. I have it within my power to destroy everything you treasure and the best bit is, I don't even have to raise a finger.' He laughed and watched, while George tried to make sense of what he was saying.

'I can get security in here within seconds and have you thrown out and I won't have to raise a finger either. If you haven't got anything else to say, I suggest you leave before I…'

'Don't be so hasty Miller. You *will* listen to what I have to say. A situation has been brought to my attention, which, if we all stay calm, could benefit everyone.' George thought for a moment and sat back down. The silence was suddenly broken by a knock at the door. Brenda then popped her head into the room.

'Can I get either of you gentlemen anything to drink?' Before Baz had time to answer, George blurted out, 'Not now, thank you Brenda,' in a brusque tone that rather took her by surprise. She said nothing and closed the door.

'Like I said, you seem to have a pretty cushy deal going on here. Your secretary's a real cutie. Probably very loyal. Do anything for you. I bet she is a good fuck.' George's glare sprang back onto his face. He stood bolt upright again and began to move towards Baz.

'George, George, George, we're not going to get anywhere very fast, if you keep popping up like a Jack-in-the-box every time I say something that offends your delicate disposition. Trust me, I will be saying a lot more that will offend you this afternoon.' He almost chuckled his way through the last sentence. Then the humour was gone. With threat and menace he leant forward. 'Now sit down. Shut the fuck up and listen.' He leant back and resumed talking in a more friendly tone. 'You will be making a massive mistake if you don't hear me out. Not that it would bother me at all. I think I am in, what is known as, a "win-win" situation. I've got you either way. But I do think you should concentrate on what I am about to tell you. At least then you can decide how and when your life falls apart.' George grudgingly sat back down again.

'There's a good boy. Now, my lad Jayden has shown me a rather interesting video he took on his phone, Tuesday morning. I won't bore you with the entire production. I think you know how the film ends anyway. I have taken the liberty to print a couple of frames off, just to jog your memory.' Baz slung the brown A4 size envelope he had been carrying, onto George's desk.

'Agreed, it's not particularly good quality, but it doesn't need to be. The moving footage is far more, shall we say, moving, sensual and erotic.' George opened the envelope and took out the contents. Printed onto regular A4 size paper were a number of images of him and Brenda. The first was them kissing in his office. *That kiss.* The second was of the two of them holding hands, walking towards the main building, looking to all the world like a loving couple. George gritted his teeth. That was a stupid thing to do, even though it had felt perfectly natural at the time. The third was a still from the confrontation between him and Jeremy, earlier that morning, showing George with his arm around Brenda's shoulder and Jeremy gesticulating at them both. George tried to stop his face from portraying the horror and panic he could feel envelop him and tried to go onto the offensive. He picked up the picture of him kissing Brenda and waved it at Baz.

'This could be anyone,' he said, with disdain, even though he could clearly see his face and of course, his office in the background. Baz shrugged his shoulders.

'Maybe, but like I told you, the full-length movie is much more revealing. Brings a tear to my eye every time I watch it.' He smiled. 'I also have footage of the two of you, going back to your place together and footage of you both leaving this morning. By way of a bonus, I also captured that rather charming little encounter you had with Jeremy, as you can see,' he said tapping the picture. 'I have to say George you certainly were her knight in shining armour this morning. Protecting her from that evil, nasty man. The dialogue in that conversation would suggest he thinks you are screwing his wife. I had a long chat with him. We got on famously. And between you and me George, he is convinced you and his wife have been at it "hammer and tongs" for some time. I don't know *where* he got that idea from.' Baz let a wide grin take over his face. 'You naughty boy George.' George looked like he was going to say something, but Baz raised his finger and put it to his lips.

'Shh. Let me finish.' There was another moment of silence. 'It's a very interesting relationship you have with her. I'm intrigued. Does she call you Mr. Miller when you're banging her, here in the office, or do you allow her to call you George, when you have your cock inside her?' George felt like he was going to explode, but he bit his lip. Baz smiled. He knew Miller was seething inside. He could see the anger and fury in his face. He also knew he had him worried. The fact that he was still sitting there, letting him talk to him like that, was evidence of Miller's consternation. This was much more fun than he had ever imagined it could be. 'Now back to business. We have a situation that I believe can benefit both of us. As I have shown you and informed you, I have photographs and film of you and your secretary engaged in behaviour that will raise a few eyebrows if they are ever made public. Kissing, holding hands, driving to and from your apartment, last thing at night and first thing in the morning. Suspicious eh? They all go to make up a rather pitiful story of a married man and a married woman, cheating on their own spouses. My new friend, Jeremy, is prepared to swear that Brenda has already confessed to him about your affair. I think with your past reputation and all this evidence, the press and the public would put "two and two together" and…well, I'll leave that to your imagination. Then of course there is the lovely Debbie Morris. I bet she would be interested in what you have been getting up to at work. Sorry. You married the girl, didn't you? Debbie Miller now, isn't it? It does seem like a bit of a coincidence, that you move your secretary into your flat the day after your wife goes away on holiday with the kids. Or am I just being a teeny-weeny bit cynical? I'm sure she is very trusting and of course, she would stand by you, in public anyway. Although it's never quite the same is it, afterwards? After all the media coverage has died down and the gutter press finds some other poor schmuck to get their claws into, there is always that nagging doubt in the other half's mind. Did he? Didn't he? You know, "no smoke without fire". I doubt any relationship, however strong, is really the same after one of these scandals. What do you think George?'

'You know there is nothing in it, Baz. I'm just protecting her from that wife-beating prick. Even a low life like you can't seriously want to mix with his sort. Anyway, all this evidence is meaningless. It proves nothing.' George flung the printed paper back onto his desk.

'Do you know what? I almost agree with you. If you were to pay an expensive barrister and show these, and everything else I have, before a judge and jury, they just might find in your favour. Fickle bunch these jurors. Trust me, I know. The trouble is George, it's not a judge and jury you have to convince. It's the general public and the press, and most of all, it's your wife. I'm guessing that might be a tougher task. Smoke and fire again. Now what I suggest is, we try and keep your liaison with Brenda quiet from Debbie and "Joe Public". It wouldn't do to have one of the country's favourite sporting celebrities reputation destroyed.'

'What do you want Baz?'

'Ah, well done George. There was me waffling on about how concerned I am for your marriage and reputation. Cut to the chase. That's more like it. So, what do I want? Well, I am struggling to make ends meet at the moment, as you can imagine. Sadly, there aren't many people out there who are willing to take on a poor bastard who has just been let out of the slammer. Even my old mate Frankie D'Costa, remember him? blew me out. What do you think about that? No old school tie thing going on there I'm afraid. Ahh well, Frankie always was a bit of a wanker, in my opinion. I guess that must be something we have in common eh? Anyway, Jayden's career has only just started and it will be a little while before he is earning the sort of wages he will need to keep his old dad in the lifestyle he deserves. What I suggest is you pay me a small signing on fee. An 'agent's percentage' you know. All above board. Shall we say 100K to start with? I don't think that would be asking too much. I know what you earn Miller and 100K is a drop in the ocean for you.'

'So that's it, is it? Straight blackmail. After all that, it's just money you want. I should have known a piece of shit like you wouldn't have the brains to think of anything more creative. I can see the similarity between you and your son. You are both the same. Arrogant, greedy and pathetic. What I can tell you, is your son will never play for this club and if I have anything to say in the matter, for any other top-flight club, for the foreseeable future. He is finished here and so are you Baz. I think it's time you left.'

'George, you have underestimated me. Of course, the money will be nice and I think that's only fair, but the second part of the deal is my favourite bit. I like to think of it as "youth development". To contradict what you just said about Jayden never playing for this club, he *will* play, on Saturday. He will start the game and he *will* play the full ninety minutes, regardless of what happens.' Baz smiled and left his words hanging menacingly in the air.

'You must be crazy. I can't do that.' Baz just shrugged his shoulders and looked helpless.

'Technology these days George, is a wonderful thing. I can download and send anything and everything I have on you and "sweet cheeks" out there, to every news station and sports editor in the world within seconds. I wouldn't even have to bother with your wife. She would see it in glorious technicolour, on the enormous TV screens I'm sure you have at your home, or where ever she is on holiday. She could snuggle up with your kids and watch as Daddy destroys everything they cherish. What a terrible end to an otherwise spotless career. On the other hand, you could rattle up the cash, play Jayden on Saturday, for the entire game and no one will be any the wiser. Everyone a winner. What do you say?' After a moments pause for thought, George spoke.

'What guarantee do I have that you won't post these images?' Baz roared with laughter and put his hands in the air triumphantly.

'That's the best bit Georgie boy. You don't have any guarantees, apart from my word of honour. You are just going to have to trust your old schoolmate. The one guarantee I can give you though, is that if you don't come up with the cash, or go against our "selection policy" on Saturday, the shit will hit the fan. I think I can guarantee you will feature heavily on the evenings news and it won't be anything to do with the result. I suspect it will herald the beginning of what will be a very awkward time for you, your wife and of course "sweet cheeks". The three of you will be all over the papers and the TV, quicker than you can say *"Nice to meet you Mr. Saunders".*' Baz smiled and stood up. 'I've obviously given you some things to think about. I will wait until after the game on Saturday. If Jayden plays the full ninety minutes, I'll know we have a deal. If he doesn't, well, you know what will happen. Don't worry about seeing me out. I know the way. Nice meeting you again Miller. This time I'm sure our liaison will be more fruitful.' Baz walked to the door and let himself out.

Two minutes later, Brenda walked in.

'Is everything okay George? Mr. Saunders popped his head around my door on his way out. He said I should come in and see if you needed a stiff drink. He called me "sweet cheeks". Cheeky git.' George was left, just staring into space, with a blank look on his face.

'George is everything alright?' she asked him again. Without moving his head, or his fixed gaze, he replied in a monotone voice,

'Yes. Everything is fine, thank you, Brenda.'

Chapter 26

Everyone a winner

After Baz had left, George found it difficult to concentrate on his work. He had been rocked by his sudden and totally unexpected appearance. Baz had been right when he said, *George looked like he'd seen a ghost*. That's exactly how he felt.

Before Baz had arrived, George was trying to come to terms with the problems he had created for himself. Kissing Brenda, he knew was a mistake, but it was something he felt the two of them could have dealt with. They could have talked it through, realised it was something that had happened in the heat of the moment and forgotten about it; a moment so trivial it would have merited no further mention; an undisclosed incident of such unimportance, it didn't even qualify as a regretful memory. Unfortunately, the episode had been filmed by Jayden, which made things far more awkward and put the incident in an entirely different perspective. Although George was furious with the boy, he had hoped he could persuade him that there was nothing to be gained by making the recording public. The only result of that would be, the end of his contract at the club and George, carrying out his threat to do everything in his power to undermine any other prospective Premier League interest. Surely the boy wasn't stupid enough to gamble his fledgling career on a petulant prank. Then there was the situation between Brenda and Jeremy. Moving her into his flat, for her own safety, seemed like the only decent and proper thing to do. Not for one moment had George considered what it would look like to the outside world, or what assumptions people would jump to, if it ever became known they were living under the same roof, let alone what Debbie's reaction would be. He now realised just how naïve he had been. But again, he was sure Debbie would understand his actions. Taken in isolation, his decision to invite Brenda to stay, should have been seen as an act of mercy and friendship and nothing else. But then Baz arrived on the scene. From the one conversation they'd had, it was clear to George that he was going to manipulate and twist the facts, to make it plain to the world that he and Brenda were having an affair. The extraordinary coincidence of Jayden being his son and the fact that Baz had "teamed up" with Jeremy had changed the whole dynamic of the drama. Now all the dots had been joined together. It would be impossible to tackle individual events in isolation. The numerous, but manageable predicaments he had been confronted with, had now merged together under Baz' orchestration and become one monumental threat to his way of life. What had started out as a difficult and uncomfortable situation, had escalated into a sinister and menacing horror story, that could wreak havoc with everything he held dear. Baz had only been back in George's life for a few hours, but in that short space of time, his entire world had been shaken to the core.

George was convinced that if Baz had turned up at any other time, his appearance would have been greeted with amusement and humour. Doubtless he and Graham would have revelled in any conflict or aggression he would have thrown at them. Just as it was back in their schooldays, the brothers would have taken great delight in going toe-to-toe with him. But he had turned up now and transformed what should have been a minor inconvenience, into a full blown and serious crisis. George leant back in his seat, nervously fiddling with his pen, searching desperately for a solution. He knew he had to be wary of Baz. He would be foolish to underestimate him. Although he hadn't seen him for more than twenty-six years, it was abundantly clear he was no longer dealing with the brash, cocky teenager he and his brother had been at war with all those years ago. Baz was now a hardened criminal who had comparatively little to lose, whereas George stood to lose everything. He would have to take his threats seriously. If he had all the footage he claimed to possess, then George knew he was in a lot of bother. As much as it irked him, he knew he had to try and placate Baz until he could come up with a plan, or a story, that would help him explain everything to his wife. He knew deep down, that was what mattered most to him. As long as Debbie understood and believed him, the rest of his problems were manageable. Any other repercussions or consequences he would be faced with, paled into insignificance compared to his family's happiness and well being. He would never do anything to jeopardise that.

Once he and Brenda had returned to the flat that evening, George headed straight to his bedroom. He left Brenda watching the TV with a glass of wine. Brenda was now comfortable and relaxed. She had found her smile again and was beginning to remember what happiness and security felt like. George on the other hand, had transformed into a man who felt like he had the troubles of the world weighing him down. He hadn't told her about Baz and his attempt at blackmail. He would deal with him in his own way and not involve her. She had enough on her mind.

He face-timed Debbie and spoke to the kids, his in-laws and finally to his wife. They spoke for nearly an hour. Debbie told him what they had been doing and what they had planned for the following couple of weeks. It sounded like they were having a wonderful time. When she asked him, what had been happening in his life, George tried to sound as matter of fact as he could. He knew he was a terrible liar but tried to keep his voice and body language as steady and as normal as possible. Debbie had always been able to see right through him. She had an uncanny knack of knowing if he ever attempted to bend or stretch the truth. He hoped the Face Time images on her phone were not as transparent as real life. He told her about the problems he was having with the young boy Jayden and that he had created quite a stir since his arrival. But he mentioned nothing about the identity of his father, or what kind of business arrangements were now planned with the ex-con. George could feel the guilt beginning to rise in him as he told Debbie everything he could, but nothing he should. It wasn't that he was actually lying to her, he just wasn't really telling her the full truth. He remembered how his mother would regularly try and impress on him and his brother, the importance of being honest. *"The truth will never get you into trouble and if it does you probably deserve it"*. They were wise words from a wise woman, but they were sentiments he was struggling to abide by. He hated himself for not being straight with his wife and he wondered if his decision would come back to haunt him in a couple of weeks. They said their goodbyes and told each other "I love you". Once they had hung up, George lay back onto the bed. He stared long and hard at his reflection gazing back at him from the huge mirror on the ceiling, willing it to come up with a solution. But sadly, his reflected image looked just as helpless and bamboozled as he did. He wondered what the next two weeks had in store. It had been a crazy few days and promised to get even crazier. What would he do about playing Jayden on the Saturday? Would compliance make his life easier, or would it just make things even more difficult in the long run? Life had suddenly become very complicated indeed.

George walked into the lounge. In the time he had been on the phone, Brenda had had a bath and changed into her bathrobe. George's mind instantly flashed back to the moment the bathrobe slid off her shoulders and the glorious vision he had been presented with. He had to get that image out of his mind. He had to control it. He knew it excited him. He wished it didn't.

Brenda was sipping her wine and looked as laidback and at ease as George could ever remember seeing her. She glanced at him over her shoulder as he went to the fridge to get himself a bottle of beer.

'You look like I used to feel' Brenda said sympathetically. 'Is everything okay with Debbie and the kids?' George sat down and nodded his head.

'Yes, they're all fine and having a wonderful time.' He paused. 'The thing is Brenda, I haven't said anything about you being here, or your situation with Jeremy.' Brenda frowned and looked concerned. She put her glass on the table and leant forward.

'George, are you sure that's wise? Why haven't you told her?' It was a good question. One he had been asking himself all day. He drew in a deep breath and began trying to convince Brenda of something, which he himself was unsure of.

'Because she would pack up and come home straight away and as much as I miss them all, at the moment that would just make things more awkward. I will tell her everything when she returns. I'm sure that's the best way to handle it.'

Brenda didn't look convinced. She picked up her wine and sat back into the sofa.

'George, I'm very grateful for what you have done for me recently. But I don't want my problems with Jeremy to impact on you and Debbie. I don't want my happiness to be at the expense of yours. I really couldn't live with myself if I thought that by keeping me safe, you and Debbie's relationship would suffer.'

George smiled at her. He knew she meant every word of what she had just said. She really was one of the sweetest, loveliest people he had ever known. She sat on the sofa, with her legs tucked underneath her and the blue bathrobe hanging loosely around her body. He felt his eyes begin to wander from her face, down towards the tantalisingly narrow gap left by the two lapels of the gown, teasingly displaying just a hint of her wonderful cleavage. Before he had a chance to develop his thoughts, he banished them to the back of his mind and raised his stare back into her eyes.

'So, for now we will leave it like that. I'm sure it is for the best and everything will be fine by the time they come home. We have done nothing wrong and have no need to feel any kind of guilt. It's a situation that has arisen and been dealt with. This way you don't get beaten up, I don't lose my right-hand man..., sorry, woman and Debbie and the kids have a great holiday. Everyone a winner.'

He sat back and gulped down a few mouthfuls of beer. Weren't they the same words Baz had used, when talking about their "arrangement", earlier that afternoon? The two issues were undoubtedly connected, but George was struggling to see how anyone could be a winner, especially him. He knew his hands were tied. He had no control over the situation. Baz and Jaydan held all the aces. He decided his only option for the time being, was to play along with Baz' proposition. Try and buy himself a little time and hope the confusion and uncertainty would clear and the threat and danger to his world would dissipate. Unfortunately, that was the best plan he could come up with; it was the only plan he could come up with! He was as worried and unsure about the future, as he had been for a very long time.

Chapter 27

The lad was in danger of getting a slap

The one thing George had been relying on, to keep his mind occupied while his family were away, was his work. But now, even the sanctuary of his managerial duties had been infected by the canker that Baz had injected into his life. For most of Friday night George lay awake, desperately trying to come up with a plan that would at least give him some breathing space. Reluctantly, he had come to the conclusion that the only way to keep Baz off of his back, would be to give Jayden a game. To conform with Baz' demands; he knew he would also have to play him for the full ninety minutes. Even without all the problems that had arisen, because of the boy's attitude and arrogance, George would still have been unlikely to pick him. But now he had no option. The fixture list, however, had been kind. They were due to play the team wallowing at the bottom of the league and struggling badly. It was a game they were expected to win and win handsomely. If ever there was a game in which George could be seen to experiment, it was this one. Lady luck had dealt him some bad hands over the previous week, but being matched against these opponents was a godsend.

Once the players had arrived, they sat down in the meeting room and George went over the tactics and strategies they would be employing. Every game was taken as seriously as the next one. Top of the table, bottom of the table, even cup games against lower league clubs were all shown the same respect and attention to detail.

George's methods were a little more modern than the ones he remembered Bernie Roswell using when he was the manager. Gone were the pointing sticks with whiteboards and coloured markers. Large, touchscreen TVs and computers had replaced the previous generation of coaching tools. George ran through his starting line-up. It was a largely predictable set of names, with one exception.

'Jayden Saunders will be playing up front, alongside David Jones.' George paused and waited to see what sort of reaction his bombshell would have. There was a ripple of movement, some players shuffling in their seats and a few mutterings. George could feel the sense of surprise in the room.

'I'm going to give him a chance to show us what we have invested in. Alf, don't think I have forgotten you. I am sure you will get a go at some point.' George smiled at the somewhat agog face of Alfie Wood, his star striker. Alf just nodded back. A few of the players sitting near Jayden, patted him on the back and congratulated him on his surprise selection. The news had come as a shock to all of them, but not to Jayden. He sat there with a smug grin on his face. His Dad had told him he would be starting the game and he also knew that, barring injury, he would be playing the full ninety minutes.

As George had hoped, his side romped to a comfortable victory. A six-nil thrashing. Alf did get on for the last half an hour, even managing to bag himself a couple of goals. But he didn't come on for Jayden. He stayed on and David Jones was substituted much to his disbelief. The game had been so one-sided, Jayden was able to show off his skills and acquitted himself rather well. George's decision to play the sixteen-year-old was hailed as a brave but ultimately successful gamble. Aside from his caustic personality and corrosive relationship with just about everyone he had come into contact with, Jayden's ability was plain to see. Doug had been right about that. The lad could certainly look forward to a bright future if he knuckled down and put in the hard work and commitment required. As George had found out at an early age, talent wasn't everything and was certainly no guarantee of success. He would have to put in the time and effort if he were to prosper at this, or any other club. Otherwise, he would be out on his ear, (although Baz might have something to say about that).

Jayden's successful debut, along with all of the plaudits he received from both players and commentators after the game, did little to dampen his ego. Interviewed by numerous sports channels and journalists, he showed no humility whatsoever. He brashly predicted, on national television, that he was the future.

Before leaving the ground after the match, both Jones and Wood, as well as a number of other players, approached George to voice their, less than complimentary, opinions on their new superstar. He was arrogant and rude. Woody even suggested, in his heavy Macclesfield accent, that the lad was in danger of getting a slap, if he continued to talk to him like he had been. George reassured them he would have a word with him. He suggested they put it down to overexcitement and the exuberance of youth. But he knew it was nothing to do with that. He was, sadly, *a chip off the old block*. An unpleasant and loathsome human being, just like his father. George wished he had someone like Terry Bridges playing for him. Terry wouldn't have taken any nonsense from the brat. He would have knocked some sense into him, one way or another and probably had a pop at Baz as well for that matter. During all his years in the game, George had encountered many hard cases, both on the field and in real life, but he had never known, or met anyone as fearsome, or as terrifying as Terry Bridges. Terry had been, and still was, a good friend. But he was no longer part of the club. Maybe if he had been on the coaching staff, things would have been different. George let his mind wander and pictured a confrontation between Terry and Baz. He smiled to himself. In George's imagined stand-off between the two hard men, he didn't fancy Baz' chances against his old captain and team-mate.

George spoke to Debbie on the Sunday afternoon and once again said nothing about either Brenda or Baz. Having decided to take that approach, he knew he had to stick with it until she returned home. He knew it was imperative to keep Baz happy and playing his son, as instructed, seemed to have done the trick; for now, anyway. He would have two more weeks, to either think of a solution, or have one present itself to him. If the worst came to the worst, he would sit Debbie down and explain everything. The truth. He was hopeful that she would believe him and trust him, enough to understand what and why he had done everything he had, in the time she had been away.

Chapter 28

Sleeping with Moneypenny

Just after 10 o'clock on the Monday morning, George's door swung open and in marched Baz.
'Morning Miller.' Before George could answer, Brenda came flying in.

'Excuse me, Mr. Saunders, you can't just come barging in here without an appointment. 'I'm sorry George …….Errr…Mr. Miller.' She hastily corrected herself. Brenda looked flustered and a little cross; George looked shocked and surprised. Baz looked amused at the commotion his unexpected arrival had caused. He grinned at the disgruntled secretary.

'That's alright, sweet cheeks. Don't worry about it. Me and George here, have got some business to discuss.' Brenda's expression suggested she was about to explode with rage. The man's audacity and total lack of respect for both George's privacy and her station had taken her completely off guard. And calling her *"sweet cheeks"*, well that was the last straw. She looked at George with incredulity, waiting for his reaction and hoping for some form of solidarity.

'George?'

'That's alright Brenda. I will see Mr. Saunders now. Thank you.' She glared at Baz, who smiled and winked at her, which made her even angrier. Brenda left and shut the door. Baz sat himself down.

'A good result on Saturday, Miller. Think you'll agree my boy shone out like a rare jewel. I think I've done you a bit of a favour, getting you to fast track him into the first team. So much so, I have been reconsidering this signing on fee you are going to pay me. After Saturday I think it only fair we up the price to let's say, 200K. It's still a bargain in today's market.' Baz lent back in his chair and clasped his hands together, resting them on his chest. He smiled at George, whose face was showing all the signs of panic, worry and anger. He had his old enemy cornered and they both knew it. Baz was enjoying this much more than he had ever thought possible. 'I think you and I are going to work very well together. Now that's not a phrase I thought I would ever say to one of the Miller boys,' he laughed.

'Now look Baz, just because the lad played well, doesn't mean anything. And as far as the money is concerned, I won't be able to …….' Baz interrupted him.

'Listen Miller. You don't seem to understand. I'm not *asking* you. I'm *telling* you. The signing on fee is now 200K. I will give you a few days to get that together. Jayden will start the game on Wednesday and he will play the entire match. It's as simple as that.'

A look of astonishment burst onto George's face.

'But Baz, I can't risk him on Wednesday. The game is too important. I need to play my best eleven. I would be mad to consider him. It's too much of a gamble.' George could see his reasoning was having no effect on the smiling hyena sitting before him. 'Maybe we can come to some other arrangement. I could…' Baz raised his finger and pointed it at George.

'He starts and he plays the full ninety.' Baz leant forward in his chair. 'I'm guessing you haven't said anything to your wife yet about 'sweet cheeks" out there. I'm guessing she is still in the dark about all of this. You know, the passionate kissing in the office, the sleeping arrangements. Which suggests to me that you are terrified of her reaction when she finds out what has been going on behind her back. Now, I'm not the brightest button in the box, but I'd say that rather points to you having something to hide. Something grubby and unsavoury on your conscience.' He grinned, raised his eyebrows and sat back in his chair. 'If I'm reading this situation correctly, you are just a little bit scared that your marriage and happy family life is on the verge of disintegration.' He glanced over his shoulder towards Brenda's office. 'And now you are wondering what it will look like when wifey discovers "Moneypenny" out there, has been sleeping with you, at your flat, for nearly a week and you haven't even mentioned it.' He shook his head in disbelief. 'What a terrible pickle you seem to be getting yourself into, George. It's just as well you are dealing with me and not that hothead Jeremy. If it were down to him, all these rather upsetting rumours would already be on the front pages. You can thank your lucky stars you have me on your side, keeping him in check. Anyway, I've got some more good news for you that might help make up your mind concerning *our* selection policy for Wednesday. I have on here,' he waved his mobile phone at George, 'a clear recording of our conversation last week. The one where I told you to play Jayden. Now I don't know how lenient the powers that be, running this club are, but I'm not sure it is a conversation you would want replayed to anyone upstairs; or come to that, any of our friendly journalists. Oh, and just so you know, I'm recording this one as well. Seems to me Miller, you have little choice, but to do exactly what I tell you. The consequences for your marriage and your job, are really too awful to imagine.' A contented grin spread across his face. 'Anyway, got to go. Can't sit round here all day. As enjoyable as this has been, I have another appointment to keep. I'm having a drink with my new mate Jeremy. He really is *very* cross with you George, for stealing away his wife. But like I said, I will do my best, on your behalf, to keep a lid on him. We don't want that poor, rejected husband, ruining our little business deal. Do we? Don't get up, I will see myself out. We will talk again very soon. And I will have that 200K by the end of the week. Either that, or I *will* take the gag off of Jeremy and leave him to tell the world what you've been getting up to with his wife. A combination of his vitriol and my evidence will be more than enough to bury any future you were looking forward to.' Baz stood up, shrugged his shoulders, raised his eyebrows and looked almost apologetically at George. 'It's up to you!'

Just when George thought it couldn't get any worse, it had. He should have realised Baz would have recorded that conversation. Now there was clear evidence of him succumbing to threats. Allowing his professional judgement to be influenced by a blackmailer, to the detriment of the club. How could he have been so stupid. He felt himself tumbling out of control. He didn't know where this would end, or how he would come out of it, but he knew he had never been in so much trouble in his life before.

By Wednesday afternoon, George had received so many complaints regarding Jayden Saunders's behaviour, he had lost count of them. It seemed the boy was intent on upsetting everyone he spoke to. That evening, George's team was at home to the side top of the league. He would be expected to field a full strength eleven.

George hosted his usual pre-match meeting, going over the opposition's strengths and weaknesses, his tactics and formations and of course he's starting eleven. When he read out the name Jayden Saunders there was an audible sigh of disbelief. The murmurings and mutterings of the players increased in volume. George had to hold his hands up and ask for a bit of quiet. He wondered if he should try and explain his selection to his disgruntled squad but decided there was little point. Nothing he could say would placate them. He looked out into a room of angry faces. He knew none of them agreed with, or understood, his selection. To a man they were all appalled at his choice. The only face that was grinning was Jayden's. He rocked back in his chair and appeared to enjoy the ever-increasing howls of disapproval being voiced by his team-mates. Unlike Saturday, there were no pats on the back, or voices raised in congratulation at his selection. Jayden sat there in isolation, an island of happiness in a sea of bad-tempered frustration. George would have loved to explain to each and every one of them, why he was persisting with the brat. He wanted to tell them he agreed with their sentiments and considered the *"little shit"* just as odious and loathsome as they did. But of course, he couldn't. He tried to settle them down and finish the meeting, but it was clear he had lost the room's attention and he feared, a lot of the room's respect.

The players filed out of the room, some of them shaking their heads. Jayden was the last to leave.

'I've given you another chance tonight, but I ……..'.Jayden cut in.

'No, you haven't. My Dad has. He told me I would be playing tonight and I already know I will be playing the full ninety minutes. It's nothing to do with you anymore, *George*.' Jayden patted George on the cheek, in a truly patronising way. 'I know you don't like me. Well, it might come as a shock to you, but I don't really care much for you. Didn't think much of you as a player and think even less of you as a manager. My dad is running my career and thanks to your insatiable thirst for pussy, you will just have to go along with it. Truly, I think he hopes you screw up and he will let it be known what a fuck-up you have made of your life. But until then, I get to play and you get to do what you are told.'

He patted George on the cheek again, this time a little harder. Jayden walked out of the room, barging his shoulder into George as he passed him. What little control George had commanded, was now gone. He had to think of something in the next nine days before Debbie came home. He began to feel like every decision he made was the wrong one.

The TV analysts and all the pundits had been baffled by George's decision to start with a sixteen-year-old boy in such an important fixture. Their bafflement had been compounded by the fact that the young lad had had a stinker of a game. He couldn't do anything right. His touch was dreadful and his ability to contribute to the overall team performance was woeful. But what no-one could understand was George Miller's reluctance to take the boy off. To substitute him and get more experienced players onto the pitch, to save the lad any further embarrassment. The crowd was getting at him and he looked out of his depth. He was as poor that night as he had been impressive the previous Saturday. What had started out as a courageous move by the manager had failed. The crowd trusted George and were prepared to applaud him for his unusual and brave selection. But the gamble hadn't worked this time and in the end the exercise had developed into, what most saw, as a cruel exposure of a young man's frailties and short comings. The criticism George received was as much about his insensitivity to the young man's feelings, as it was to his failings. George had been asked some difficult questions by the interviewer after the game and had failed to come up with any convincing or plausible answers. For the first time he could remember, either as a player or as a coach, the team had been booed off by their own supporters. But he knew they were not booing the team. They were booing him. He felt wretched. He felt like a traitor. And tomorrow he would have the morning papers to deal with. He knew the sports editors would have a field day at his expense.

Chapter 29

Even to Graham it sounded fishy

Graham and Kerry arrived home from their ten days in the Maldives on Thursday night. They too, like Debbie, had delayed their departure, to enable them to attend Doug's funeral. By the time they walked through the front door, it was nearly eleven o'clock. They were both exhausted.

They were now both semi-retired and enjoying a stress-free existence. They had both been successful in their business dealings and ventures. Kerry had his own fashion label and his clothes were in great demand. His "Zampa" range of men's and women's clothing sold alongside some of the giants of the fashion world and for equally extravagant sums of money. Graham had also been very successful. His investment company had broken into the American market twelve years earlier and he now had offices in London and San Diego. The money had rolled in.

They had both handed the reins of their respective empires over to their trusted lieutenants, to deal with the day to day running, while they spent most of their time enjoying themselves.

It was the first week in April and this was already their third overseas adventure of the year.

They had both retained their enthusiasm and appetite for keeping fit. There was a friendly rivalry between them that always pushed them both to their limits. Graham had stopped playing football some years earlier, but had replaced it with numerous other activities. They ran, cycled and swam together, constantly trying to outperform each other. They had taken up kickboxing, tennis and squash. Their lives were devoted to leisure and holidays, but there was rarely an hour in the day when they were sitting down relaxing. It was all go.

They had bought a large house in South Buckinghamshire, only a few miles from where George and Debbie lived. Although they were close by, they saw very little of each other. With Graham and Kerry constantly jetting off around the world on holiday and George and Debbie always tied up with either the kids, or George's football, there never seemed to be enough time for them to sit down and chat.

Like George, Graham and Kerry had kept their flat in central London, where they had lived when they first met. It was a colossal, converted warehouse. It had so many wonderful memories for them both. It was a convenient place to crash if they had been out in London and couldn't face the journey home to the shires.

'I'll make the tea' Kerry said as Graham slumped onto the sofa.

While they had been away, they had done their best to avoid contact with the outside world. They had read no newspapers and watched very little TV. Apart from the occasional glimpse at their mobile phones (and they were kept to a minimum) they were blissfully unaware what had been happening. The Martians could have landed in London or New York and neither of them would have known. It was a real change of pace for them both, Graham in particular. Only a few years ago, he couldn't imagine starting his day without reading every newspaper available, from cover to cover. He had kept himself up to date with everything good, bad and ridiculous that was happening in the world, from the financial markets, to the sports fields and the politics of the day. It would have been unthinkable for him to go without his daily intake of global events for a single day, let alone ten. But life with Kerry had taught him that sometimes, the most important things are right in front of you and should be given all your attention.

Graham wondered what his family had been up to while he and Kerry had been away. He knew his Mum and Dad would be tucked up in bed and probably fast asleep by now, but his brother George would almost certainly still be up. It was always interesting to find out what had been happening in George's life. He'd quietened down a lot since his bachelor days. Since he had met Debbie again twelve years ago, his lifestyle had become less hectic. He had settled down and become more of a family man. Once he was married and the kids had arrived, the drinking, gambling, womanising rogue that so often adorned the front pages of the daily newspapers seemed to vanish into the mist. Since his playing days, George had kept a relatively low profile as far as the media was concerned. His reputation as being one of the wild boys of sport had slowly faded. There were now younger and more extravagant sporting heroes taking their place on the front pages. Scandals, infamy and disgrace seemed to go hand-in-hand with being a sports' personality, just as it had been back in George's day. But there were many in the legions of reporters and journalists that had good memories and they were just waiting for *that* 'George Miller' to resurface and give them another story.

Graham called his brother. George answered immediately.

'Hi Graham. I assume you've got home safe and sound. When are you off next, tomorrow?' he laughed.

'Yes, just got home. No, we are here for a bit now and no more travelling for, well at least another three weeks. So, what's been happening in your world? Anything interesting?' George let out a loud ironic laugh.

'You could say that, yes. But it's too complicated to talk about over the phone. If you fancy meeting up for a beer, I will tell you all about it. Think you will be both shocked and surprised.' Graham could detect a note of trepidation in his brother's voice.

'Everything is okay, isn't it George'? There was a pause.

'No not really.' The tension and worry in George's voice was now very plain to hear.

'What is it? What's wrong? Is it Debbie or the kids? Mum or dad?' Graham's voice had lost its tone of jovial curiosity and had now become more serious and inquisitive, worrying about what had made his brother sound so deflated.

'I'm about tomorrow night if that suits, or have you got other plans for your Friday night?'

'No tomorrow is fine. We don't have a game until Monday.'

Graham suggested meeting at George's home, but George explained they had the painters and builders in while Debbie and the kids were away.

'I haven't been there since they started and can only assume the place is a mess at the moment.'

'Okay then, I'll come to the flat.'

'No. Don't come to the flat. Brenda is staying there at the moment.' There was a pause in the conversation. George could almost hear Graham's mind ticking.

'What do you mean, staying there? Where are you living then?'

'I'm at the flat as well.' There was an even longer silence as George waited to hear what Graham's reaction would be.

'What? You mean you are both living there together? But…..'

'Like I said Graham, it's complicated. I will explain all tomorrow. Why don't we meet in the "Broken knee bar"? I'll see you about seven. Oh, and in the unlikely event you talk to Debbie, please don't mention anything about it. Alright?'

'Okay,' agreed Graham. But George could hear the confusion and concern in his voice. Graham repeated the conversation he'd just had to Kerry.

'We have arranged to meet at seven o'clock, if that's okay with you.' Kerry nodded and looked thoughtful.

'I think it might be better if you meet him on your own. Sounds like a brother to brother talk to me.'

'You could be right' Graham said, still mulling over the scant and perplexing information regarding his brother's situation. What was Brenda doing at the flat, with George, while Debbie was away? As hard as he tried, he couldn't imagine a scenario that made those circumstances palatable. The only rational reason he could think of, knowing his brother as he did, didn't bare thinking about. Even to Graham, it sounded very fishy.

Chapter 30

The "Broken knee bar"

The "Broken knee bar", as the brothers called it, had been through numerous reincarnations since that fateful evening twelve years ago, when it had earned its name. It had always been a favourite haunt of George's. He had spent many enjoyable hours in there over the years, with many beautiful women. But the evening that stuck in both his and his brother's mind was the one when Graham announced to George that he and Kerry had decided to get married. It was an evening full of happiness, excitement and celebration. Between them they consumed two bottles of Laurent Perrier Rosé champagne, although George had limited his intake to just two and a half glasses. Graham had demolished the rest. Unfortunately, Graham couldn't hold his drink as well as his brother and had become quite tipsy. After returning from the Gents, he stumbled and tripped on one of the small steps and fell head long into George's troublesome right knee. The sequence of events that followed and the decisions the brothers had to make still haunted them to that day. They had been forced to pull 'The Switch' for the first time since they had been at school. Swapping identities, like they had when they were younger. Then it was for fun. Doing it at the age of thirty would prove to be one of the most dangerous and potentially foolhardy adventures the brothers had ever undertaken. Ultimately, they had been successful and had saved George's career and reputation. They both knew that without the successful 'Switch', George would not be in the position he was now. Those memories of twelve years ago still sent shivers down both their spines. The brothers had to be constantly on their guard and watch what they said. Even after all those years, one slip of the tongue could prove to be disastrous, as Graham nearly discovered at Doug's funeral.

During those twelve years, the decor and layout of the interior had changed a number of times, as new management came and then left. The most recent refurbishment had changed the geography completely. Gone were the small secluded alcoves, that George favoured; those dark little recesses that offered their residents a modicum of privacy. That area had now been absorbed by the larger and relocated bar. The dance floor was larger and there were more tables available. The whole ambience was brighter and somewhat less seedy than it had been all those years ago.

On his way to meet his brother, Graham wondered if Brenda would be there as well. He hoped not. He needed to talk to him alone. As much as he was looking forward to telling him all the wonderful things he and Kerry had been up to in the Maldives, he was also desperate to know why George was living in the flat with Brenda. He had an awful feeling his brother was about to tell him some very bad news. If that was the case, Brenda's presence would make a frank and honest discussion almost impossible.

Graham walked into the club and immediately glanced at the spot where his infamous swan dive had taken place. He shook his head and smiled. He saw George sitting at a table. He was relieved to see him sitting on his own. He was deep in thought.

George ordered two more beers and without delay, began to tell Graham the events that had unfolded since they had last met at Doug's funeral. Graham sat quietly and listened intently. He told him about the awful things Jeremy had done to Brenda and the bruising on her neck and face and the realisation that he needed to get her away from her psychopath husband before she ended up on a slab. He told him of the re-emergence of Baz and his attempts at blackmail. He even came clean about the kiss and the possibility that Jayden had recorded it all on his phone. He made no mention of the moment Brenda presented and offered herself to him in all her naked glory.

'Baz says he has recordings of our conversations regarding Jayden's selection. He also has dash-cam footage of Brenda and I leaving the club together arm in arm and going to the flat. He has us leaving the next morning and going into the club hand in hand. Then there is the scene with Jeremy, where he accuses us of having an affair. He says he has footage of us kissing in my office, but I haven't seen that yet. He showed me a still frame, which isn't particularly good quality, but says the "full movie", as he likes to call it, is far more revealing. He and Jeremy are now bosom buddies by all accounts. Baz told me that Jeremy is itching to announce to the world that George Miller has stolen his wife. Apparently, Jeremy is prepared to swear that Brenda has already confessed to him about the affair, which of course she hasn't. I think Jeremy is just an irritant at the moment. He hasn't got the balls to do anything. It's Baz who is the real worry.' Graham took a swig of his beer and leant forward in his chair, staring deeply into his brother's eyes.

'George. Tell me honestly, have you and Brenda....?'

'No. No we haven't.' George fired his answer back, in an almost aggressive tone. 'I swear. I know what it looks like and I know it's not good, but I promise you, Brenda and I have never….. well, you know. Never! Baz says as long as I keep doing what he asks he will keep his evidence to himself and keep a lid on Jeremy. But it's becoming almost impossible. I played Jayden, as I was told to on Wednesday and he had a shocker. I'm losing control of the situation and I'm not sure what to do for the best. I have to keep this under wraps until Debbie gets home. Now it has gone this far, if I suddenly tell her about Brenda and the kiss it will look like I am trying to cover my tracks and have something to hide. With hindsight I should have told her straight away, but I didn't. Now I think my only option is to wait for her to come home and deal with it face to face. Once she is back, I will explain it to her, like I have explained it to you and hope she trusts, believes and understands me. What happens after that, I don't know. All I want is her love and trust. Nothing else is really important. If I lose the job, or even face some kind of censure from the FA, I don't care, as long as Debbie is by my side. I will deal with Baz and Jeremy after that and take whatever consequences I have to. Baz wants me to meet up next week to discuss what he calls "terms". He wants me to transfer 200K into a bank account once Jayden has set one up and he has told me that

Jayden is to play the full ninety minutes again on Monday. I somehow need to buy another weeks grace, but I don't think I will be able to. I tell you Graham, Baz is a real psycho. I wouldn't put anything past him.'

'I see,' said Graham. 'Blimey, you've got yourself into some tight spots in the past, but this one is right up there with the best of them. I hope you're right when you say you think Debbie will understand. I hope she does too. But to be honest George, as your brother, and no one trusts you more than I do, even I might have trouble believing your story when confronted with that amount of evidence, circumstantial as it is. Is there no way you can reason with him? Surely, he must have his price. A one-off payment to forget it all and just fuck off, back under the rock he crawled out from. I could get the money sorted. Even double it if that would help. At least it wouldn't be traced back to you, if anything else happened.' George let out a long sigh.

'I honestly don't think it's about the money at all. That's just a handy little smokescreen. I think he just wants to crush me and destroy everything I have.'

'Is there anything I can do to help? What if we both confront him? Even with his mates, Frankie and Robbo, they used to shit themselves when they came up against the two of us at school' he said with a smile. 'Maybe, together we can intimidate him into backing off.'

'Nice idea,' said George, 'but Baz is a different animal now. He's a very dangerous man, with a grudge. He wants nothing more than to avenge the vendetta he has been stewing over for the last twenty-six years. And now he thinks he has the means to repay the debt. There is one thing you could do for me though. How would you feel about Brenda moving into your flat for a few days? I think it would be better if she wasn't at mine when Debs gets back. It wouldn't be for long. A week at most. Until we decide what's best for her'.

'No problem at all. I will check with Kerry, but I'm sure we have no plans to use it in the near future. She can stay as long as she likes. When would you want her to move in?'

'Debbie is back next Friday, so could we say Wednesday after work, about 7 o'clock?'

'Perfect, that will give us a chance to clean the place up a bit and put some clean sheets on the bed. We will do that this weekend. I'll meet you both at the flat, Wednesday evening, to show her where everything is.'

'Thanks Graham. I owe you another big one.'

George went on to describe his first meeting with Baz. How his eyes were immediately drawn to the two-inch scar that snaked around his left eye. The scar left by the swinging door that had smashed into the side of his head, twenty-seven years earlier, after Graham burst into the small room back at school.

'He kept gently rubbing it with his fingers. Reminded me of Bloefeld stroking his white pussycat in the Bond film. It must have been a constant reminder to him, all the time he was inside. I'd like to think every time he touched it, he thought of us and that blood spattered room. It must have driven him crazy all those years.'

The two brothers drank more beer. They recalled how the small room had resembled an abattoir at the end of that particular confrontation, covered with Baz' blood.

Whatever the predicament the brothers found themselves in, they always managed to extract some humour from their past adventures.

Chapter 31

No caller ID

George was relieved he had managed to find somewhere for Brenda to stay. Somewhere she would be safe and comfortable. Once again, his brother Graham had come to the rescue. But Brenda wasn't the problem that was causing him most angst. He knew he was in deep trouble. Baz, and to a certain extent Jeremy, had forced him into a corner that appeared to have no way out. Unintentionally, he had let it get to a point where he had few options left. He was damned whichever way he looked at it.

It was good to share his troubles with his brother. It always made him feel a little better about his dilemmas, but this time, Graham would be of no physical help whatsoever. During their conversation, Graham had also said something that had compounded George's anxiety. When Graham said, even *he* would have trouble believing

George's story, he knew he was in dire straits. Maybe he was expecting too much from Debbie. Maybe even *her* trust and belief in him would be stretched beyond reason.

George called Debbie over the weekend. They were having a wonderful time. It did cheer him up to hear the happy voices of his children, excitedly telling him what they had been doing and what they had planned for the last week of their holiday in the sun. Speaking to Debbie always made him feel good. But this time he struggled. He wanted to tell her what he had been going through, but it was too late. His decision to tell her nothing about Brenda moving in on that first night, was now proving to be a huge mistake. He told Debbie everything was fine and that he was doing okay. The words almost got caught in his throat. He found it so difficult to lie to her and he hated himself for doing it. He told her as many truths as he could, in an attempt to dilute the untruths coming out of his mouth. He told her several times how much he was missing her and how much he was looking forward to seeing her the following Friday. He told her he loved her. As difficult as some of the things he had said had been, that was easy to say. It was always easy to say.

'There is something I want to discuss with you when you get home darling. It's nothing to worry about, but it is sort of important. Maybe we could do it after the kids have gone to bed.' Debbie sounded intrigued and asked him what it was all about.

'It's not something I really want to talk about over the phone. It can wait until you get back. Please don't worry, it's nothing to fret over. Everything is fine, I promise.'

George managed to convince her not to concern herself. Unfortunately for him, he had failed to convince himself.

Before the Monday night game, George once again stood before his team and coaching staff to go over his plans for the match. For the first time he could ever remember he felt an atmosphere of hostility coming back at him from the gathered players. He felt uncomfortable in front of them. He felt like an outsider. He knew he had to try and ignore the negative vibes and the looks of disinterest on most of their faces. There were the usual mutterings and murmurings as Jayden's name was once again read out in the starting eleven. George noticed several players shuffling in their seats, shaking their heads and looking down at the floor in disbelief. He realised there was nothing to be gained by trying to explain his decisions, not that he could explain them anyway. He was the boss after all and what he said, went. Except it wasn't what he said. It was what Baz had said. He ploughed on with the briefing but found it hard to inject any enthusiasm into his speech. He was as downcast as the rest of the room. Except for one. Jayden's smile became broader and broader as he could sense George's and his team-mates growing discomfort. George knew that his reputation and the respect he had built up over the years as a player and now as a manager had all but vanished.

He watched the game in a semi-trance. He couldn't find any enthusiasm within himself to encourage or cajole his team. His hands were tied. He felt useless.

It was a poor match. When the sides came off at half time, there were no rallying cries or heroic speeches to lift morale. George could feel the hole he was standing in slowly start to fill with earth. He was being buried alive. He knew it wasn't just the combined efforts of Baz, Jeremy and Jayden that were making his life so unbearable. It was also the players and the crowd who were adding to the stress and tension. He sat in the dug-out and watched as the game resumed. His eyes followed the action, but his mind was somewhere else. He felt detached from proceedings and divorced from the bond he had always felt towards the team. He was living a nightmare that was spiralling out of control and there was nothing he could do to stop it.

'Get a fucking grip Miller. This is shit.' George heard a man's booming and angry voice blurt out from the crowd. He glanced over and looked into the sea of hostile and frustrated faces to see where the *advice* had come from. It could have been any one of them. The combination of passion and rage pouring from the irate supporters jolted George out of his trance. The second half was barely five minutes old. He suddenly stood bolt upright, as if he had just been struck by lightning. He had a steely and determined look on his face.

'David Jones. Get out there please.' Jones stripped off and made his way to the touchline. When the numbers went up on the board there was a short moment of surprise followed by a huge roar from the crowd. The green number ten stood beside the red number forty-two. Jayden's number. Alf Wood looked relieved. He assumed it would be him that would make way, as it had been for the previous few games. But the greatest look of surprise was on Jayden's face. He looked absolutely astonished. He made no move towards the touch line, he just waved his hands at the management team telling them they had made a mistake. But it was no mistake. George walked to the edge of the pitch and beckoned for the youngster to come off. Saunders was still gesticulating wildly at his manager when a couple of his own players started to usher him towards the bench. There was no love between the boy and his comrades. In their efforts to remove him from the playing surface, a number of scuffles broke out. They wanted him off and he was not going to go. Ultimately it was the referee that had to step in and guide the reluctant player off the pitch. There were no high fives between the change of personnel and no arms around the shoulders or pats on the back from the coaching staff. Jayden was escorted straight down the tunnel and away from the cameras, but not before he had hurled even more abuse at George. As the young boy was dragged away, George watched on, with a look of contempt, knowing that would be the last time Jayden Saunders would ever play under his management. Whatever the consequences were to be, because of his actions, he would have to endure them. And, although the results of Baz' wrath and the backlash of his temper were uncertain, George felt a glow of emancipation, as if shaking off the shackles that had been weighing so heavily around his neck. A gesture of defiance and a reclamation of his self-respect and his dignity. For the first time since Baz had marched into his office, he was in charge of his own destiny; for better or worse. It felt good.

The substitution had immediate effect. The side began to gel together. There was a renewed passion within the team. Five minutes after coming on, Jones set up Alf Wood, who scored with a thunderous header. Moments later, Wood repaid the compliment for Jones to slide one in from six yards out. Team spirit coursed through the players and once again they looked hungry and keen. George had never seen such a transformation in the side's attitude before. The atmosphere in the ground was electric again and the crowd came back to life. The victory was sweet and by far the most satisfying moment since his return to the club. Back in the dressing room he addressed the players.

'Gentlemen. Thank you for that performance. I know you have had some issues with my selection over the last few games and to be honest, I do understand how you feel. For what it's worth, I think I can say we have seen the last of Master Saunders for the foreseeable future.' There were a few cheers and a smattering of applause. 'I think we, or should I say you, have tonight proved to me what my best options are. Thank you for your patience. Now we have the buzz back I want to keep it if that's okay with you.' George looked straight at Alf and David. With huge grins on their faces, they both nodded enthusiastically.

By the time George got back to the flat it was already midnight. Brenda had left him a note. *"Am exhausted so have gone to bed. Great result. Well done. See you in the morning".* He poured himself a large whiskey and slumped onto the sofa. He felt a sense of relief that he had put an end to the Jayden Saunders issue and that he'd managed to get such a reaction out of the players. He hoped he had been able to rescue his reputation and regain some of the team's respect. He was proud of himself for what he had done; but what *had* he done? He had ended his torment and appeased his conscience by doing what he knew to be right; taking Jayden off. But by easing one problem he had almost certainly made his other predicaments ten times worse.

George placed his phone on the table and stared at it. He knew it would very soon burst into life and he would have to deal with a torrent of abuse and threats from a furious Baz. Sure enough, five minutes later, the mobile's ringtone shattered the silence in the room. No caller ID. He knew who that was.

'Hello Baz. I've been expecting you.' Baz was incandescent with rage. He sounded like he had been drinking.

'What the fuck did you think you were doing? I told you he would play the full ninety minutes. You know the consequences.'

'Baz, I did it for his own good. He was having a nightmare and the crowd were getting at him. Leaving him on was doing more harm to his future than good.'

George cursed himself for trying to justify his actions to Baz. He had been brave enough to substitute Jayden at the time, but now that courage had deserted him. He was almost begging Baz for his understanding and forgiveness. But Baz was in no mood to listen to reason or apologies.

'You and I have got things to talk about. Money for one. Your little prank tonight has cost you a lot of cash. It's the last time you will disobey me Miller.'

'Baz we can't go on like this. We need to sort something out. I've been thinking about what you said regarding a signing on fee and I think that is fair. Name your price and we can draw a line under this forever. What do you say? I can give you 250K, in cash if you like.' He knew he was being disgustingly obsequious and he felt his skin crawl while he was saying it. He just needed to buy himself a few more days. Anything to keep Baz quiet until the weekend.

'I say I will decide what happens and when. You're not going to get off that lightly Miller. I know the money doesn't mean anything to you. It's the other stuff that will really hurt you. That's what you're shitting yourself about. I will explain the next phase of our arrangement to you on Wednesday night. Meet me in the alley behind Peckham Station at 9.30 and I will tell you exactly what you are going to do next and how much you will need to transfer into Jayden's account. And if anything else goes wrong I will make, not only you, but your entire family suffer.' Baz hung up.

It was a quarter to one. George called his brother. He could tell he had woken Graham, but he needed to hear a friendly voice.

'Sorry mate I know it's late. I've just spoken to Baz.' He told Graham about the substitution and the threats Baz had made. Graham felt as dejected as George. It was always painful knowing there was nothing he could do to help.

'Kerry and I went up to the flat on Sunday. It's all clean and tidy and there is fresh bedding and towels for Brenda. I forgot to leave a chocolate on the pillowcase though.' They both laughed. It was a rare moment of humour. 'I will be there to meet you and show Brenda around.

'That's great brother, thank you so much. We should be there between 6:30 and 7 o'clock if that's okay with you. See you then.'

Chapter 32

Paula and a rather large knife

The contrast between George's and Brenda's moods on the Tuesday morning was stark. Brenda was back to the sparkly, happy, young woman George remembered from years before. The weight had been lifted from her shoulders and the knowledge that her troubles were all behind her had given her a youthful glow. She had been living in George's flat for nearly two weeks and the difference in her demeanour and humour was clear. It was lovely to see. George, however, was the antithesis. He cut a forlorn figure. As every day passed, he began to feel like a condemned man approaching the hour of his execution. He was still hoping a solution would present itself, but time was running out. He knew Baz' temper had been stretched to the limit and the dreaded showdown with Debbie was edging nearer with every second. The flesh on his face hung heavy.

Too heavy to be able to smile. His eyebrows were set in a permanent frown. He felt sick.

Brenda almost skipped into his office with a mug of tea and a plate of biscuits, still blissfully unaware of the menacing threats that were hanging over him.

'I've got some good news' she said as she presented him with his chocolate hobnobs. George looked up at her and did his best to look interested. Any good news would be welcome at that moment he thought.

'I've spoken to Jeremy. I've never heard him sound so contrite. I told him I need some time on my own and I am going to stay with some friends out of town for a few days. He said he understood and told me how sorry he was for everything he had put me through. He blamed it on the pressure he has been under at work. He said he should never have taken his frustrations out on me and that he now knows what an arse he has been. He promised it would never happen again and that we should go away for a holiday somewhere sunny and expensive. He sounded calm and collected. His voice reminded me of when we first met. There was even a trace of affection hidden in there somewhere.'

George looked at her in disbelief. The frown that had sat so comfortably on his face moments before returned and he glowered at her.

'You're not telling me that after all you have been through, you are seriously considering going back to him?' Brenda smiled as she saw the incredulity on his face.

'Of course not. What do you take me for? I know I'm not the brightest star in the sky, but give me credit for a little intelligence, please. I'm certainly not that stupid. I wouldn't go back to that sadistic, two-faced wanker for all the money in the world. I just played him along, so I could be sure he wasn't going to try and find me and hassle me constantly. I told him that if he gives me a few days peace, we can sort everything out and get on with our lives. I didn't mention that they would be separate lives, or that I would be speaking to a solicitor about divorce proceedings. I said I needed to pick up a few clothes and some other bits and pieces and would pop over sometime this week. He was okay with that. He even offered to pack a bag for me if I told him what I wanted. But I said I would do it. He told me to take as much time as I needed, but that he was missing me and couldn't wait for me to come home again and begin what he called the 'healing process'. That *we* should both think about where *we* had gone wrong and what mistakes *we* had both made and try and understand each other's point of view; but most of all, forgive each other. Can you believe the gall of the man? He wants me to understand why he beat me up and raped me and then he is going to forgive me! What an arsehole. I know what his "healing process" will involve. I've had enough of that to last me a lifetime, thank you very much. Don't worry George,' she said shaking her head, 'after the last couple of incidents, I don't ever want to see, or speak to him again. He can rot in hell for eternity for all I care.' George looked a little more relieved.

'Thank God for that.'

'I thought I would get my stuff tomorrow afternoon if that's okay. Would it be alright if I left a little earlier than usual? I want to be sure Jeremy isn't there. He is rarely home before 7:30, so if I could leave about 5:00 I could be in and out before he returns from work.' George agreed.

'I will come with you, just in case. I've told Graham we will meet him between 6:30 and 7:00 at his flat, so that fits in perfectly. He can show you around and tell you where everything is.'

On Wednesday morning Brenda parked her car next to George's, outside the club's main entrance. She had packed all her belongings and the bits and pieces she had accumulated at George's flat over the past couple of weeks. She was sad to be moving out. She had enjoyed her time living with George. The safety, security and peace of mind, the views and of course the rather luxurious lifestyle that went with a Riverside penthouse dwelling, were all things she had loved. But it was the company she loved most of all. She would certainly miss that. Knowing that her forbidden fruit was sleeping down the hallway still made her body tingle. She knew it was just a fantasy, but it was one she was happy to lose herself in every night. While her own fingers gently aroused her, she would shut her eyes and imagine George's touch slowly bringing her to fulfilment. She had loved being close to him both day and night, but she understood the reasoning behind her move. George had saved her from a fate worse than death. He had protected her and guarded her from all her troubles. She knew she loved him and she knew she would always want to be more than just a little sister to him. Maybe it was a good idea to move into Graham's flat. Apart from George's marriage there was also her own sanity to think of. She was becoming more frustrated every night. So near and yet so far. It was as painful as it was wonderful. Staying at Graham's flat would give her a chance to refocus on her life and decide what she was going to do, where she would live and how she would deal with Jeremy.

Jeremy was unaware of Graham's flat and would hopefully leave her alone while she prepared for *her* version of the "healing process". He wasn't stupid. He knew that anything he did to Brenda would incur the wrath of George. He knew that his wife's new guardian angel was itching to teach him a lesson. To pay him back for what he had put her through. Jeremy didn't have the balls to take on George. He was probably aware that any misdemeanour on his part would have Miller champing at the leash to get to him. Both Jeremy and Brenda doubted she would be able to hold him back next time.

George had a busy Wednesday ahead of him. Apart from the day to day running of the team and selection issues for the upcoming fixture on Sunday, he had a meeting with Chris Ewens to discuss some of his plans for the following season. He was due to leave with Brenda at about 5pm, drive to her house to pick up her things, then meet Graham at his flat around seven. After that, he had his meeting with Baz in the backstreets of Peckham. He had no idea how that would pan out. He knew what he had to do though; try and buy himself a few more days of grace. Do whatever Baz wanted. Agree to everything. Throw himself at Baz's mercy if need be. Anything to placate him until the weekend, when he could speak with Debbie. All the mounting problems he had would hopefully disappear once he had explained everything to her. The only thing he really cared about was his family. That's what he needed to protect. The job, reputation and everything else were secondary. If he could convince Debbie that his motives were honourable and his actions and conduct had been gallant and faithful, he would let everything else take its course. Then he would deal with Baz and Jeremy.

George's meeting with Chris was at two o'clock. Just as he was about to head upstairs, his phone rang. It was his dad. George frowned at the screen. His dad had never called him at work before.
'Hi dad. Is everything okay?'

'Hello son. Yes, everything's fine. Sorry to trouble you at work. I didn't mean to disturb you. I just thought you should know we have just been paid a visit by one of your old school friends. A man called Barry Saunders.' George shivered with fear and felt the breath leave his lungs. 'Is that Baz, the thug that used to hang around with the De Costa boy?'

Baz' words about making his entire family suffer echoed in George's head.

'Oh shit. What happened? Yes, that's him. Are you alright? What did he say?'

'Calm down son. Everything is fine. He seemed pleasant enough to start with, asking about you and Graham. I started to put two and two together and when I asked him if he was known as Baz at school, he became a little more aggressive. He tried to invite himself into the house, but I wouldn't let him. He asked if he could use the toilet and started to push his way forward. There was a little commotion and your Mum came out of the kitchen to see what all the fuss was about. She had been chopping up vegetables to make some soup. She had rather a large knife in her hand. The sight of that stopped him dead in his tracks. He said he was just passing and wanted to see if we still lived at the same address. He said he would call back another time when we weren't quite so busy. His eyes kept flashing to the blade in Paula's hand. What's going on son? Are you okay? I got the impression he wasn't the nicest bloke in the world.'

Baz had upped the ante. George felt his blood start to boil. Harassing and blackmailing him was one thing, but trying to intimidate his parents was something he was not going to tolerate. He assured his father that everything was under control and that he shouldn't worry.

'Best not to open the door to him again though. I'm meeting up with him this evening and I will tell him not to bother you again. Everything will be settled by this weekend.'

'Alright George. As long as you are okay. Don't worry about us. We can take care of ourselves.'

George had no way of contacting Baz. He would have to wait until he saw him that evening. But this had now gone to another level. If Baz was going to involve his Mum and Dad, then all bets were off. He had crossed the line. Who would be next, Debbie? The kids? Baz had unknowingly relinquished any power he held over George. That evenings meeting was now guaranteed to be a fiery affair. One in which George would be the aggressor and Baz would become the prey. Baz was in for an almighty shock

Chapter 33

A dungeon of unhappiness

That afternoon's meeting with Chris Ewins went well. George found more to like about the man every time he spoke to him. They had discussed many subjects. Topics that George was keen to talk through and examine with great passion. The future of some of the players. Who George wanted to keep and who he thought should move on; and who he wanted to replace them. It would be his first real opportunity to stamp his mark on the team. To recruit the sort of players he thought would be able to take the club back to the top. He even put forward the idea of asking Terry Bridges if he would be interested in a return to the club, in some form of coaching role. Chris thought that was a great idea.

Jayden's name was eventually mentioned. Chris was keen to find out how the youngster was fitting in and if George saw a future for him at the club.

Chris was aware of the friction between Saunders and some of the other players and wanted to know George's opinion. George remained ambivalent on the subject. He didn't want to be drawn on whether Jaydan should stay or go. He told Chris that the boy's future was still in the balance, although he knew in his heart, Jayden Saunders would never play for him ever again, whether it was at this club or any other. He suggested they meet again in seven days. He would give the boy's future his full attention and have a definite answer for him the following week. George found it difficult to concentrate on Jayden, when all he could see in his mind was the image of Baz, standing at his parents' front door and trying to barge his way in.

At 4:15 George popped his head around Brenda's office door.

'Hi Brenda. I've finished my meeting with Chris. There is nothing for me to do here, that I can't do at home, so do you want to make a move now?' Brenda looked at her watch.

'That would be great. But you don't have to come with me. Jeremy will still be at work.'

'I'm coming with you, and that's final. Just in case.'

A little earlier than planned, George followed Brenda's car out of the club and over to the house she had bought with Jeremy. The traffic was surprisingly light. Probably due to the school holidays that were now in full swing.

Brenda parked her car outside her house. The street was narrow and only allowed for parking on one side of the road. George lowered his window and leant across to speak to Brenda.

'I'll park up there somewhere, then walk down. Leave the front door open for me.'

He slowly crawled up the road looking for anywhere he could leave his car. There were a few spaces, but none large enough to accommodate the bulk of his Range Rover. He was just about to turn around and head back towards Brenda's house, when he saw a man in a large Mercedes pull out. He was about a hundred yards further down the road but contented himself the space would be the best he would find. He squeezed the car into the vacant gap, locked it and began his long walk back to Brenda's.

Brenda turned the key and opened the front door. She had walked through it hundreds of times before without even thinking, but this time she paused. It felt different. She felt a wave of uncertainty and panic come over her. She took a deep breath and crossed the threshold. As she did so, she shivered. It was colder inside than it had been outside; or was that just her imagination? She put the snib on the door and pushed it to. Her eyes searched the gloomy hallway. Everything was still and quiet. Memories and images raced through her mind, but none of them were good. Every room in the house had witnessed some form of atrocity or violent act. She could hear the ghostly echoes of herself screaming and pleading for him to stop. She could hear the countless ornaments smashing against the walls, thrown in uncontrollable fury. Hatred and anger still hung menacingly in the air as the memories of Jeremy's outbursts and temper came into her mind. She could still hear his voice shouting at her, booming through the house. This place she once thought of as home, was now no more than a dungeon of unhappiness. A torture chamber in which she had been physically and mentally abused by a man she once thought she loved. Another shiver wriggled its way down her spine. She would pack her things as quickly as she could and leave, shutting the door for what she knew would be the last time.

She edged her way from the front door towards the staircase. The eerie silence of the house only disturbed by the creaks from the floorboards. They were louder than she had ever heard them before. She rested her hand on the newel post, which also groaned as she pulled on it. It was as if the house was warning her, murmuring to her, reminding her of her past traumas. She looked up the stairs. Straight across the landing was their bedroom door. It was shut. She took another deep breath. She could feel her heart beating and the butterflies in her stomach. The stairs creaked loudly with every footstep. She had never really noticed it before. She felt like she was in a scene from an Alfred Hitchcock movie, or wandering through Miss Haversham's mansion in Great Expectations (without the cobwebs of course). She told herself not to be so silly and melodramatic. She skipped up the last few stairs and across the landing towards her bedroom door. Even the handle managed to emit an unusual groan as she turned it. She would do what she had to do and then leave. Closing the book on her woefully inadequate, married life. The bedroom door creaked as she slowly opened it. It was as if the entire house was singing out to her in an effort to scare her. It was succeeding. She walked in. Everything was as it had been two weeks earlier. Everything neat and tidy. The bed was made and the curtains were open, letting in the late afternoon sunshine. She bent down and pulled the large suitcase out from under the bed.

'What a lovely view. That's what I have been missing most.'

The voice shattered the silence. Brenda jumped up and felt her heart miss a beat. She had heard no warning creaks from the floorboards to suggest she was not alone. The fanfare of moaning timber that had announced her arrival onto the landing had fallen silent. There had been no such flourish to welcome the second set of footsteps. Her blood instantly froze in her veins and she had a sudden urge to pee. She knew the voice. She turned around and saw Jeremy standing in the doorway. She sucked in an involuntary gulp of air and let out a strange unintended whimper. She dropped the suitcase and felt herself begin to shake. She had no control over it. She clasped her hands together in an attempt to lessen the trembling.

'Jeremy what are you doing here?' I thought you'd still be at work.'

She tried to force a smile onto her face and keep her voice as steady as possible, to give him the impression she was calm and relaxed. But she could feel her face start to twitch. The smile was an unconvincing one. And her high pitched and unsteady voice betrayed the fear that was stampeding through her body. She felt the trembling and the shaking increase.

'I thought I should be here just to make sure you were okay. I've been worried about you. I thought I might persuade you to reconsider and stay here with me so we can talk things through and get back to normal.'

Jeremy stepped into the room. Brenda instinctively took a step backwards. Jeremy slowly edged towards her. Brenda slowly backed away, but after three steps she was up against the wall. She had nowhere else to go.

'What's the matter darling? You look ever so .....' He considered his next word. 'Guilty!' His face contorted into a snarl and he spat the word out through gritted teeth. 'Have you got something to feel guilty about? Are you hiding something from me? Do you want to confess your evil ways?'

His voice was harsh and aggressive. It was a voice she had become familiar with over the years, especially in the bedroom. His teeth were clenched, as were his fists. He walked slowly towards her, his eyes fixed menacingly on hers, his top lip curling like an angry hyena.

Brenda was on the verge of wetting herself. For a brief moment she wondered if she should put up her hand and ask him if she could be excused and go to the toilet, like some timid little schoolgirl. But she thought better of it. Jeremy stood next to the suitcase lying on the floor. He bent down and picked it up, examining it as he turned it in his hands.

'The big suitcase, I see. Lots of room in here. Were you planning to go away for more than a couple of days then?'

'I… I… I…'

She couldn't speak. Hysteria had taken hold of her. Jeremy screwed up his face again and hurled the suitcase at his petrified wife. Brenda tried to duck, but the fear had left her paralysed. The corner of the case crashed into her collar bone and then into the wall, gouging out a fist sized divot in the plaster. The brass clasp on the front grazed her cheek and opened up her flesh, releasing a curtain of blood that ran down her face.

'So, what is this? Are you moving in with that arsehole permanently? My new mate Baz has told me all about you and Miller. He has shown me a recording on his phone of you two kissing, holding hands and leaving work in the middle of the morning, arm in arm and driving back to his flat. Now what the fuck do you think that tells me? It tells me I have been right all along and that my wife is a slut and her boss is a home wrecker. Baz says it's been going on for years. Everybody has known about it for ages. Everyone except me. Oh and of course, Miller's stupid wife.'

'Jeremy it's not like that I promise you. He is a happily married man. He just let me stay with him until things calmed down with you.'

'Calmed down with me!' Jeremy yelled. His face was now bright red and the veins were bulging in his neck. He stood directly in front of her. Not for the first time, she felt his venomous drool, spray onto her face. 'I wouldn't need to calm down if my wife wasn't screwing her boss. Happily married, is he? Well, that won't be for much longer. Anyway, I have calmed down.'

In a flash, he had his right hand around her neck and began forcing her up the wall. It was a scene that had been enacted many times previously. Brenda, as she had done before, started to shut down. Her eyes rolled back and she could feel her body going limp. She felt the floodgates open and the warm flow of urine cascade down her legs, soaking into her tights and running into her shoes.

'So, you can forget about moving out and you can stay here with me. You've got an awful lot of repenting to do. And you can start right now.'

'Please Jeremy, don't do this again. Let me go.' Her voice strained and struggled to fight its way out of her constricted throat.

'You, my dear, are going nowhere. You are staying here and you *will* learn your lesson.' Brenda was now no more than the ragdoll she had become so many times before. Jeremy released his grip on her neck and shook her violently by the shoulders, crashing her head into the wall. The tears flowing down her face mixed with the blood on her cheek. He threw her onto the bed and began to unbuckle his belt.

'No Jeremy. Please,' she begged.

But he was not listening. He never listened. Brenda tried to call for help. She shouted out George's name, but little sound came out of her bruised and battered throat. She tried again, this time with a little more volume, but still not enough to find its way out of the room. Jeremy stopped. He frowned at her with a quizzical look. He buttoned up his trousers and walked out of the room towards the top of the stairs. He could hear voices. Male voices. He craned his head towards the conversation. He recognised both. He could hear the voice of his neighbour, Greg Palmer. The second voice was also familiar to him. Miller. George bloody Miller. The look of confusion on his face turned to panic and fear poured from his eyes. He looked down at the front door. It was ajar. The penny then dropped. She had left it open for him. She had bought him with her. Jeremy turned and watched as Brenda slowly got up from the bed.

'You bitch. You brought him with you. To my house!' Brenda took a deep breath and with the last ounce of strength left in her body, she screamed.

'GEORGE!!'

This time the volume was there. A terrifying screech that echoed and reverberated around the bedroom, over the landing, down the stairs and out of the front door. Jeremy's panic grew. He had to get to the front door and close it before Miller came in. He turned and made his way to the top of the stairs. Brenda was already standing and ran towards him. She threw herself at him in an attempt to stop him descending the stairs and shutting the door. Her outstretched hands crashed into his waist, knocking him off balance. Brenda was spent. It was her last act of defiance. She fell to the floor, landing on her shoulder. The pain again shot through her. She lay there, still and unconscious.

Chapter 34

Greg Palmer was a very large human being

Walking back to Brenda's house, George could feel the wind getting up. The sky was dark and foreboding. The weathermen had predicted a violent storm that evening. It looked like it was already forming in the angry, black clouds above his head. He could see that Brenda had left the door ajar. Hopefully she had managed to collect most of her things in the time it had taken him to walk back from his car. He was just as keen as she was to finally shut the door on her cruel and tormented married life. As he approached the front gate, he heard a voice.

'Excuse me.' George turned around. 'You're George Miller, aren't you?'

'Yes.'

'Ah, hello my name is Palmer. Greg Palmer.'

The man offered his hand and George shook it. Greg Palmer was a very large human being. He must have been in excess of twenty-five stone.

He continued. 'I knew Brenda worked for you. She always talks very highly of you whenever anyone asks what you're like.'

George smiled and nodded. He didn't really want to get involved in a conversation with this man. It looked like it was about to chuck it down with rain and he wanted to get Brenda settled into Graham's flat before he met Baz in Peckham.

'Thank you. That's nice.' George was just about to carry on into the house when Greg piped up again.

'I'm a big fan you know. I don't get to many games these days. Not as many as I used to. Bit of a squeeze' he said, patting his enormous gut with both of his hands. He almost seemed proud of it! 'I remember you when you were a player. Bit of a rascal, weren't you? But everyone loved you. Especially after you won the Champions' league for us in Barcelona. That just about guaranteed your immortality. I was there you know. That night in Barcelona. Had a great time. Crazy to think that was twelve years ago. Where does the time go?'

'Yes, it only seems like yesterday' George agreed.

There was a moment's silence. George was sure his new friend Greg was about to regale him with more sporting and memorable occasions from his slimmer, youthful days, but George had other things on his mind.

'Lovely to have met you Mr Palmer I…'

'Oh, please call me Greg.'

'Lovely to meet you Greg. I must be …' Before he could finish his sentence, a bloodcurdling scream came blaring out into the street.

'GEORGE!!'

It was Brenda. Both George and Greg immediately turned their attention to the house. George rushed through the gate, down the garden path and burst through the front door, his eyes desperately searching for her. He looked down the hallway and into the kitchen, but there was no movement or sound. While he frantically scanned the downstairs, he heard footsteps from above. He glanced up and saw Jeremy standing on the landing between the top of the stairs and the bedroom door. Their eyes fixed together for a brief second. George saw a look of shock and panic in Jeremy's eyes. Just as George was about to run up the stairs, he saw Brenda fly out of the bedroom and hurl herself at her husband, clattering into the back of his legs and barging him forward. He saw Brenda fall and disappear from sight. George felt a nudge behind him and realised Greg had finally caught up and was standing by his shoulder. They both watched in horror as Jeremy stumbled forward towards the edge of the stairs.

As he desperately tried to steady himself, his knees buckled and he started to fall. There was nothing to stop him. As he lurched forward he reached out his arms, trying to grab hold of anything that might arrest his descent. But it was too late. He spilt over the precipice of the landing, head first and succumbed to the forces of gravity. His skull crashed into the balustrades halfway down, with a sickening, snapping noise, as the thin spindles splintered and shattered under the force. Jeremy's body rolled and somersaulted all the way down. His head smashed into the heavy newel post at the foot of the stairs, just by George's feet. The final, thunderous impact cracking the skull like an eggshell. Within seconds, the stair carpet was drenched in his blood. George took a step backwards to avoid the quickly-spreading crimson tide from staining his shoes. Jeremy lay there in a crumpled heap. He had landed in a most peculiar position. His head, having revolved almost 180 degrees, was wedged between the newel post and the last spindle. His face stared up at them with a wide and glassy look in his eyes. The rest of his body was still, but in a curious and unnatural pose. His left arm was clearly broken between the elbow and wrist. Two jagged bones having stabbed their way through the flesh halfway up the forearm. His right leg was also sticking out at a bizarre and disturbing angle. It was a grizzly sight. Blood was beginning to emerge from his nose and from his ears too. George looked down on the tangled mess but could find no sympathy or concern for the bloody, piece of shit at his feet. It was Brenda he was worried about. He vaulted over Jeremy's body and ran up the stairs. He saw Brenda lying on the landing floor, half in and half out of the bedroom. He looked back down the stairs. He could see Greg searching for a pulse on Jeremy's blood-soaked neck. George picked Brenda up in his arms and carried her back into the bedroom. He laid her on the bed. Her eyes were closed. There was blood on her cheek and blood beginning to seep through her blouse near her left shoulder. Her skirt was soaking wet.

'Brenda. Brenda can you hear me?'

He brushed the hair off her face and untangled it from the claggy blood on her cheek. She opened her eyes, but they were distant. George craned his head towards the door and shouted down to Greg.

'Call an ambulance.'

'Already on it' came the voice from downstairs. Moments later, George heard slow, heavy footsteps on the stairs. Greg peered around the door.

'Oh my God. Is she okay?'

'I think so. That bastard down there has been treating her like this for years. She's only just raised the courage to leave him. That's what she was doing here. Collecting her things, then moving out.' Greg's face was full of sympathy.

'We did have our suspicions. The shouting we used to hear coming from him and the language; it was shocking.' He shook his head in condemnation. 'But she never said anything. Even when we asked her if she was alright, she always said everything was fine. Well, she won't have to worry anymore.'

'Too bloody right she won't,' said George, 'She is never going anywhere near that cunt again. If he ever even raises a finger to her in the future I swear I will…..' Greg cut in.

'He won't be raising a finger, or anything else for that matter, to anyone, ever again.' He lowered his voice and whispered, 'He's dead.' For a second George was astonished. Then he was glad. Then he was disappointed. Disappointed because the stairs had robbed him of his retribution. Jeremy had been lucky. He had got off light.

Greg went back downstairs and waited for the ambulance and the police to turn up. Brenda's fixed stare remained focused somewhere between this world and the world she escaped to, whenever Jeremy lost his temper.

'It's okay,' he whispered to her, gently stroking her forehead.

'Has he gone?' she whispered timidly.

'Yes, he has. He has gone forever. He fell down the stairs. It looks like he has broken his neck or fractured his skull in the fall. Both hopefully' he added in a whisper to himself. 'He's dead.' Brenda's look of fear became one of horror.

'Dead? Dead? Then I killed him' she wept. 'It's my fault. I pushed him. That's what made him fall. I killed him.' She burst into tears.

'Brenda, look at me and listen to what I have to say.' He placed his hands on her cheeks and pointed her eyes directly at his. 'You didn't kill him. Do you understand. You did not kill him. You didn't push him. He fell.'

'But I did push him.'

'No Brenda. You didn't. Now look at me.' He focused her eyes back on his. He held her face tighter. 'You have to remember what I am telling you.' She nodded. 'You came here to pick up some things. He surprised you and beat you up. When he realised that the door was open and I was outside, he raced to close it. In his haste he tripped, lost his balance and fell. That's what both Greg and I saw. No one pushed anyone. Do you understand?'

As he tried to force the information into her brain, he realised he was shaking her a little harder than he had planned. The look of fear had come back into her eyes. George stopped shaking her and pulled her head into his chest, cradling her gently. Brenda cried out in agony.

'It's my shoulder. It's so painful.' George rested her head back on the pillows.

'I'm sorry Brenda. I'm so sorry. But you have to tell me you understand what I have just told you. And that is what you must tell the police. He beat you up and ran towards the stairs and the next thing you knew you woke up here. Tell me you understand.' Brenda burst into tears.

'I think I've wet myself,' she cried. George had felt the dampness of her skirt and tights when he lifted her into his arms.

'Don't worry about that. You can get changed while I go and speak to Greg for a minute. He left her lying on the bed, still sobbing. George walked downstairs. Greg had found a blanket and laid it over Jeremy's body. The blood stains from his scalp and left arm had soaked through the makeshift shroud. They were clearly visible and getting bigger. George felt like giving the carcass a kick as he stepped over it, but he thought better of it with Greg watching.

The two men chatted and went over what they had seen. As George hoped, Greg had been just too late to see Brenda's lunge at Jeremy. All he saw was his neighbour, floundering at the top of the stairs, before losing his balance and falling to his death. George agreed with him that that was all he had seen too. George told Greg he had found Brenda unconscious, lying on the bedroom floor. Greg had no reason to question or doubt his story.

'Stay here until the ambulance arrives. I'll go and sit with Brenda.' Greg agreed and George climbed the stairs once again. On entering the room, he realised Brenda hadn't moved. She still lay there in her wet skirt and tights.

'George, I can't move. It hurts too much. My shoulder is agony,'

He carefully eased her blouse away and saw why. Massive bruising and swelling had appeared all around her collar bone. Blood was weeping from the broken skin at the epicentre of the wound.

'There are some clean pants and tights in the top draw over there and another skirt hanging in the wardrobe. Please George, will you get me out of these things. I don't want anybody to see me like this.'

He found the clean clothes and as gently as he could, removed the soiled garments. He gave her a quick wash with a flannel and then dried her off as best he could with a towel. She remained still and silent as he softly patted the towel between her legs and thighs. There was nothing remotely sexual or arousing about his actions for either of them. There was only sadness, helplessness and gratitude in Brenda's eyes and only sorrow and tenderness in George's. He helped her put on the clean pants, tights and skirt, then kissed her softly on the forehead.

Chapter 35

A lifetime would be nice

The police and the ambulance arrived within fifteen minutes. George immediately told the paramedics not to waste their time with Jeremy, but to come upstairs and attend to Brenda. After a brief inspection of the corpse confirmed George's diagnosis, they ran up the stairs to find Brenda sitting up on the bed.

The paramedics gave her a thorough examination and listened to her story. They put her left arm in a sling, fearing she had either broken or fractured her collar bone; probably when the suitcase had hit her. They had tended to the wound on her cheek and noted the bruising to her neck and throat.

A man in a raincoat and a WPC in a high-viz jacket knocked and entered the bedroom.

'Mr. Miller?' the man inquired.

'Yes.'

'I'm Detective Inspector Cooper and this is WPC Adams. I wonder if I might have a word with you downstairs.'

'Of course.'

Brenda was reluctant to relinquish her hold on George's hand as he went to stand up. A look of panic and fear spread quickly across her face.

'Don't leave me George. Please don't leave me on my own.'

'I'll only be downstairs. These lovely people will look after you. Don't worry. I'll see you in a minute.'

He gave her a reassuring smile and gently slipped his hand out of her grasp, then followed the detective downstairs. Jeremy's body was still grotesquely posed in its ghoulish, twisted, contorted shape, still melodramatically gazing into eternity. The blanket had been removed and a photographer was flashing away with his camera, capturing the cadaver from every angle. George sneered at the corpse as he stepped over it, still having to suppress the urge to give it a kick.

The inspector asked George what he had seen. He asked him what he had been doing there and questioned him about his relationship with both Brenda and the deceased. George tried to keep his answers brief and as simple as possible, giving as little detail as he could, without seeming evasive. The Inspector nodded and grunted at each of his replies whilst the WPC wrote down notes. From what George could gauge from the policeman's responses, it seemed he had more or less repeated exactly what Greg Palmer had told him.

'I will of course need you to come down to the station and make a formal statement if you don't mind. Mrs Higgins too, as soon as she is well enough. It shouldn't take too long.'

After what felt like an age, Jeremy's body was removed. Zipped into a body bag, with far more reverence than he deserved, then driven away. Moments later, Brenda was escorted down the stairs, strapped into a cradle and supported by the two paramedics. They were taking her to hospital for tests and x-rays. She was still very shaken and in a state of shock. George took hold of her right hand.

'They're taking me to hospital George. Please don't leave me. Please stay with me. Promise you won't go.'

'Of course, I'll come with you.' He looked at the policeman, 'If that's alright with you inspector.'

'Yes, I think that's fine. We can take your statements once Mrs Higgins has recovered. The WPC will travel in the ambulance. I'm afraid you will have to make your own arrangements Mr. Miller.' George nodded.

'I have my car parked up the road.' He tried to break away from Brenda and let the paramedics take her away, but she clung on to him with an iron grip.

'Don't leave me George. Please.'

'It's okay Brenda. There is no room for me in the ambulance. But I'll be following behind. I will be there when you get to the hospital and I will stay with you for as long as you like.' Reluctantly, Brenda released her grip and forced a smile.

'A lifetime would be nice,' she whispered.

Chapter 36

Call me, as soon as you can

George jogged to his car. It had started raining heavily. The storm the forecasters had promised was in full swing. The wind was howling and whipping up the disgorged leaves, driving them and the deluge into George's face. He shut the door and sat in the dry and calm sanctity of his car. He looked at his watch.

'Shit,' he whispered to himself. It was 8:30 already. He searched for his phone. There were a couple of text messages from Graham. He called his brother.

'Hi Graham. Really sorry to mess you about. There's been an incident. That's why we aren't with you yet.'

George watched as the ambulance drove past him, it's blue lights flashing in the gloom and ever-increasing murkiness of the evening.

'Hang on mate I'm putting you on hands free.' George slotted the phone into the Bluetooth connection and pulled the Range Rover out into the road, slipping in behind the paramedics.

'Are you still there? We went to Brenda's to pick up some things for her to move into yours. Jeremy was there, waiting for her. I got waylaid by a neighbour, just long enough for Jeremy to beat the shit out of her again. Anyway, the long and the short of it is, Brenda is on her way to hospital and I'm following her there now.'

'Shit! And what about Jeremy? What kind of mess is he in? I'm assuming you *"persuaded"* him to stop the assault.'

'Jeremy is on the way to the morgue.' There was an eerie silence. 'Hello Graham, can you hear me?'

'Yes, I can hear you. The morgue!! Fucking hell! He's dead? Did you kill him?'

'I bloody would have done, but no. The stairs saved me the bother. He fell, in a rush to shut the front door and stop me coming in. It looks like he broke his neck, or fractured his skull, but who gives a shit? The arsehole is dead and bloody good riddance. Anyway, that's why we haven't arrived at yours yet.'

'Don't worry about that. Is Brenda okay?' George told him what he knew and what had happened.

'Weren't you supposed to be meeting up with Baz this evening?'

'I was, but I promised Brenda I would be there at the hospital. And I'm not going to let her down. I don't have time to go to the hospital, see Brenda, then go and talk to Baz. He will just have to wait. Probably just as well. I think the mood I am in right now I would tell him exactly where he could shove his evidence. Then beat the living shit out of him, just for good measure. It looks like Brenda's stairs have saved me the trouble of smashing Jeremy to a pulp and Jeremy has stopped me doing the same to Baz.' George then told Graham about Baz' visit to their parents' house and his threat to make his entire family pay for his insubordination. George could hear the anger in Graham's voice.

'Jesus. *You* might not get a chance to kill him if I get hold of him first. Where were you going to meet him?'

'I'm supposed to meet him in the little alleyway behind Peckham Station at 9:30 this evening, but I won't make it now. I will just have to see what he has to say tomorrow and try my best to ride the wave. To be honest with you, I'm tired of it all. I'm fed up of feeling threatened and scared and having to kowtow to that bastard. Maybe this business with Brenda and Jeremy has been the final straw. I'm just going to have to deal with whatever comes along.'

'Do you want me to go and talk to him? At least it might contain his anger. If nobody turns up, he is more likely to fly off the handle and do something daft. I can be there in half an hour. I promise I'll keep calm.' George was unsure, but figured he had nothing to lose. Graham was right, if nobody turned up, it was likely Baz would release everything he had, immediately. Although his alliance with Jeremy was now no more, he potentially still had enough evidence to cause George and of course Debbie, a great deal of heartache.

'Anything you can do would be great. But be careful. He really is a nasty piece of work. If it looks like he is starting to lose control, get out there. This is my problem. Not yours.'

'It was, until Baz went to mum and dad's. Now it's *our* problem.' They agreed to text each other later and compare notes on what had turned out to be, an unexpected evening for them both.

George parked his car and ran through the torrent of rain into the main entrance of the hospital. Brenda had been wheeled in, still strapped into the cradle and had been sedated. George found the WPC who had travelled with her. He asked her question after question, desperately seeking assurances as to Brenda's welfare, but all the policewomen would say was "she is in good hands Mr. Miller. I'm sure they will let us know as soon as they have something to tell us". They sat in the waiting area. It was packed. As he sat there quietly contemplating the events of that evening, George began to notice a number of people nudging each other, cupping their hands over their mouths and whispering to their neighbours and occasionally nodding or pointing in his direction. Not surprisingly, he had been recognised. Mobile phones began to pop up, occasionally letting off the flash, confirming his fears. Then one by one, they began to walk over for a chat, an autograph and the obligatory selfie. He tried his best to be civil, but he wasn't really in the mood to be pleasant to strangers and he didn't want to discuss football with anyone. He had always been polite and chatty with the fans, but now wasn't the time or the place. A lady from behind the reception desk walked over to him and asked if he would follow her. To the disappointment of the crowd that had formed around him, George stood up and excused himself from the excited throng. She showed him and the WPC into what looked like an office, off the main corridor.

'I thought it might be a bit quieter in here Mr. Miller,' she said. 'I'm sure those people didn't mean to be rude or intrusive. We don't get many celebrities in here you see. Anyway, make yourself comfortable. I will call you as soon as there is any news on Mrs Higgins. Can I get either of you a cup of tea?'

They waited and waited. George looked at his watch. It was now nearly eleven o'clock. He wondered what was happening with Brenda. Then he wondered what had happened with Baz. He looked at his phone. There was a text message from Graham. It simply read, *Call me, as soon as you can.* George was about to make the call, when a doctor entered the small room.

'Mr. Miller?' He asked.

'Yes doctor.' He plunged the phone back into his pocket.

'Mrs Higgins is asking for you. You may go in and see her, but only for a few minutes. She's heavily sedated so you might not get much sense out of her.' George and the policewoman followed the doctor down several corridors and finally into a small room. Brenda's was the only bed in the room. The WPC sat outside while George went in to speak with her.

Brenda was propped up on numerous pillows. She had a tube in the back of her hand and her left arm was strapped across her chest. The cut on her cheek had been cleaned and thankfully, hadn't needed stitches, but the bruising around her eye and on her neck had blossomed into an exhibition of colour. She had an oxygen mask over her nose and mouth. She looked like she was sleeping. George felt the fury and the sadness grip him again in equal measures. It was a cocktail of emotions he was getting used to. Even though Jeremy was dead, George still managed to feel an intense hatred for him.

He sat by her bed and held her hand.

'Brenda. It's me, George. Can you hear me?' he whispered. She slowly opened her eyes. He felt her hand grip his tightly.

'Everything is okay. Don't worry about a thing. You are safe here in hospital and there is a policewoman just outside the door. You need to sleep now. I'll be back in the morning. Just remember what happened earlier.' George glanced at the door. It was shut. They were alone. 'Jeremy beat you. He ran to the top of the stairs and fell. You had nothing to do with it. Do you understand?' Without answering, she shut her eyes. George felt her grip on his hand weaken. He bent down and kissed her, unsure if she had heard him.

'See you tomorrow my sweet, sweet girl. Sleep tight.'

After George had left the room, the doctor told him that Brenda had sustained a fractured collar bone, some nasty bruising and had a bit of a bump on her head. She had concussion from the beating and they were going to keep her in overnight. They would reassess her condition in the morning. The WPC assured George that there would be someone sitting outside her room at all times and would let him know if there were any changes. He told her he would be back about 8 o'clock the next morning, but to call him, regardless of the time, if Brenda awoke and asked for him. Another check of his watch told him it was just past midnight. It had been a hell of a night. He said his goodbyes and walked to the car. The storm was still crashing down. The potholes in the car park had turned into lakes and the wind pushed and bullied him as he made his way across the ever-swelling lagoon. It was too late to call Brenda's parents and he didn't want to worry them by waking them in the middle of the night. There was nothing they could do anyway. Their daughter was stable and being looked after by the best people available. He would call in and see them the next day and assure them all was fine. He shut the car door and phoned his brother.

'Hi Graham. I've just come out of the hospital. How did you get on with Baz? Did you manage to see him?' He could hear a tremble and uncertainty in Graham's voice. He was slurring his words; he sounded drunk!

'I don't know George. I think it might have gone horribly wrong.'

'What do you mean?'

'George, I don't want to talk about it on the phone. Can you get over here to the flat? As soon as possible. I don't think I should drive.' He could sense fear in his brother's voice; a dread and an anxiety he couldn't ever remember hearing from Graham before.

'I'll be there as quickly as I can.'

Chapter 37

Three hours earlier

Graham knew the streets of Peckham well. The one-way system was a pig if you didn't know the area. One wrong turn and you could be driving around the guts of SE15 for hours. He parked his car in one of the backstreets, the other side of the bus station. It would mean he had a five-minute walk in the pouring rain, but at least he was pointing in the right direction when it came to going home. Just in case he needed to make a quick getaway.

He clicked the key twice, locking the car and setting the alarm. He hunched his shoulders and turned the collar of his coat up to protect him from the foul weather. He thought about what he would say to Baz and how he would handle him. On the one hand he had to keep calm and try to placate him. Promise him anything he wanted, to try and buy George a few more days, but inside,

Graham's anger was still burning. The thought that this gangster from their past had been to their parents' house and tried to intimidate them was eating away at him. He would love to be able to take out some of his anger on his old school adversary, but that would have to wait. It all depended on Baz' state of mind. *He* would have to be the one who dictated the mood and the direction of the conversation.

Graham looked both ways as he crossed over Rye Lane. There was nothing coming. The main thoroughfare running through the heart of Peckham was deserted. Bereft of people, bereft of life. The biblical storm had turned Peckham into a ghost town. Graham half expected to see some tumbleweed blow down the middle of the road. His walk turned into a trot, skipping over, and trying to avoid the numerous puddles that had formed. He passed the train station and turned right into the narrow alleyway that ran behind the shops on Rye Lane. Baz had chosen well. It was dark and it was secluded. There were no streetlights and certainly no CCTV cameras. The narrow backstreet funnelled the wind and rain between the walls of the buildings with increasing power and force. One gust was so strong it almost knocked Graham backwards. He was a few minutes early. He took what shelter he could in a small doorway, probably the back entrance to one of the shops on the Main Street. He cast his eyes up and down the desolate landscape. There were no voices, no music, no ringing phones, no sound at all, except for the incessant whistling and gusting wind and the hammering of the rain. He listened to the different sounds it made as it clattered into the metal bins and the black plastic rubbish bags strewn about. The splashing of the drops as they added to the swollen rivers and lakes that had already formed. He heard the sound of an unhinged gate creaking open, then smashing itself shut as another gust toyed with it's fragile wooden frame. A high-pitched screech, from two cats fighting, cut through the bass-like drone and percussion of the downpour.

Graham checked his watch again. It had just gone 9.30. There was still no sign of human life. He wondered if Baz had thought better of coming out in such abysmal conditions. Maybe he had decided to stay in the dry and warmth of his flat or the pub, amusing himself with the thought that George would be standing out in all this weather, waiting for him. Graham decided to wait there for another fifteen minutes. If he hadn't turned up by then, he would leave and let George speak to him.

The screeching cats had obviously decided their disagreement could wait until a dryer time. The weather proving too much, even for the South London strays. It was 9.40 and Graham was cold, wet and becoming increasingly grumpy. Through the relentless pounding of the rain, he heard the sound of footsteps. The clip-clip, splash-splash of shoes making their way towards him. They became louder. Graham screwed his eyes in the direction of the noise. Into the dark, black hole that was the far end of the alleyway. The feet were not running. They were walking; a slow and steady pace. No effort was being made to reduce the exposure to the rain. The flashing neon lights from some of the shops on the main road gave a tantalisingly brief hint of what lay hidden in the darkness. Slowly a figure emerged. Unconcerned and unmoved by the deluge that was falling on him. Baz. Another hurricane force blast of wind burst down the constricted lane, accompanied by a curtain of rain. Then a voice.

'Miller. Miller, where are you? Graham watched as he moved closer. 'Miller,' he shouted at the top of his voice, managing to relegate the sound of the weather into second place. Graham stepped out of the doorway and into the street. They stood face to face, six feet apart, like two gunslingers from the old Wild West.

'Hello Baz.' Baz stopped walking. He stood still, although Graham detected a slight swaying in his posture. It looked like he had been drinking.

'I fucking told you what would happen if you disobeyed my orders. Taking Jayden off on Monday night has dropped you right in the shit. I've got enough evidence on here,' he said, patting his breast pocket, 'to ruin you. I'm going to take great delight watching you crash and burn and seeing you squirm and try to explain to the world that you are an innocent man. Watching you lose your job and seeing your family life fall apart is what I have dreamt of for years.' Baz took a step closer to Graham. The faint burst of neon illumination briefly lit up Graham's features. Baz looked puzzled. He didn't recognise the beard or the full mop of soaking hair.

'What's going on? Where is Miller? Who the fuck are you?'

Graham smiled.

'You mean you don't recognise me Baz?' After a few seconds, the confusion turned to surprise and then hatred.

'You!' he growled.

'Yes, Baz it's me. The other Miller. George asked me to come in his place. Something cropped up and he couldn't make it. It had something to do with your new pal Jeremy, I think. He wanted me to talk to you. To tell you that he was sorry for what he did and to explain to you that it was with the boy's best interests at heart. He said it won't happen again. He told me to tell you he would sort out your money by next week and that Jayden would get another run in the side. He wanted me to ask you not to be too hasty. To give him another chance. He said everything will be fine if you give him another week.' Graham was almost choking on his words. He knew George had no intention of paying Baz a single penny, or obeying anymore of his "orders". The only thing George wanted was to add to the scars on Baz' face, as did Graham, but diplomacy had to be tried as a last resort, for George's sake.

Baz looked confused. He knew George was worried about his wife and the public seeing the evidence he had, but he wasn't expecting such a sycophantic capitulation as this. The Miller brothers had never backed down or given in. This was not like them at all. He began to smell a rat. The rain was still blasting into both of them. Baz stroked his scar as he thought about his next move. He remembered an old adage he had often relied on: *If you are uncertain which way to turn, don't do what you think is best, do what you think your enemy most fears.* Baz smiled. He had made up his mind. He knew what he was going to do. He would see Jeremy tomorrow morning and they would pool what they had on Miller and together would release it all for the press and public alike to ponder. He had had enough of stringing George along. It was time to go in for the kill. He'd had his fun and managed to screw with George's mind. It was now time to show the world what George Miller, national hero, adored sporting icon and famously loyal family man, an inspiration and a role model to so many people, had been doing, as soon as his poor, trusting wife's back was turned. He would throw him to the wolves.

'Well, you can tell your brother that as far as I am concerned, everything is already fine. It's him that's in deep shit. He wants another week? Ha! I'm not even going to give him another day.' He patted his coat pocket again. This little lot is going off to the world's media and I will look forward to watching events unfold tomorrow morning.' Baz started to turn and walk away.

'Wait a minute Baz. There must be some kind of arrangement we can come to. How much do you want, to destroy the evidence you have and fuck off out of our lives forever? If it's money you want just name your price. I can give it to you. Whatever you want. 300K, 500K. Tell me.' Baz started to laugh. He turned around and walked right up to Graham, their faces only inches apart.

'You really don't get it, do you Miller? Yes, a few quid would be nice, especially if I could manage to squeeze it out of George, or even you for that matter. I've got an idea how much you are both worth and it makes me sick. 300K, 500K, wouldn't even make a dent in your bank balance. Anyway, Jayden will soon be earning six figure weekly salaries, so the money won't be a problem for either of us. So, you see it was never about the money. I don't need your fucking money.' He poked Graham in the chest. 'It's always been about revenge, not blackmail. I want to crush him and grind him into the dirt. The irony is, if this *had* been about money, he might have stood a chance of surviving it. But it's not and it never has been. All your money and his combined wouldn't stop me from exposing him and dragging his name through the gutter. That Mr. Miller is priceless. He's going to lose it all.' Graham stared into Baz' sneering eyes as the raindrops ran down their faces. He hadn't changed that much since their school days. A little more weather beaten maybe, but ultimately, he was still the same piece of shit he had always been. Graham knew he wasn't going to be able to talk him around. Everything Baz had said made perfect sense. The money was and always had been, a sideshow. A smokescreen behind which, the more sinister aspects of his plan could hide. He had just been playing with George, always knowing what the outcome would be, once he got bored with his little game. He knew Baz had decided to play his hand. There was no more need for diplomacy. It had been tried and it had failed. There were no more rules. The gloves were off. By playing his "Ace" Baz was now fair game and vulnerable to all of the pent-up anger that had been brewing within the Miller boys. He was now nothing more than a target. Graham felt the anger once again start to burn in his veins. He had made up his mind that Baz was not going to walk away from this unscathed. If nothing else, he would make him pay for intimidating his parents.

'You always were a piece of shit, Baz. Nothing has changed.'

'Nothing has changed yet. But by tomorrow morning, what will have changed is the happy and contented lifestyle of George Miller.'

'I see you still have my autograph on your face. I gave that to you twenty-seven years ago. Do you remember?' Graham jabbed his finger onto the scar, causing Baz to wince with pain. Baz' eyes narrowed and the familiar snarl came back to his face. Graham could see he had hit a raw nerve.

'I do remember. I remember everyday. Every time I look in the mirror. Every time I touch it, I promise myself that one day I will pay you back. It looks like lady luck has given me the chance to do just that, tonight. A two for one offer. Your brother's happy life will be in tatters tomorrow and now I have the chance to get even with you. This could be the best twenty-four hours of my life.'

'Well, I hope you thought of me and remembered how much us Miller boys enjoyed giving it to you. Maybe it's time to give you one over the other eye.' Graham shoved Baz in the chest with both hands, knocking him backwards.

'You fucking Millers. I'm going to enjoy this.' Baz reached into his coat pocket and pulled out a knife. The nine-inch serrated blade glinted in another burst of flashing neon from the main street. 'Maybe it's my turn to give you something to remember *me* by.' He swung the blade in front of Graham's face, first one way and then the other.

Graham stepped back, his foot disappearing into an ankle-deep puddle of water.

'You never scared me at school Baz and you certainly don't scare me now. You're nothing but a coward. Always hiding behind a knife or a gang. You've never had the balls to front someone down without an edge. You're nothing.'

Baz waved the blade passed Graham's face again and again. It was close enough to hear the hiss of the steel as it flashed past his eyes. Graham was backing away, keeping out of arms reach, but he knew sooner rather than later he would have nowhere to go, unless he turned and ran. And that wasn't going to happen. Again, the serrated teeth carved their way through the pouring rain, only inches from Graham's face. Then Baz lunged. A full on thrust towards his stomach. Graham's kickboxing had honed his reactions, he was sharp. He stepped to his right and watched as the blade flew past him. He grabbed Baz' wrist with his left hand and punched him square on the nose with his right. Baz' head recoiled from the blow and blood immediately began to flow from his nostrils. The two men grappled with each other; Graham's right-hand clutching and squeezing around Baz's throat, Baz trying in vain to throw haymakers at Graham's head with his left fist. They lurched from side to side in a drunken waltz. Another water filled pothole caused them both to stumble and the two of them splashed to the sodden ground. Both men's concentration was focused on the knife as it jerked and twisted in Baz' hand. Graham repeatedly smashed the back of Baz' hand onto the small kerbstone running along the alley. With every bone breaking crunch, Graham could sense Baz' grip on the weapon weakening. With blood oozing from his crushed knuckles and fingers, Baz slowly relinquished his hold on the handle. The knife slipped into the gutter and disappeared beneath the water. Graham rolled himself off his side and into an upright position, until he was straddling Baz. He still had hold of his right wrist and with his right foot, managed to pin Baz' left arm to the floor. He had him at his mercy, but in Graham's heightened state of arousal, there was going to be precious little of that. He sent a crunching blow into Baz' face. He felt the cheek bone crumble beneath his fist. Momentarily, Baz' body went limp. His arms had stopped thrashing and he lay beneath Graham, still and stunned. A second later, Graham could feel movement coming back into Baz' limbs. He delivered another fearful blow in exactly the same spot as the first. There was little resistance. The bone had all but disintegrated. Baz went limp again. Graham looked down on the bleeding mess below him. He felt his nostrils flare and his lip curl as another torrent of rain washed the blood away from Baz' wounds.

'This one is for me you cunt.' He hit him again. 'This one is for George.' Another blow. 'And these are for my Mum and Dad.' Graham smashed his fist again and again into the bloody morass of what little remained of Baz' face. The old scar had ruptured and was spewing out blood just as it had all those years ago. The human being lying in the gutter was unrecognisable. The eye socket had been smashed and his left eye sat loosely in its mooring. The cheek bone and nose were crushed beyond form. His jawbone had been broken and his teeth had splintered. The jagged edges of his incisors, canines and molars had sliced through his lips and the flesh around his mouth. Flaps of skin danced in a grotesque display, constantly animated by the ferocious downpour. As heavy as the rain was, it couldn't wash away the blood that was pouring relentlessly from what was left of Baz' identity. Graham looked down at what he had done. He felt himself returning to his senses, as if the demon within him was leaving his body. His breathing had slowed and was now more regular. It was like he had emerged from a trance. He struggled to believe he had inflicted so much brutality on another human being. Even Baz! He felt a wave of nausea wash over him. For the first time since he had spoken to Baz, he became aware of the rain falling on his head and the wetness of his clothes. He shivered as the driving wind and rain reminded him of the bleak and dark place he was in. He looked at his right hand. There was blood all over it. He unclasped his fist and held it out in front of him watching as the rain slowly washed it clean.

Baz hadn't moved. Graham started to panic. He was certain he had killed him. Surely no one could take a beating like that and survive. If he did live through it, he was going to need some major surgery to rebuild that face.

Graham stood up. He knew he had to get out of there as quickly as possible. He glanced up the alleyway. There was still no sign of life. He began to walk away, but couldn't help taking one last glance over his shoulder at the body, lying prostrate and lifeless. As he watched the fast flowing river of rain water coursing down the alley, washing over Baz' freakish and deformed features, he felt a huge sense of shame engulf him. The cultured, intelligent and civilised man he had always believed himself to be had mutated into a barbaric, depraved animal. Someone or something he didn't know; something he didn't want to know. He needed to conceal the atrocity the beast within him had created. He couldn't leave it there. The first person to pass by would find it and raise the alarm. The deserted streets would quickly be filled with police, ambulances and curious onlookers. Out of sight, out of mind. If he could hide it, it might also give him enough time to make his escape unnoticed. He walked back and grabbed Baz by the lapels of his coat and dragged him towards the bins. He was too heavy to pick up and drop into the large Biffa bin. It was full anyway, but the overflow of rubbish had created a small mountain of black and yellow sacks to the side. Graham began to pull some of the bin liners away from the pile. A number of rats suddenly squealed and ran off in every direction, causing Graham to stumble backwards with fright. He landed with a splash on his arse. He took a deep breath and gathered himself. He heaved Baz' body into the resulting cavity and took one last look at him. Rubbish lying in a pile of rubbish. How very apt he thought. Graham began to pile the bin liners on top of the lifeless body when he became aware of a noise coming from within the mountain of refuse. Was Baz regaining consciousness? He cleared a couple of the bags away, revealing the gargoyle beneath. The noise was coming from within his coat. His mobile. Graham plunged his hand inside and found the phone. On the screen was the word *Jayden*. It was his son calling him. Graham put the phone in his pocket and entombed Baz once more in the stinking garbage. One last glance both ways confirmed that no one had witnessed the carnage or the cover up of the previous few minutes. Graham made his way back to his car. He decided to keep away from the main streets, the lights and any CCTV cameras that might capture his image. He sunk deeper beneath the collar of his coat and kept his eyes fixed on the ground. The roundabout journey back to his car took nearly fifteen minutes, but he was convinced he had made it unseen. Again, he looked around. There was no one. He took out Baz' mobile and removed the SIM card. He then broke the device into a thousand tiny fragments, stamping on it with all his might. A nearby drain swallowed all the pieces before Graham toasted the SIM card on his car's cigarette lighter. He watched as it slowly shrivelled and smoked on the red-hot element. It was the first time he had ever used it. It left a terrible stench in the air. A movement across the street snapped Graham's attention away from the smouldering evidence. He saw two eyes looking at him, twinkling in the reflection from the orange light of a nearby lamp post. The eyes glared at him with a curious intensity, watching his bizarre actions. Graham stared back. His initial fright at being discovered had gone. The inquisitive fox on the opposite side of the road had no interest in what he was doing and moved on. So did Graham. He needed to get back to his flat as soon as possible. On the drive home he became aware of just how wet he was. His coat and trousers were dripping and he realised he was sitting in a pool of water. He started to shiver and could feel his hands trembling as they held onto the steering wheel. He kept having to tell himself to slow down and concentrate on his driving. The last thing he needed was to be pulled over by the police or photographed by a speed camera.

By the time he parked outside his flat the shaking and the feeling of nausea had subsided. But he needed a drink. A good strong drink.

Chapter 38

A forgettable, loathsome irrelevance

The first thing Graham had to do was get out of his wet clothes. He was soaked to the skin. He stripped himself down and headed for the bathroom. On the way he called Kerry.

'Hi Kerry, it's me. There's been a change of plan. Brenda won't be staying here tonight and George is in a spot of bother. It's far too complicated to explain right now, but I'll fill you in tomorrow when I get home.'

After towelling himself down, he wrapped himself into his thick, warm bathrobe. He picked up a bottle of brandy and a glass and plonked himself down on the sofa. His mind was a confused tangle of thoughts. So many ifs, buts and maybes. He poured himself a long drink. He held his hands out in front of him. They had started to shake again. He had to concentrate to get the cognac into the glass and had to hold the glass with both hands to prevent himself from spilling any. The first two fingers of brandy slammed into the back of his throat and made him shudder. He could feel the burning liquid slide down his throat. He closed his eyes and his body convulsed as the alcohol assaulted his system. He poured himself another and again slugged it back in one. He thought about calling George. It was nearly eleven o'clock. He didn't know what had been going on with his brother. It sounded like he had had a rather extraordinary evening too. He decided against phoning him but sent him a text. It simply read *'Call me as soon as you can'*. Graham poured himself another drink. He knew he would pay a heavy price for his consumption in the morning, but at that precise moment, the morning seemed a long way away.

While he was waiting for George to call, he began going over in his mind what had happened. He was desperately trying to convince himself that he had seen, or felt, signs of life in Baz as he had buried him beneath Peckham's unwanted shit. Had he felt movement in his chest when he took out the mobile phone from his inside coat pocket? Maybe. Maybe not. He berated himself for not thinking to search for a pulse, or any sign of breathing, before he left the scene. He felt nothing but hatred and loathing for Baz, especially when he thought of him bullying his parents, but the idea that he, Graham Miller, might have killed him and in such a savage manner, made him feel sick. He looked at his right hand and made it into a fist. Had that really ended another man's life? He recalled the image of Baz, lying amongst the bin bags, barely recognisable as a human being. Surely no one would be able to survive that kind of beating. He tried to justify his actions. The mitigating circumstances of self-defence. He was being threatened with a knife. His life was in danger. Surely, he was within his rights to protect his own life. But he knew he had gone way past that. He had defended himself and rendered his assailant senseless. It was the unrestrained violence that had followed, that was in question. He considered himself a well-educated and peace loving man, but having reached the age of forty-two he had discovered he was capable of becoming a wild, untamed and vicious animal, with no trace of compassion or feeling. It was a terrifying thought.

It was just after midnight when Graham's phone pinged into life. The sudden blast of the ringtone in the still and silent flat made him jump to attention. It was George.

'Hi Graham. I've just come out of the hospital. How did you get on with Baz? Did you manage to see him'?

Graham didn't know what to say. It certainly hadn't gone well. But he was unsure as to just how badly it had gone.

'I don't want to talk about it over the phone. Can you get over here to the flat? As soon as possible. I don't think I should drive.' George told him to sit tight and he would drive over. He would be there as soon as he could.

Just after 12:30 the two brothers sat facing each other across the table in Graham's lounge. George was sipping on a whiskey, his brother was slugging back another brandy.

'So, what happened?' asked George, eager to discover why his brother appeared so agitated. Graham drew in a deep breath and swallowed another mouthful from his glass. His voice was already beginning to slur from the effect of the alcohol.

'I think I killed him George.'

'What?' George looked staggered. The events that had taken place back at Brenda's house had been extraordinary. Enough drama for a lifetime, let alone one evening. And now here was Graham telling him he thought he had killed a man. Had the world gone completely crazy? Graham then proceeded to give his account of everything that had happened in the dark alleyway behind Peckham Station. When he had finished, he hung his head.

'I just kept hitting him and hitting him and hitting him. With each punch his face seemed to disintegrate even more, until there was hardly anything left that looked like a man. I had lost all control. It was as if I had been possessed by some psychotic maniac. I have never felt an anger like it before. I just couldn't stop myself.'

George could see the glass in Graham's hand begin to shake again. Graham started to shudder. He looked up at George. There were tears forming in his eyes.

'What am I going to do?' George tried to move the conversation away from the beating.

'Before the fight, did he say anything about the so-called evidence he had?'

'He kept referring to what was on his phone. He kept tapping his breast pocket and telling me that everything he had was on that. I took the phone and smashed it to pieces, then dropped it down the drain. I burnt the SIM card. Whatever he had on that phone has gone, unless he saved it onto anything else. But I guess we won't know that for a while.'

Graham looked at George with pleading eyes, as if he were seeking Divine guidance.

'I actually think I beat a man to death tonight.' George tried to calm him down.

'You don't know you killed him. You probably only knocked him unconscious. Anyway, if he is dead it's no great loss to humanity. You have done the world a favour.' George's words didn't have the desired effect. 'Look Graham, there isn't anything we can do except wait. Whether Baz is dead or alive, we will find out sooner or later.' George was right, but that didn't help Graham's state of mind.

George told Graham what had happened at Brenda's house. Graham listened to the description of the brutality that Jeremy had inflicted on his wife, before George saw her push him down the stairs to his grisly death. As barbarous and cruel as Jeremy had been to Brenda and as sensational and shocking as his fall and death, George's story failed to take Graham's mind away from the broken and bloody horror he had left in that pile of rubbish.

They talked through the night. The brandy and whiskey were replaced by numerous cups of coffee. There were so many questions that remained unanswered and so many doubts and fears that went with them. There was one thing they knew for certain. It had been a night like they had never experienced before.

By 7 o'clock neither of them had had any sleep. George had showered, freshened himself up and was going to head back to the hospital.

'I'll call you later if I hear anything. Why don't you grab yourself a couple of hours sleep, then head back home to Kerry? Maybe say nothing at the moment until we know what has happened.

Let's keep your rendezvous with Baz and my vision of Brenda, pushing Jeremy down the stairs, to ourselves.

'That sounds like a good idea to me,' Graham replied. George popped a couple of extra strong mints in his mouth to kill off the last remnants of his "whiskey breath" and headed back to see Brenda.

On arrival, he noticed a new face sitting outside Brenda's room. Another WPC. He introduced himself. The young policewoman started to blush.

'Ah yes. Mr. Miller. Carol … sorry WPC Adams said you would be here this morning. I think your friend Brenda…err, Ms Higgins, is feeling a little better today. She is awake if you want to go in.'

Brenda was sitting up in bed. Her eyes were open and she seemed more alert than she had been the previous evening. She still had the oxygen mask on her face and a drip connected to the back of her hand. The sling still held her left arm across her chest and the bruising and swelling around her face and neck had become even more evident. As soon as she saw him come through the door a smile flickered across her face. She removed her mask.

'George.' She held out her right arm and pulled him into her embrace. He hugged her as gently as he could. He could feel her body once again begin to tremble. Even through her happiness at seeing him, she had started to sob.

'George, what's going to happen? I've been having flashbacks and dreams all night. I think it's the drugs they've been giving me. I keep reliving those awful last moments with Jeremy.' She lowered her voice to a whisper. 'I killed him George. I killed him!' George went over the story once again, lowering his voice and constantly glancing over at the door to make sure they weren't being overheard.

'Listen Brenda. I saw it all. And so did Greg Palmer and we have both told D.I. Cooper the same story. As far as he is concerned, you were upstairs unconscious and Jeremy, in his haste to shut the front door, tripped and fell. It's as simple as that. You have to stick with that story, otherwise you will make me look like a liar and I don't want to get in trouble with the police. My bad boy days are over. You know that.' He gently caressed her cheek with his fingers. Brenda forced a smile.

'I do, more's the pity,' she grinned.

'Here, I've got you some grapes, some chocolate Hobnobs and some orange juice. Call me if there is anything else you need. I have to go into work now, but I'll be back later. I think it would be better if you went to stay with your Mum and Dad for a while after this. Now Jeremy is no longer a threat, you will be better off with them fussing over you, than rattling around in Graham's flat. Have you called them yet?' She hadn't.

'I'll do it now,' she said waving her mobile at him.

'Tell them I will pop into see them on my way to work and will tell them everything.'

'Thank you, George. Thank you for everything.'

He drove to Brenda's parents' house. Over a cup of tea, they talked about their daughter and their ex-son in law. George didn't tell them what he had learnt about the violence that had been going on over the years. It wasn't his place. But he did get the distinct feeling that neither Mr, nor Mrs Cousins, thought very highly of their daughter's choice of husband. The shocking news that their son-in-law was dead was greeted with disbelief and amazement, but there was little or no sign of sadness or sorrow. Not surprisingly, their questions and concerns were all about their baby girl. Jeremy had ceased to be a worry. Less than twenty four hours after his death, Jeremy had become a forgettable, loathsome, irrelevance.

Chapter 39

Killed by a number 63 bus

Having spoken to Brenda's parents, George finally arrived at his office just after 11 o'clock. He told the girls on reception that Brenda wouldn't be in for at least a couple of weeks, maybe more. Janice suggested she could stand-in for Brenda while she was away. George gratefully accepted her offer, but he wondered what she would make of Brenda's unique "filing system". He had a game to prepare for on Sunday and was looking forward to finally burying his head in his job. For the first time in a while the selection of his starting eleven was purely in his own hands. Having regained control of the decision-making process, he realised how simple it was to put his strongest team out. The first two names were easy. Alf Wood and David Jones up front. He looked at the piece of paper he had just written on and smiled. He felt the excitement and the energy again. He had forgotten how much he enjoyed his job. He had no way of knowing how the next forty-eight hours would pan out, but for some reason, he felt like a weight had been lifted from his shoulders and a cleansing, fresh breeze had gently blown away all of his worries. What had happened to both Jeremy and Baz had at least bought him the few days he needed to be able to explain the situation to Debbie once she had returned. All the confusion about what to say and what to keep secret had now evaporated. The fog of uncertainty had cleared in his mind. Jeremy was dead and Baz, going on what Graham had told him, was unlikely to complicate matters for at least a few days. He could tell his story without fear of contradiction or the contaminated and concocted "evidence" Baz had been so excited about. He had only one course of action open to him and that was the truth. He just had to pray that Debbie believed him.

George's phone rang. It was Bob Hunter his assistant. He told George that Jayden had failed to turn up for training. Bob knew he was a troublemaker and had exchanged views on the boy with George a number of times.

'Little toe-rag isn't here. Thought I should let you know.'

'Thanks Bob. No problem. He wasn't going to figure in the squad anyway.' George wondered if Jayden's absence had anything to do with what had happened to Baz the night before. It really didn't matter one way or another as far as he was concerned. They could both rot in Hell.

Janice knocked on George's door. It was just before 1 o'clock.

'Excuse me Mr. Miller. There are a couple of gentlemen who would like to see you.' George raised his eyebrows in a quizzical look.

'They're policemen,' she continued, suddenly looking a little apprehensive. George nodded, and tried to give the impression he was expecting them.

'Thank you, Janice. Show them in.' He tried to remain cool and collected. He knew he would have to talk to the police again sooner or later, but it had taken him a little bit by surprise, them turning up at his place of work. He assumed they would have asked both him and Brenda to make their statements down at the station. He quickly ran through the series of events in his mind and tried to remember what he had told D.I.Cooper. Everything he had said was true, it was just what he had failed to mention that he had to be clear about. He took a deep breath and prepared himself for his cross-examination. Janice showed the two men in. George's confidence was immediately rocked. He was expecting to see D.I.Cooper. But both these men were unknown to him.

'Sit down gentlemen. Can I offer you any tea or coffee?' The policeman declined and Janice shut the door behind her.

'What is it I can do for you?' George asked, trying to appear calm.

'I am Detective Inspector Church and this is Detective Sergeant Malloy.' They both showed George their warrant cards. George gave them a cursory glance, before they were whipped away and replaced back in their jacket pockets.

'Mr. Miller,' Church continued, 'do you know this man?' He pulled out a ten by eight black and white photograph from the leather folder he was carrying and slid it across George's desk. Straight away, George recognised it as Baz. By the look of his pose, it had been taken while he was in prison. He felt a shiver of uncertainty ripple down his spine. He had to refocus. This wasn't about Brenda or Jeremy. He tried to switch his concentration to the other main event that had happened the previous evening. His heartbeat quickened. George picked up the photo as nonchalantly as he could and looked at it. His eyes immediately went to the scar snaking its way around Baz' left eye. It brought a smile to his face. He looked up at the policeman, who were waiting for his answer. He pushed the photograph back across the desk towards them.

'Yes. I do know this man. His name is Barry Saunders, although I know him as Baz. Why do you ask?' George was having to make a real effort to appear unmoved and unflustered by these new and unexpected questions. He had to try and remember everything Graham had told him, but at the same time behave as if he knew nothing of Baz' ill-fated trip to the backstreets of Peckham.

'Did you know him well Sir?' Malloy joined in the conversation.

'I've known him on and off for over thirty years. We were at school together. He left when he was fifteen or sixteen, I think. I hadn't seen him again until a couple of weeks ago. I believe he spent a lot of his life, since school, being looked after by you chaps. It appears he was at large about seventeen years ago, long enough to father a child. A son, Jayden. I signed Jayden earlier this year. I wasn't aware at the time the two were related, until Baz made himself known to me a couple of weeks ago.'

'What was your relationship like with Mr. Saunders? Would you say it was a friendly one?'

George wondered where the questioning was leading. He wished they would get to the point and tell him just what they wanted.

'Certainly not. We didn't see eye to eye at school and we certainly didn't see eye to eye this time around. I have never liked the man and never will. Does that answer your question? Anyway, why are you asking me about Baz? What's this all about? Is he back in trouble again?' George quietly congratulated himself on his steady nerve.

'Are you aware that Mr. Saunders died last night?' George felt his entire body convulse as a shockwave rampaged through him. The words George had been hoping not to hear, hit him like a sledge-hammer. His heart started to pound faster and he could feel the beginnings of a sweat forming on his brow and his top lip. So, it was as Graham had feared. He had actually beaten him to death. Now he really had to think about what he said. He knew the shock of Baz' death had been plain to see, but how did the detectives interpret his somewhat stunned demeanour? He swallowed and took a deep breath.

'Died?' he said, with all the astonishment his fear allowed. 'How?'

'When I said died, Mr Miller, I meant, *killed.*' The last word hung in the air with an almost accusing ring. The detectives sat motionless, both staring intently at George as if trying to decipher every twitch and muscle spasm on his face. Waiting for a reaction.

'Killed? You mean murdered?' George asked, in a voice that had lost all of its confidence. He already knew how, but what did the police know about who and why? Ignoring his question, Malloy continued the interrogation.

'Mr. Miller, where were you between 9:30 and 11:30 last night?'

'What? Me?' George asked incredulously.

'Yes, Mr. Miller. You. We know you were due to meet with Mr. Saunders at 9:30 in Peckham. Did you keep that appointment?'

George's mind was racing. What did they know? He had to keep one step ahead of them. Give them no information he didn't have to. He knew he had a cast iron alibi, but the panic of hearing Baz was in fact dead, made the situation not only more serious, but far more dangerous.

'Between 9:30 and 11:30 you say.' He paused for a moment and tried to gather his thoughts. 'I don't think I can give you exact timings of my movements last night. It was an evening full of shocks and surprises. I can tell you where I was between 6 o'clock and midnight but I can't be sure of accurate timings in between.'

'Please go on Mr. Miller.' Malloy already had a notebook and pen in his hand, poised to take down George's testimony.

'I was here most of the day, then at about 4.30pm I drove to my secretary's house. She wanted to pick up a few of her things; clothes, toiletries and a few personal items. She had decided to leave the prick she was married to. He had been beating her up for years and she finally found enough courage to walk out on him. I went along as insurance. Just in case. But I got waylaid by a neighbour. While I was outside talking to a Mr Palmer, the neighbour, we heard a scream and both rushed in. Jeremy, the husband, in his haste to get to the front door, fell and tumbled down the stairs. I'm no medical expert, but I think he broke his neck. Brenda, my secretary, was upstairs unconscious. The neighbour called the police and an ambulance. We were there until about 8.30ish. D.I.Cooper was the man we spoke to at the scene. When Janice told me there were two Detectives to see me, I assumed one of them would be him. Anyway, Brenda was taken to hospital. I followed the ambulance and waited there until she had been seen. I sat with a nice young WPC, Carol Adams I think her name was, until about midnight. Then I left. I returned to the hospital this morning at about 8 o'clock and stayed for about an hour. After that I visited Brenda's parents and explained to them what happened, then came here and have been here since 11 o'clock, or there abouts.' Once he had finished his story, George sat back in his chair, satisfied with his account, and smiled at the two confused looking policemen. It was certainly not what they had been expecting to hear.

'I see,' said Church. He looked at Malloy, who took out his phone and walked into the lounge outside the office.

'So, you didn't see Mr. Saunders at all last night?'

'No. I had more important things to worry about. I have no way of contacting him so could do nothing about it. I assumed he would get bored of waiting, call me and arrange another time. Baz Saunders was not top of my priority list.'

'What about his son, Jayden? You have a contact number for him presumably. Why didn't you call him?' George leant forward and rested his arms on his desk.

'Inspector, I had a lot going on in my head. Death and violence may be a day-to-day occurrence in your occupation, but seeing a man fall down a flight of stairs and break his neck is not something that I regularly get to witness. My secretary was upstairs unconscious, having been beaten up by that bastard. No, I didn't think to call his bloody son.'

George was becoming angry at the questions. He was confused and unsure of where the policemen's inquiries were going. He was worried that the two unconnected events would become entangled with each other and in the confusion, he might say something that would either drop him in it, or worse still, drop his brother in the shit. He took another deep breath and tried to compose himself.

'Is there anything else I can help you with?' He was keen to bring the interview to an end. The confidence he had felt at the beginning of their chat had gone and he was feeling decidedly jittery. And he knew it showed.

DS Malloy came back into the office. He shrugged his shoulders and nodded at Church.

'I've spoken to D.I.Cooper Gov and he's confirmed it. Just as Mr Miller said.' Church sat in quiet contemplation. George and Malloy waited. George leant back in his chair. He thought about what he had been asked and about his answers. He had momentarily become angry but had pulled himself together and as far as he could remember, had said nothing that either wasn't true or that they didn't already know. The silence dragged on.

'Mr. Miller, was Mr. Saunders blackmailing you?' The question took George by complete surprise and further jolted his composure. Whatever the police did, or didn't know, they were obviously aware of the *situation* between him and Baz. He thought long and hard about his answer.

'He was trying to.'

'In what way, may I ask, Mr. Miller?'

'He said he had evidence of me being unfaithful to my wife.'

'And did he?'

'Of course not.'

'How can you be sure?'

'Because I haven't been unfaithful. It's a bit difficult to have evidence of something that hasn't even happened, I would suggest. Don't you think?' D.I.Church smiled.

'Yes, I suppose it would be. Mr. Miller do you think this is what he was referring to?' He gestured to Malloy who opened the leather folder again pulling out a tablet. He punched his fingers on the screen a number of times and then handed it to George.

George sat in horror as he watched the recording that Jayden had taken on his phone. He really did have the "full movie". George shuffled uncomfortably in his seat. The recording started with him slowly lowering the polo neck of Brenda's sweater, before sensually kissing her neck. He saw her head tilt back and an expression of ecstasy spread across her face. The sound did nothing to ease George's guilt, as Brenda let out a moan of pleasure. He didn't recall hearing that the first time around. It was plain to see she was enjoying the experience. Surely, he hadn't spent that much time kissing her neck. It seemed to go on forever. Eventually he lifted his lips away from the base of her neck and replaced the heavy roll of wool. He felt a moment of relief, once his head pulled away, but he knew there was worse to come. Sure enough, he saw Brenda raise herself onto her tip-toes and put her arms around his neck, pulling his head towards hers. Their lips brushed together. Since the event had happened, George had tried to justify it, by convincing himself that Brenda had kissed him and he had simply been an unwilling and surprised bystander. He felt his heart sink, as he watched himself place his arms around Brenda's waist and pull her into him. Their mouths momentarily locked together in the most passionate of kisses. Again, the recorded action on the tablet seemed to go on much longer than George had remembered. Jayden's off camera cough bought the kiss to an end. He had kept on filming as they continued to embrace. Both had a look of horror on their faces, as if caught red-handed, committing a crime. George looked into both his own and Brenda's expressions and all he could see was *GUILT*. He glanced up at the policemen, who again sat motionless, staring back at him. George reluctantly returned his attention back to the tablet. Presumably, Jayden had edited Baz' evidence together. The scene cut away from the kiss in the office, to George and Brenda walking out of the main entrance and into his car. He was more or less carrying her. The footage then showed his car driving to the flat, with the two of them inside. Then, George leaving half an hour later on his own, only to return that evening. The two of them, driving back to the club the following morning, with Brenda clearly visible, sitting in the passenger seat, putting on her makeup using the vanity mirror. George watched as he and Brenda walked hand in hand towards their office, for all the world, looking like two young lovers. It then caught every moment and every syllable of his confrontation with Jeremy, including all of his insults and insinuations. That was the final scene. The "full movie", as Baz had called it, was over. George paused for a moment.

His worse fears had now been confirmed. Baz did have all he had boasted. And cut together, it looked far more damaging than he could have ever imagined. The evidence he had just witnessed, was so awful, he started to doubt his own innocence. He was pretty sure that if Debbie had been shown the footage, she would have struggled to believe his story. If the roles had been reversed and it had been Debbie trying to convince him that there was nothing to worry about, he knew he would find it hard to accept. He hated himself even more. He dropped the tablet on his desk and looked up at the two policemen, fearing they had already condemned him as a philanderer and nodded.

'Yes, I suppose that is what he was referring to; and yes, I know it doesn't look good. But I have never cheated on my wife and this footage doesn't prove anything.'

'You are, of course, right Mr. Miller. On its own, this footage proves nothing, as far as you and your secretary are concerned, although I also appreciate, it's not something you really want your wife to see.'

'How did you get hold of this?'

'It was on the boy's computer.'

'What will happen to it now? It's not something I want made public, for obvious reasons.'

'No, quite. Well, once we have no further use for the material, it will be erased. I have advised the young lad to do the same. Now we know he has it, any attempt to use it, for extortion or blackmail, will obviously have us crashing down on him from a great height. If it is ever used by a third party, for the same reason, we will know where they obtained it and again, that will mean Jayden Saunders having to answer a few awkward questions. For his own good, we have strongly recommended he delete the recording.' George nodded; almost gratefully.

'So, Mr Miller, if we can go back to last night. What was the purpose of your meeting with Mr Saunders?'

'He said he wanted to talk. That he had something to show me. Presumably that.' George gestured at the tablet. Church raised his eyes to the ceiling as if in deep thought. Then he looked George square in the eye.

'If you were confident, as you said you were, that he had no real evidence, why on Earth, would you agree to meet him? Especially on a filthy night in Peckham.' George was momentarily stumped. He felt the sweat begin to form on his top lip, yet again.

'I wanted to make it clear to him that I wasn't interested in anything he had to say. That I didn't want any more dealings with him. I didn't want the situation to get out of hand in my office. I wanted to explain to him on neutral ground. If he was going to get nasty, I didn't want it to be linked with this place. Listen inspector, Baz and I go back a long way. There is a lot of history and a lot of unfinished business between us, in Baz' mind anyway. He wasn't the type of person who would let things go. He wanted to destroy me and everything I have. He was prepared to do anything to achieve his goals. He threatened me and my family. I can look after myself Inspector, but I won't stand by and have my wife and children intimidated. He even went to my parents and tried to put the frighteners on them. He is a scumbag.'

'Was,' said Church. George frowned.

'Sorry, inspector.'

'Was. He *was* a scumbag. He is no longer a scumbag, that is for sure.' George let out an unintentional laugh at the Inspector's observation.

'So, do you know who killed him?' George asked, in a tone that could only be described as uninterested curiosity. D.I.Church looked at him with narrow eyes.

'*Who*, killed him?'

'Yes. Who? You said he had been killed. I assumed you meant murdered.'

Church's frown deepened.

'Why would you assume that Mr Miller?' Again, George felt the accusing eyes of the two policemen burrowing into him and wished he hadn't asked the question.

'I..I don't know. I just thought…' He didn't know what he thought. To his huge relief, Church put an end to his floundering.

'Mr. Saunders was not murdered Sir. He was killed by a number 63 bus. We think he had been drinking. He stepped out into the road, obviously unaware of the Double Decker and fell straight under the front wheel. Terrible mess. There wasn't much left of him really. We found his wallet and some personal effects and contacted his son. Dental records were of no use as his head had been completely squished to a pulp. However, the severed arm recovered from the scene and the fingerprints taken, confirmed his identity. We are still waiting on the DNA results, but I think it's safe to say Mr Barry Saunders is no longer with us. Chap called Donnelly was driving the bus. Only just started working for the bus company. Poor man; terribly shaken up as you can imagine. Not his fault though. Anyway, Jayden his son gave us some samples which we are confident will match. He's been very helpful. Nice young lad. That's how we knew about the meeting and the blackmail.'

'Jayden told you about the blackmail?' George asked.

'Yes. He was a little vague as to the details, but when we asked him, he said he had nothing to do with it. Is that true?'

George could still feel the shockwave reverberating through his body. A 63 bus. So, Graham hadn't killed him. Baz must have regained consciousness and wandered under the bus unaided. While D.I.Church recounted his grisly story, George had felt a smile start to appear on his face. Graham was not a murderer and Baz had done a wonderful thing, falling under that bus and disappearing from humanity forever. George's mind started to wander. His thoughts turned to Jayden. The boy had denied taking part in the blackmail and intimidation his father had perpetrated, probably knowing that any connection between him and a police investigation would do irreparable damage to his embryonic career. The young lad clearly had more brains than George had given him credit for. By distancing himself from his father, he had left the door open, for what would probably be, a glittering career.

'Mr Miller. Is that true?' Cooper asked again, jolting George from his thoughts.

'I think so. As far as I know inspector, the young boy knew nothing of his father's plans. I'm pretty sure it was just the warped mind of a man set on revenge. How is Jayden?'

'He seems to be holding up. I'm sure the reality of the situation will hit him soon.'

'Don't worry inspector, everyone here at the club will do everything they can to help him through this.' George was surprised at how sympathetic he had managed to sound.

'Oh, there is one other thing Mr. Miller. We didn't find Mr. Saunders mobile phone. Jayden said he definitely had it with him when he left their flat. The boy mentioned to us, that his father had evidence of a different kind that he was planning on using against you. He said he had recorded some conversations with you on his phone. Is that correct?' George paused for thought again.

'I don't know what he recorded inspector. We did have a couple of conversations. They covered a number of subjects, but what he was planning to use against me, I can't be sure. He demanded money, which I refused to pay him. He wanted assurances about his son's future, but I couldn't give him any. Do you have these recordings? If you would let me listen to them, maybe I could help shed some light on them.'

'Unfortunately, the recordings were only on his mobile phone. The boy said he hadn't saved them onto anything else. We've searched and searched but can't find any trace of it. Would you know anything about that at all Sir?'

'Like I told you inspector. I was elsewhere. All I know about what happened last night is what you have just told me. This has all come as a massive surprise. As for his mobile phone, I neither know, or care, of its whereabouts. I know there was nothing incriminating on it, because, I had done nothing to incriminate myself. In fact, if you do find it, I would be interested to hear just what my old school friend Baz regarded as incriminating. I can't say I'm happy that Baz is dead. Of course, I'm not. But I'm also not particularly upset at the news either. He was an odious, vicious and demented human being. Personally, I don't think the world is worse off without him. Now, if you don't have any more questions, I've got a game on Sunday to prepare for.' Church and Malloy looked at each other and stood up.

'Thank you, Mr. Miller. You've been very helpful. We may need to speak to you again if anything else comes to light.'

'I will be here most days. Always pleased to help in any way I can gentleman.'

As soon as they had left George called Graham and gave him the news they'd both been praying for.

Chapter 40

Beautifully choreographed deaths

At last, it was Friday. The day George had been both dreading and yearning for. The day of reckoning and hopefully, the day he got his life back. It had been eighteen days since Doug's funeral and seventeen since Debbie and the kids had gone to see her parents in Mallorca. What had taken place in that time still left George feeling dizzy and bemused. He was still trying to come to terms with everything that had happened. The horrifying discovery that Brenda was being brutally abused at home and his need to protect her, as a friend, from any further harm. The moment of weakness when he had *allowed himself to be kissed by her*, in what was anything but a platonic manner and the bad luck and bad timing of that kiss, taking place, as Jayden Saunders watched on. Experiencing first-hand, once she had moved into his apartment, how much Brenda really did love him and even more worryingly, his reaction to those emotions. The inconceivability of Baz turning up again and being Jayden's father. The scheming and vitriol of Baz and Jeremy's plotting in an attempt to destroy everything that was precious to him. The threats and the implied violence towards the people he held closest to his heart. And finally, the unconnected, but beautifully choreographed deaths they were both to meet on the same night. It had been eighteen days the like of which he had never experienced and hoped he would never experience again. A hurricane had blown through his life and thrown everything he had taken for granted into doubt. Like an unforeseen storm at sea, his life had been blown onto the rocks and had been in danger of sinking without trace. But just at the last moment the skies had cleared and the waters calmed. For all the bad luck and malevolent daggers that had been relentlessly stabbing him in the chest, he now felt a calmness and a composure that had been unimaginable only days before.

His first task of the day was to pick up Brenda from her Mum and Dads' house. She had been allowed home from the hospital the previous evening. They would then go to see D.I.Cooper at the police station to give him their official statements. After that, George would drop her back to her Mum's, go to work and concentrate his mind on the match coming up on Sunday. Then home, to await the arrival of his family back from holiday. It seemed crazy to George that Debbie was still blissfully unaware of any of the extraordinary events he had experienced. It was a mind-boggling story and would take some telling.

When Brenda stepped into George's car, she still had the bruises and the scars of her final encounter with Jeremy. Her face was still puffy under her left eye and her lips and neck showed the bruising he had inflicted on her. Her makeup was once again working overtime to conceal the horrors that marked the last moments of her married life. Her left arm was still bound in a sling and strapped to her chest. She gave George a smile. Even through all her makeup and despite the damage done, her smile was warm and the twinkle in her eyes sparkled.

George repeated what he had seen and what he had told the police. He begged her to say the same and back him up. It was a chapter in her life that needed to end, not to be drawn out for years to come with court cases, charges of manslaughter, or God forbid, a prison sentence. Reluctantly she agreed. She was equally keen to move on and start her life afresh. One thing Brenda did tell George, was that it hadn't been the suitcase that had fractured her collar bone. She knew she had done it when she fell, after pushing

Jeremy. Again, George told her to forget that ever happened. The suitcase had caused the injury and she had all but lost consciousness, after calling his name.

George told them exactly the same story he had at the house.

'Mr Miller, you said you found Mrs Higgins lying unconscious on the floor when you went upstairs. Can you be precise, as to exactly where you found her?'

'I've already told you. She was lying on the floor, by the foot of the bed.'

'Are you sure about that sir?'

"Yes, I am positive. Why do you ask?'

When Brenda was asked the same questions, she told them she remembered being strangled, struck and shaken and having her head banged against the wall. She recalled Jeremy hurrying to try and shut the front door and she remembered screaming out for George, but after that, had no recollection, until George picked her up off the bedroom floor and placed her onto the bed. The rest of it was all a blur, until she woke up the following morning in hospital.

'Well, you see Mr Miller, we found traces of urine out on the landing, close to where Mr Higgins fell. In fact, there was a patch of carpet that was rather sodden! We know that Mrs Higgins,' he paused… 'lost control of her bladder, quite understandable in the circumstances and wondered, if you may have been mistaken about where you found her.' George shook his head.

'No inspector. I am certain I picked her up from inside the bedroom. I did however help Brenda change out of her wet clothes and into fresher, drier ones. She didn't want anybody to see her like that. Now I think of it, I do remember throwing the wet garments out of the room and onto the landing, before putting them in the washing basket in the bathroom. Maybe that's what your people discovered.' Again, George quietly congratulated himself on his quick thinking.

'Well yes, I suppose that could explain it. Thank you, Mr Miller.'

Cooper seemed satisfied with their accounts and thanked them both for their time. He wished Brenda a speedy recovery from her injuries and even wished George good luck for the match on Sunday.

The time they spent at the police station had been mercifully short. They had been interviewed separately but were now back together in George's car. They both repeated what they had told D.I.Cooper and were both happy that their stories matched. Brenda was keen to accompany George into work. She said she felt fine, but he insisted she spend a few more days at least, at home recovering.

'If you feel strong enough, you can come back next Friday and then you will only be allowed to make the tea.' His voice dropped to a whisper. 'Janice is a lovely girl, but her tea…..!' He screwed up his face. 'But definitely no sooner. That's an order.'

Once he had dropped Brenda off at her Mum's, he drove himself to the club. An afternoon of nothing but footballing matters would be exercising his brain. With both Baz and Jeremy now permanently out of the equation, he began to feel the fog and uncertainty begin to lift. He knew he still had the biggest and most daunting hurdle in front of him. Convincing Debbie that everything was okay would still be tough, but now he didn't have to worry about any outside influences distorting the truth and trying to undermine him. The damning evidence of the *full movie* and all the other incriminating material Baz had amassed was gone. The explanation he would give his wife would contain only what he decided to tell her. Everything Debbie would learn about what had been going on in her absence would be George's version of events. Having seen the evidence Baz was planning to use, he knew he had dodged a bullet. His fate was now in his own hands. His destiny solely reliant on his rendition and portrayal of the drama and turmoil that had plagued him over the previous seventeen days. He was still nervous about the outcome, but knew he was in a far better position than he had been only forty-eight hours earlier.

The atmosphere at training was relaxed and jovial. Like it had been, not so long ago. The banter was back and so was the camaraderie. The lads were laughing and joking, even pulling George's leg, about some of his recent dubious decisions. But it was all done in jest and good humour. It felt like the dark cloud that had been hanging over the club, the players and George, had been blown away.

At 4 o'clock George called his players together. He knew the news about Jayden and his father would eventually spread. It probably already had. He informed them of Baz' demise and how it had happened. He told them Jayden had been excused from duty for the rest of the season and that they wouldn't be seeing him again for some time. There were no cheers or celebrations at the news. The players managed to keep their emotions to themselves, but George could feel a sense of relief that the main protagonist in all of the unrest felt around the club, had *temporarily* vanished. In his mind, George knew it was permanent.

George wished them well and said he would see them on Sunday morning. Still wearing his tracksuit, he jumped into his car and began his journey home.

Chapter 41

The importance of being honest

The traffic through South London, over Vauxhall bridge and then on to the road-work infested A40 was slow. It always was. His sat-nav told him the journey would take just under two hours. About par for the course. In those two hours George went over in his mind how he would explain to Debbie what had happened to him during the time she had been away. It was an extraordinary story; almost unbelievable in many ways, with so many twists and turns, a Hollywood scriptwriter would have been proud of the plot. But this wasn't Hollywood. It was far more important than that. This was real life. His life. So many crazy and unpredictable things had happened over the last eighteen days. The world in which he resided had been turned upside down. Everything he had taken for granted was under threat. Everything he feared was a possibility and everything he possessed seemed to be slipping through his fingers. Until now. Now that both Jeremy and Baz were dead, he wondered if he had to tell her anything at all. The two main threats to his happiness and his career were gone. Without them, was there any need to go into every detail? The evidence Baz had collected and edited together of the kiss and the journeys to and from the flat, was now hopefully irrelevant. The police had no interest in the footage and had advised Jayden to erase whatever he still possessed. The police had made it very clear to the young lad that, if he made any attempt to make the images public, or make financial gain from them, he would likely face prosecution for extortion or blackmail. Although Jayden was as evil and twisted as his father, George convinced himself he wasn't stupid enough to gamble his career on the need to avenge a father he had only known for a couple of weeks. The stink and the negative publicity that would surround the boy would make it very unlikely any other top club would want to be associated with him, certainly in this country, anyway. His glittering career would be over before it had begun. He would surely have no future in the professional game. The recordings on Baz' phone concerning Jayden's selection, had been dealt with by Graham. By smashing and disposing of Baz' mobile, all traces of those conversations had been destroyed. So, assuming that none of the so-called evidence would ever see the light of day, what exactly should he tell Debbie? He couldn't bear the thought of lying to her or keeping anything hidden from her. Honesty and trust had always been very important to them both. He knew that deceit and mendacity had no place in their marriage. Deception was not an option. Apart from being very bad at it, he knew the guilt he was feeling over what had happened, would be nothing compared to the regret and remorse he would permanently have to carry around with him, for being untruthful to her. In his mind, that was as much of a crime as being unfaithful. He knew he couldn't, and wouldn't, lie to her.

As he crawled along with the slow-moving traffic, approaching the ever-present lane closures at Acton, he realised, that although the rather convenient deaths of both Jeremy and Baz had made his life easier in some ways, they had made absolutely no difference to what he had to admit to his wife. He knew he couldn't afford to leave out a single detail. Anything he omitted now could one day come back to haunt him. There really was only one route to take. The only route that paid his relationship with his wife the respect it deserved. The truth. The whole truth and nothing but the truth. The importance of being honest had never been more *important*. He would of course be gambling everything on her reaction. If Debbie didn't believe him, or suspected anything untoward had happened, he would doubtless pay a heavy price. But if he told her everything and she did believe him, they could close the book on this uncomfortable chapter in their lives and move on. As nerve wracking and as scary as that prospect felt, he knew it was the only way.

Chapter 42

He had just lit the blue touch paper

George received the phone call he had been longing for, as he pulled his Range Rover into the driveway. It was Debbie. The plane had landed safely and they were at the baggage reclaim, waiting for the carousel to deliver their luggage. Once they had collected their bags and met up with their cab driver, they would be less than an hour away. It was wonderful to hear her voice and to know she was so close. For a brief moment the excitement he felt at seeing his family again temporarily evicted the nerves and tension that had been resident in him for the past couple of weeks. He had become pragmatic about the outcome of his heart-to-heart with Debbie. He knew there was only one course available to him and that was the truth. The lack of any other real alternatives had eventually put him at ease. He was still worried and nervous about how she would react to what he was going to tell her, but he knew it was the best and the only option he had, to keep the love and the trust they had always treasured. If they were going to survive and move on from what had happened, it needed to be with no doubts, no skeletons and no unwanted or unexpected surprises lurking around the corner. Living a lie would have been unbearable. That thought was more unthinkable than any reaction Debbie might give him. He remembered when they were younger how Paula had constantly told him and his brother about the importance of being honest. He tried to not to dwell on the negative. Think positive he told himself.

Showered and changed, he wandered around the house checking everything was neat and tidy and in its rightful place. Mr Bell and his boys had done a marvellous job, as usual, with the decoration and the building work. The entire house looked new and fresh. The smell of paint had been banished by the cleaners, who had come in the day after James Bell had finished. Everything had been washed, dusted and cleaned. A large vase of flowers stood proudly on the lounge table and others had been placed in the kitchen and in the hallway. The fresh air and sunshine that had been let in, had transported the blooms scent all over the house. George had always loved his Riverside flat, but this was his home now. His family home. It felt good to be back.

When he had mentioned to Debbie that there was something on his mind he wanted to talk to her about, during their last phone call, she had sounded intrigued and wanted to know more. George had explained that it was nothing to worry about and would be better if they discussed the issue face to face. It hadn't stayed in her mind for very long. All she could think about was wrapping her arms around him and putting her lips against his.

George heard the hissing and the crunching of tyres on the gravel driveway. It was them. He rushed to the front door and opened it. Before he had a chance to put on his shoe's he saw his children burst out of the back doors and run towards him with their arms open wide and huge beaming smiles on their faces.

'Daddy! Daddy!' they both screamed. As they reached him, they both dropped the small rucksacks they were carrying and flung themselves at their father. George bent down and braced himself for impact. They both hit him at the same time and very nearly knocked him over. They wrapped their arms around his neck and he curled his arms around their waists. They weren't small children anymore and it took all of his strength to stand. He hugged them tightly and kissed them both. Then he saw Debbie get out of the car. Every time he laid eyes on her, it felt like he was seeing her for the first time. The thrill and excitement, always the same. She was beautiful. She was sexy. She was stunning. She managed to take his breath away every morning he woke up next to her, every evening he said goodnight to her and every minute he was lucky enough to see her in between.

She had a healthy-looking tan on her skin, as did the children. The Spanish sun had obviously been a lot kinder to them than the London weather had been to him in the previous three weeks. Debbie smiled at him. The smile that warmed him to the core every time. George relinquished his hold on his children and let them slowly slide down his body and onto the ground. He walked up to Debbie and hugged her tightly. The enormity of what lay ahead suddenly hit him. He could feel the beginnings of a tear welling up in his eye. He had to control his emotions. He didn't want to have to explain himself until they were alone and the children had gone to bed.

The kids had already run into the house. George's lips brushed against Debbie's. It had been nearly three weeks since he had tasted her mouth on his.

'God I've missed you,' he said. 'I've missed all of you.' Debbie grinned.

'All of me, or all of us?' she said with a suggestive twinkle in her eye. George laughed and glanced down at her bronzed body.

'Both,' he said.

'I've missed you too Mr. Miller.' She glanced down at him. 'All of you.' They both laughed and hugged again.

Once the driver had helped George carry the bags into the house and driven away, they went inside.

'How were Neenee and Nanna?' George asked the kids. Neenee and Nanna were Debbie's parents. They had been given those names, initially by Matthew when he was young and first started talking. Debbie's mum and dad had always thought they would be 'Grandma and Grampa', but it wasn't long before they realised they had no say in the matter. As Matthew's evolving ability to form words and make associations, encompassed family members, for some reason known only to him, Neenee and Nanna were Christened. There was nothing else to do but accept their names and go along with them. By the time Emily came along their identities as grandparents were well established. Neenee and Nanna would be their names from then on.

They excitedly told their father about the many adventures they had had on their holidays. Their voices, becoming increasingly louder and more frantic with each story. George listened and smiled as the two children became ever more animated. It was lovely to know that they had enjoyed themselves so much. But all the time, in the back of his mind he knew the moment of reckoning was fast approaching. He could feel the nerves and the anxiety begin to build within him. After having something to eat, the two youngsters began to fade fast and the yawns became more frequent. There were a few mild protests when Debbie told them it was time for bed, but the day had been long and exhausting for them all. By 9 o'clock they were in bed and fast asleep.

Debbie poured them both a glass of red wine and sat down on the sofa next to George, playfully nuzzling herself into his embrace and gently stroking his inner thigh.

'So, Mr. Miller what is it you wanted to talk to me about?' she asked. 'Is it important, or can it wait?' She slid her hand up from his knee and started to gently caress him. Instantly, George's body reacted in the way they both knew it would. GOD, he had missed her. But what he had to say, had to be said and there was nothing that should delay his story. *Even that.* George softly took her hand away from his groin and turned to face her. He took a sip of his wine and tried to focus his mind on the sequence of events that had rocked his world since she had been away. The moment had arrived. He knew the next ten minutes or so would have a massive bearing on the rest of his life. Every second of worry, panic, nausea and fear he had experienced over the past seventeen days would now hopefully be washed away by a careful, truthful, heartfelt recollection of everything that had reduced his life to a living hell. He put down his glass and held his wife's hands.

'An awful lot has happened since you have been away and just about all of it has been bad.' Debbie's playful and sexy mood vanished. She sat up. Her eyes narrowed and the lines on her forehead deepened. A worried frown appeared on her brow. It had been a blunt opening line. George's face conveyed the nervousness he was feeling. He certainly had her full attention.

'What's wrong? What do you mean, *bad!?*'

'From the day you left, things started to unravel. A series of events took place over the following few days, that were not only surprising, but truly shocking. They all combined to make my life hell. Initially, I thought it best to say nothing to you. I didn't want to worry you or ruin your holiday. The last thing I wanted was for you to jump on a plane and come rushing back. I thought I could manage everything and that all of the problems would disappear naturally. But I was wrong. I was *so* wrong. Instead of disappearing, they became bigger and far more threatening than I could ever have imagined. I know this sounds crazy and I *will* try and explain, but having *not* told you about what was happening straight away, it became impossible to then tell you, as things unfolded. I didn't know what to do for the best. I tried to keep a calm head and a clear mind, but ultimately, I panicked. The longer it went on, the worse it became and the more

I felt myself sinking. My darling, I'm not exaggerating when I tell you that these past seventeen days have been the most stressful and awful days of my life.'

Debbie was now engrossed and hanging on his every word. She didn't quite know what to expect when he started the conversation, but she certainly hadn't bargained for something as serious as this.

'Before I tell you the full story, you have to believe me when I say everything I did and everything I said was with the best intentions. I genuinely didn't see the story unfolding in such a negative and potentially destructive manner.'

Debbie had no idea where this was going, but she knew she would have to listen carefully and had already realised that humour, or light-hearted interruptions from her would not be needed, or welcome. She stared worryingly into his eyes.

'What on Earth has happened?' she asked, now needing more information as quickly as possible, to get her heart rate down. 'Is everything okay? Are you okay?'

'Yes, I think so. I mean, I hope so.' George took a deep breath. 'On the Tuesday you left, I went into the office as usual. From the moment I saw Brenda, I knew something was wrong with her. She looked haunted and was quiet and flat. I know you don't know her very well, but believe me, she is normally a real live wire; full of beans and energy and always smiling and laughing. Always happy.

Just like you.' Debbie smiled and squeezed his hand.

'She is when she is around you George, but I suggest that is because she is in love with you.' That wasn't what George needed to hear. That wasn't going to make his task any easier.

'Oh, come on, don't be so ridiculous' he said as dismissively as he could.

'George, on the few occasions I have met her, it is plain to see in her eyes. The way she looks at you. The way she glows when she is near you. Trust me I know, because you have the same effect on me. Brenda may not mean to show it, but to me at least, it is as obvious as the nose on her face. Married or not, she still holds a torch for you and to be honest I don't blame her. Being stuck with that wet fish Jeremy for a husband, it's only natural the poor girl yearns for someone better. Fortunately for me, you are already accounted for.'

Debbie forced a smile, but she could see George's expression had remained unchanged. Her light-hearted attempt to diffuse the tension in the air had not succeeded. She could tell this story had a way to go and judging by George's demeanour, it was going to get worse before it got better. She clasped his hands in both of hers.

'Come on darling, what's worrying you? Tell me.'

'Well, it turned out that all was not happy in the Higgins household. When I saw her sitting in her office the day after Doug's funeral, I did think she was wearing more make up than usual. But when she bought me in a cup of tea, ten minutes later, it was clear to see why. That morning, it looked like she had applied her foundation with a brickie's trowel. It looked awful. On closer inspection, I thought I saw the tell-tale signs of bruising under all the camouflage. I asked her what was wrong and she burst into tears. I comforted her. She was wearing a heavy, white knitted, polo neck jumper, which concealed most of the carnage. I looked at her neck and saw bruising and finger marks around her throat. It was horrible. I held her in my arms while she sobbed. She told me the abuse had been going on for some time and that she had decided to leave Jeremy. She had planned to do it gradually, collecting her things, bit by bit and storing them in her office, until she found somewhere to rent. She didn't want to arouse his suspicions, for fear he would try and stop her. She was in a terrible state. While I held her, she kissed me. Whether it was out of gratitude, fear, or just the emotional mayhem in her mind, I don't know.' George looked into Debbie eyes and saw the concern and pity she felt for Brenda.

'It wasn't a peck on the cheek. It was on the lips. It did rather take me by surprise and I have to admit, it took a couple of seconds for me to pull away. I was sort of lost in the moment.'

George could feel his heart beating just a little faster. Having watched the recorded kiss, he knew this was *a little white lie*. He forgave himself. Debbie's concern and pity slowly ebbed away and a thoughtful and worried frown gradually appeared on her brow.

'As soon as I pulled my lips away from hers, I noticed the young lad Jayden Saunders standing there watching us. He had walked straight into my office through the open door and had been observing us the whole time. I gave him a rollicking and chastised him for his lack of manners, but that only made things worse. He laughed at me and made some pretty dreadful insinuations about me, Brenda and the fact that you had just gone on holiday. I was so angry I nearly hit him, but fortunately, managed to reign myself in.' George took another deep breath and tried to gauge Debbie's reaction. Her face betrayed little emotion. Apart from a desire to get to the end of the story as quickly as possible.

'Just when I thought it couldn't get any worse, it did. The following day Brenda was late for work. During the entire time I have known her, she has never once been late for work. When she eventually arrived, I barely recognised her. She looked like a zombie. She was a mess. Physically, mentally and visually. When I approached her to ask her what had happened, she actually collapsed into my arms. I carried her into my office and she told me she could never go back. That bastard not only beat her, but raped her in the most brutal and appalling way. She was distraught.' Debbie's frown had gone and been replaced by a look of sheer horror.

'That poor girl. How is she now? Where is she now? Where is she living?

'I'll get to that in a moment. The only thing I could think to do was get her away from him as quickly as possible. Somewhere I could be sure he wouldn't be able to get to her. Somewhere I could guarantee her safety. So,…. I invited her to stay at the flat in London.' He paused again and waited for her reaction. He had just lit the blue touch paper. If there were going to be any fireworks, they would be from hereon in.

'Of course,' Debbie immediately said, with far more understanding than George could have hoped for. 'So, what was, or is, the problem? It all sounds pretty horrific. But why are you looking so …. on edge?' It was the end of the prologue. The scene had been set. The next chapter was about to begin and the story start in earnest. He knew the story. He just hoped it had a happy ending.

Chapter 43

Animalistic abilities

George took a large gulp of his Rioja and refocused. So far so good, but that had been the easy part. He continued with his story.

'On the Thursday, Jayden's father came to see me. I was hoping he would help me calm the lad down and get him to show more respect to everyone. He's a cocky little shit at the best of times. Anyway, his father had recently been released from prison. It turned out he had spent most of his adult life behind bars. Unfortunately, any hopes I had about him being a calming influence on his son were dashed as soon as I met him. His name was Barry Saunders.' George paused and looked at Debbie, as if he were expecting some sort of reaction. She shook her head and frowned. The name meant nothing to her.

'And?' she said shrugging her shoulders.

'Barry Saunders. You and I remember him from our school days as Baz.' There was the first bombshell. The look of shock on Debbie's face was instant. Her mouth fell open and her eyes widened.

'Baz? That piece of shit that used to hang around with the De Costa boy? You're joking!'

'Afraid not. Baz was back in our lives. It would appear that his time away had done nothing to soften his attitude towards the two brothers who had always got the better of him and his mates at school. His hatred for me and of course Graham, hadn't so much diminished, as festered, over the years. As soon as Jayden told him about walking in on me and Brenda and seeing us kiss, Baz saw it as a way to blackmail and put pressure on me. He presented me with this.'

Tentatively, George handed Debbie the print from the brown envelope. The print taken from Jayden's phone, that Baz had presented to him on their first meeting. George could feel his heartbeat increasing. He watched for any flicker of emotion. He thought he recognised a look of sadness and disappointment on his wife's face, as her eyes washed over the blurry A4 print of her husband kissing his secretary. He waited to see if she was going to say something, but she remained tight-lipped.

'He told me the boy had a video of the entire scene on his phone, *but as far as I know, that doesn't exist*. Baz said he followed us from the club to the flat when I first drove Brenda there. Then back to the club the following morning. He convinced himself that the two of us spending the night together, was proof of an affair. By that time Baz had met and befriended Jeremy. He persuaded him that Brenda and I had been carrying on with each other for years and that it had been common knowledge. Jeremy was happy to believe him and he too was intent on spreading the news of our infidelity. They both threatened to tell their story to the press and post videos on social media. They also threatened to send you messages, making up God knows what lies. I think they were relying on the "no smoke without fire" attitude from both the press and from you. Any images they might have had would all have been innocent. But I don't think some members of the *"sporting journalists-mud-slinging club"* would have worried too much about that. I just couldn't take the chance. You know what they are like. Never let the truth get in the way of a good story. But most of all, I was worried about what you would have thought. You had been away for a few days by then. I hadn't said anything to you about it, because I didn't want you to worry. I thought it was a situation that would blow itself out. Mainly because there was nothing in it. Just someone trying to help and protect a dear and vulnerable friend. But once Baz turned up, it was too late. Firstly, it wasn't a conversation I wanted to have over the phone and secondly, telling you then would have sounded more like a guilt-ridden attempt at a cover-up.' Debbie again looked puzzled. She was still holding onto the print of her husband kissing a woman that wasn't her. She glanced down at the image again.

'So, where did you stay while Brenda was at the flat?' Debbie's face betrayed the fact she already knew the answer to her own question. But she desperately wanted George to give her a different one. Their eyes remained fixed on each other. Her breathing became noticeably heavier and her voice conveyed the dread and fear in her heart.

'You were at the flat too, weren't you?' Her face sunk and the colour drained away from her tanned cheeks. She looked like she was about to burst into tears.

'Of course, I was. I couldn't live here. The place was full of dust sheets and rubble. And besides, I didn't think it was a good idea to leave Brenda on her own. If Jeremy had followed her or tracked her down, he probably would have given her even more grief.' The look of confusion and surprise had gone. Debbie's only facial expression was now one of terror. Maybe she did now know where this story was leading. She felt a shiver pass through her body and realised that her hands had started to tremble.

'Originally, the plan was to find Brenda somewhere to stay after a couple of days. To keep her out of Jeremy's clutches. But the fear of him tracking her down and perpetrating even more violence upon her was too overwhelming. Things had become so bad, I really don't think it was beyond the realms of possibility, that he could have killed her. The risk of that happening was just too great and unthinkable. Maybe the Police could have stepped in to protect her, but when Baz turned up and started with his threats and insinuations, it became impossible to know what to do for the best. I knew if I involved the Police, Baz would then put all of his lies into the public domain. With Jeremy backing up everything he said, the footballing world, the public and worst of all you would probably have formed a judgement and an opinion based on my previous "offences" when I was younger. As Baz' threats became more violent and absurd it seemed that the safest thing to do was to stay where we were. Jeremy was happy and eager to tell the world that Brenda had already confessed to an affair. It was all building up. The "mountain of evidence" was all lies and vitriolic imagination. The only way out was for me to explain it to you like I am doing now, face to face. But I needed time. I needed to wait for you to return home. I decided to play along with whatever Baz wanted, as long as it would buy me that time. The thought of you hearing it from Baz or the press was unthinkable. To have you suddenly cut the holiday short and fly back into all of that controversy and press coverage would have given all those terrible and untrue rumours credence. I tried to talk to Baz and explain that nothing had happened, but he didn't appear very interested in the truth. He just saw it as a way to get his own back for all the wrongs that had happened to him, both at school and since. I then committed my biggest mistake. A decision I made to buy myself time, only succeeded in dropping me further into the shit. In order for Baz to keep silent, he told me he wanted me to play Jayden in the next few matches. He wanted him to start each game and be guaranteed the full ninety minutes, regardless of his performance. I never really gave Baz much credit for any intelligence, but I have to admit, whether he meant it or not, forcing me to play the boy and recording those conversations, was a stroke of genius. After that he had me by the balls. Jayden's unexpected run in the first team and my inexplicable decision to keep him on, even when he was clearly having "a mare", would have confirmed any evidence he had. And that would have been the end of my career. I was sinking fast. He had me every which way. The more I thought about it, the more I came to the conclusion that there was only one thing that mattered to me and that was you and the kids. I went along with playing Jayden. If my career was to be condemned because of what had happened, then so be it. But I couldn't, wouldn't, lose my family. I decided to go along with Baz' rules until you came back.'

'Well, here I am. I'm back. So how many days did Brenda live with you at the flat and where is she living now?'

'Two weeks. She was in the process of moving out on Wednesday night just gone.' Debbie was struggling to control her breathing and she could feel her lip beginning to tremble. She felt a tidal wave of tears preparing to pour out of her eyes. She was preparing herself for some extremely bad news. The first tear plunged down over her cheek.

'George, please finish this story. You are beginning to frighten me. What's going on? What's happened? Are we ....' George squeezed her hand and raised it to his face, kissing her fingers. A tear rolled down his cheek.

'We are fine. Please, just hear me out. There isn't much more to go.' He sucked in another deep breath and prepared himself for the last lap.

'I felt I was falling deeper and deeper into the abyss. I was even stupid enough to offer Baz money to fuck off. I'm sure he recorded that as well. I played Jayden for a few games. The discontent and the atmosphere within the team were awful. Eventually I substituted him during the game on Monday. He was having a stinker. Baz was furious. He decided that because I had gone against his wishes, he would expose everything he had. I asked him for one last chance. I even begged him, just to buy the extra couple of days I needed, to be able to have this chat with you. We arranged to meet on Wednesday night. The same night Brenda was due to move into Graham's flat. We drove over to her house after work to pick up some of her clothes and personal stuff, but Jeremy was there, waiting for her. Before I arrived, he had already beaten her and was just about to rape her again. Brenda screamed out my name. I was outside talking to a neighbour. We both rushed in. Jeremy made a dash to shut the front door before we could enter, but he lost his balance and stumbled at the top of the stairs. He fell and broke his neck,' he left a pause, before adding, 'he's dead.'

'Oh my God. Dead?' George nodded.

'They took Brenda to the hospital. She was badly beaten and in a state of semi consciousness and shock. She had a fractured collar bone, concussion and was covered in cuts and bruises. I went with her. It meant we weren't going to be able to meet Graham at his flat. It also meant, I wasn't going to be able to meet Baz in Peckham. To be honest, at that point, I couldn't see any way out. No light at the end of the tunnel. It seemed that whichever way I turned I was screwed. When I spoke to Graham to tell him what happened, he suggested he go and talk to Baz. See if he could talk some sense into him.'

'And did he? Manage to sort things out?'

'Yes and no. He met Baz. They talked, but it was clear that Baz wasn't interested in money, or making any kind of deal. He was just playing me along. He had always meant to spread his vicious rumours, regardless of what I did. He was just having a little extra fun, watching me squirm and suffer. He wanted to destroy me and everything I held dear. He and Graham argued. They had a fight. I thought Baz was a dangerous man, but it seems he met his match, once again, in Graham. Graham gave him a bloody good hiding. I went to see Graham after I had left the hospital. He was in a terrible state. He was convinced he had actually beaten Baz to death, having left him buried in a pile of rubbish in the backstreets of Peckham. The next morning, I had two police officers come into my office. They informed me that Barry Saunders was dead. I must admit I almost puked on my desk. I immediately assumed that Graham had been right and that he had killed him. But he hadn't. Apparently, Baz had recovered from the beating and regained consciousness about an hour later. Sometime after the fight, Baz wandered into Rye Lane and stumbled under a bus. He is dead as well.'

George looked at his wife's face. Her expression was blank, as if she had ceased taking in information some time ago.

'Brenda and I did live in the flat together for two weeks. We thought it best if she moved out of our flat and into Graham's. But since Jeremy is dead and no longer a threat to her, or her Mum and Dad, she's going to live with her parents while she recuperates. There is nothing connecting Graham to Baz. The police know nothing of the meeting between them, or the fight that ensued. They know about Baz' attempts to blackmail me and that I was due to meet him on the evening he died. But I have a cast iron alibi. I was in the hospital with Brenda, in the company of a WPC who can vouch for me. So here we are.'

They stared into each other's eyes for a few moments in total silence. Debbie, showing the shock that George's story had merited, and George hoping for a reply or a reaction, to his epic tale.

After what felt like an age, Debbie spoke.

'Well, I can understand why you wanted to wait until the kids had gone to bed,' she said, with great understatement. Debbie began to ask all the questions that had been building up in her mind, as George's story unfolded. 'How is Brenda now? How was Graham? Did Kerry, or John and Paula know anything about what had happened? What had the police said to George about any further investigations?' All of her questions were sympathetic and understanding. But George knew she had questions in her head that she hadn't asked. Such as, what had really gone on in that flat for the two weeks he had been alone with a woman who was desperately in love with him? She knew how Brenda felt about George. How fond she had been of him in the past and how obviously smitten with him she still was. She also knew George. Since they had been re-acquainted twelve years ago, he had never even looked at another woman. But she knew there was always a chance that the old *bachelor George* might someday re-emerge.

Once he had answered all her questions, he decided he would do his best to answer the questions she had been afraid to ask. He described what had happened in those two weeks. How they had shared dinner and the odd glass of wine. How they had watched TV, chatted about the old times and what the future held in store.

'Brenda was staggered when I told her you were unaware she was staying at the flat. She even threatened to leave, unless I told you. She knew how it would look and said she didn't want to be the cause of any problems between the two of us. She said she would rather take her chances with Jeremy, than upset you. I gave her my reasons for not telling you and promised her everything would be okay. I'm not sure I really managed to convince either of us that what I was saying was true.'

He told her how every night they kissed each other on the cheek and said goodnight. Walking in separate directions down the hallway to their respective bedrooms. He told Debbie that although he had feelings for Brenda, they were the feelings he would have for a younger sister. He told her that every night without fail, he would lie in his bed and think of her and the kids and how much he missed them. The only scene he omitted to mention during their time in the flat together, was the episode when

Brenda's bathrobe fell to the floor and she offered herself to him on that first evening. He could still see it clearly in his mind. How she walked over to him, naked and fell to her knees before him. That memory was still fresh and worryingly exciting. But he had overcome the urges he felt at that time and would do his best now to banish those images to the back of his mind.

'Brenda is a sweet girl and I would be lying if I said I wasn't really fond of her. But I have you and I would never do anything to jeopardise my life with you and the kids. You must believe me.' George looked pleadingly into her eyes.

When he had finished, he felt exhausted. He felt like he had been in the witness box, giving evidence for hours. It was now the judge and jury's turn to give their verdict and then, the sentence.

'Ever since I have known you George, you have been good at somethings and terrible at others. Some of the things you are good at have made our lives at school, in Newcastle and back here, for the past twelve years, so unimaginably exciting and erotic. You're a good man and a good father. However,' she paused. George's heart sank. 'The one thing you have always been terrible at is lying. You know I can always tell when you stray from the truth. George you are the worst liar I have ever met!' His face collapsed and he felt breathless.

'But I'm not lying to you, I promise.'

He looked and sounded like a five-year-old boy, trying to persuade his mother of his innocence. His voice was desperate. Had all his honesty been in vain? Another lengthy and heavy silence punctuated their conversation and increased the tension in the air. Debbie's solemn face eased itself into a smile. She took hold of his hands again in hers.

'I know you're not. Trust me George, I would know if you were. I can see through you George Miller like a pane of glass. I've always been able to. That's something else I love about you.' She kissed his fingers. 'Another thing that you are good at is honesty and truth and apart from your more physical talents, I think that is what I treasure most. Thank you for being so open with me. I'm sure it would have been easier to have skirted around some of those incidents.' She glanced down at the A4 piece of paper lying on the sofa. 'I love that we have no secrets. I love you.'

They squeezed each other's hands. The tension that had been building with every new revelation evaporated and disappeared in an instant. George felt every muscle in his body relax and he was acutely aware of the broad grin that was spreading across his face. He started to laugh and cry at the same time. Tears of relief flowed down his cheeks. It was clear that the events of the last couple of weeks had been weighing heavily on her husband's shoulders. Debbie looked into George's watery eyes. It was easy to understand the joy that had engulfed him. She could only imagine what she would have felt if she had faced a similar predicament. The thought of losing George was just too awful to even contemplate. She was in absolutely no doubt that what he had told her was completely true, honest and sincere. She knew his love for her was as strong as her's for him and she knew nothing, or no-one would ever be able to come between them.

'Now, having excelled yourself at storytelling, truth and honesty, how about taking me to bed and excelling at some of your more animalistic abilities. I've missed you, George Miller.'

Hand in hand they gently walked up the stairs and into their bedroom, popping their heads around the children's doors on the way up. They were both fast asleep.

Chapter 44

Private, Personal and Confidential

Three days after Debbie had returned home, a letter arrived. A handwritten envelope addressed to Mrs. Debbie Miller. In the top left-hand corner, written in large capital letters, were the words "Private, Personal and Confidential".

Debbie looked at the envelope with a tinge of caution. After all she had heard from George about what had been going on while she had been away, any mysterious contact was likely to arouse suspicion. The story George had told her had been incredible to say the least. Beatings, blackmail, threats and ultimately, the deaths of the two main protagonists were more akin to a Hollywood blockbuster. Although George was pretty sure they were all in the clear, there was always the possibility that something might emerge, some shred of evidence or information, which could open up the whole sordid business once more.

The events that had taken place whilst she had been in Mallorca were barely believable. But she had believed her husband. George, whom she trusted implicitly, had opened himself up to her, in what was clearly a desperate attempt to come clean on a situation that could so easily be misconstrued. Debbie was convinced of her husband's honesty. She had to be. He meant everything to her. To doubt him was to question their entire existence.

George had already gone to work, happy and confident in the knowledge that the entire episode was now confined to history. The kids were back at school. She was alone in the house. She walked into the kitchen, not taking her eyes off the beautifully scripted handwriting on the envelope. She didn't recognise the calligraphy. She made herself a cup of tea and sat down. Tentatively, she opened the envelope and withdrew a number of folded sheets of paper. The pages were covered in the same handwriting as the envelope. On the first page, tucked up in the top righthand corner, was the name and address of the sender. It was from Brenda. A shiver passed down her spine. What kind of confession or revelation was she about to discover? Would there be anything in what Brenda had to say that would conflict with the story George had told her? She briefly considered tearing up the letter and throwing it in the bin without reading it. If there were to be any anomalies, it would throw doubt on everything he had said. If that were the case, she would rather not know. With her heart beating a little faster than usual, she reluctantly glanced down at the first few lines.

My dear Debbie

Please may I ask one favour from you? That you read this letter to the end and believe every word contained within it. I swear to you, on everything I hold dear in my life, that these lines are the truth. I will start at the beginning.

I love your husband. I fell in love with him on the first day we met, seventeen years ago. For the next five years, I worshipped him, as a young schoolgirl worships a pop star. I fantasised about him. I went a little bit silly, whenever he came into my office. I dreamed that maybe one day, he would ask me out, or better still, take me home with him. I was ready and eager to give myself to him completely. Back in those days, he had a bit of a reputation as a lady's man. I was convinced that sooner or later, it would be my turn. There were a number of opportunities for him to fulfil my dreams in those five years, but he didn't take any of them. On one particular night, after we had watched a match together, I was convinced it was my night. But he chose to drive me home to my parents' house, instead of taking me back to his flat. It was the most crushing blow I had ever experienced and if I'm honest, I still look back at that evening with great sadness. Thinking back though, I now realise that George was only being a gentleman. He could have easily added me to his list of conquests but chose not to. I would like to think it was because he was so fond of me and didn't want to take advantage of a smitten young girl. I might never know the real reason. After the cup win in Barcelona and meeting you again he was a changed man. He was still charming, funny, lovely and of course, gorgeous and I still loved him. But it was plain to see that he too was in love. In love like I had never seen him before. With you. In those two years before he retired, I met you a couple of times and I understood completely why he felt that way about you. You are a wonderful person and so perfect for George. No wonder he didn't have eyes for anyone else. It was then that I knew for sure, that any chance of my teenage crush coming to anything, was finished. That day too, was another hammer blow for me. The only thing that made it slightly easier, was knowing that George was happy and would be happy for the rest of his life. Because of you.

In the ten years between him retiring from playing and returning to the club as manager, I have to admit, I have thought about him most days. I think I judged every man by his standards, comparing my feelings for them with the feelings I still had for George. Naturally none of them came even remotely close. He was a tough act to follow. I met and married Jeremy, knowing that I was settling for second best, "at best". I don't know how much George has told you about my marriage to Mr Higgins, but it wasn't the most romantic of unions. I had been suffering from his mood swings from day one. I tried desperately not to let it interfere with my work, which became my only solace in life. The new managers didn't take much notice of me, as long as I did my duties. It was only when George came back, that my troubled home life was noticed. He picked up on my mood swings immediately and continually asked me if I was alright. I think he was pretty convinced that things were not good, but again, as a gentleman, didn't pry too much into my private life. It was only when things became unbearable for me, that George insisted on helping. At the beginning, I think he wanted to help me by giving Jeremy a taste of his own medicine. But I persuaded him that would just make things worse. Eventually, I could take no more. George came to my rescue and literally saved me from a fate worse than death. In a moment, of what I can only describe as hysteria while George was comforting me, I kissed him. I was lost in another world and wasn't used to anyone showing me such kindness or tenderness. I kissed him on the lips. Although it was something I had been dreaming of doing since I was eighteen years old, I have never regretted anything more (apart from marrying Jeremy, I suppose). Please forgive me. It was all my fault and I am truly, truly sorry. He insisted I stay, at what is now your flat on the river. I was so bewildered confused and frightened, I was happy to agree to anything. George took me in and made me feel safe, for the first time in years. I can't tell you what a relief it was, to know that I wasn't going to be beaten or raped most evenings.

I still love your husband, for all the same reasons I have done over the past seventeen years. Only now, I think I love him and admire him even more. During my stay at the flat, it did occur to me, that maybe my time had finally come. I was alone, with the man of my dreams. But I knew that life had moved on and things had changed. George loved me enough to save me from Jeremy, even though he knew it would look suspicious and possibly put him in an awkward position. Especially with the person he loved and cherished more than anyone else in the world. The love he showed me by doing that, is a love I could never have expected from anyone. My love for George is all about the kindness and charity he showed me, regardless of his own situation. He gave me sanctuary and peace. He literally saved my life and I will never be able to repay him for that.

During our time at the flat, we talked. We spoke about my life and where it all went wrong and we spoke of his life with you and how perfect it was.

This is the bit I want you to believe, most of all.

My love and admiration for George wouldn't let me do anything that might cause him pain or sorrow. The thought of me, being the cause of any sadness between you and George, is more hurtful to me than the thought of going back and living with Jeremy. I promise you, with all of my heart, that during my stay at the flat, George was the perfect gentleman once again.

Debbie, I still believe you are the luckiest woman in the world, having him as your husband. But I now know that George is the luckiest man in the world, having you as his wife. The two of you are perfect. Maybe one day I will find happiness like yours, or if not, close to it.

I will continue to love your husband. I'm afraid there is nothing I can do about that. But it will be as a younger sister and a dear friend.

I owe him my life and I owe you my gratitude, for your understanding and for your trust.

Thank you for reading this to the end.
I will be forever in both yours and George's debt.
Brenda.

P.S. George has no idea I am writing this letter and probably has no idea about some of the emotions I have talked about. I know the two of you have no secrets from one-another but would ask you to say nothing to him about this correspondence.
B.

Debbie wiped the tears from her eyes, folded the pieces of paper back into their original state, then walked into the study. She opened the top draw of the desk and slid out the A4 sheet of paper George had shown her whist telling his story. She folded it together with the letter, smiled to herself and slotted them both back into the envelope. She paused, then slowly tore the lot in half; then, with slightly more effort, into quarters. She walked back into the kitchen, stepped on the peddle bin and dropped the confetti of paper in with the other rubbish.

She loved and trusted her husband and couldn't imagine him being anything but true to her. She also felt a pang of sisterhood for Brenda. She tried to imagine the horrors she had experienced at the hands of the brute she had married. The physical, mental and verbal torture she had been subjected to during her marriage was unthinkable. Her life had been a living hell for years. She shuddered at the thought. She wanted to hug them both.

Chapter 45

Funeral two
(Two weeks later)

Brenda declined the offer from Jeremy's mother to accompany her in the funeral car. She had no love or sympathy for the woman. Ever since they first met, Brenda had the impression that Mrs Marjorie Higgins had thought her unworthy of her wonderful son. The relationship between the two women had been, at best, frosty. Jeremy had always taken his mother's side against her. He had never stood up for her or protected her from his mother's spite or wit. She had always been on the outside and that was where she would remain on Jeremy's final journey.

It was a small gathering. Apart from his mother, there were only about another dozen people there. Brenda presumed they were either from his work or members of the rugby club he held so dear. They were probably the same people who had attended their wedding. Even then, she hadn't really been introduced to any of them. And here they were again. The same strangers, probably hoping for a free drink and a cheese vol-au-vent. She swapped nods and sympathetic smiles when she noticed someone looking at her, but otherwise kept herself to herself. She, Jeremy's wife, was a stranger at her own husband's funeral. Having known him for five years, she realised that she didn't know him at all. He was as much a stranger to her now as he had been when they first met.

The other mourners were all dressed in black and all looked suitably forlorn. Jeremy's mother provided most of the drama. Sobbing and wailing throughout the service from the front pew. She sat on her own and looked sadly pathetic. A few hands reached out from the pew behind, patting her gently on the shoulder, trying to console the poor woman in her darkest hour. But even watching from her position a few rows back, Brenda could find no sympathy for her.

The vicar said some nice things about Jeremy, most of which Brenda didn't believe. He gave his heartfelt condolences to his mother and his grieving widow. Brenda again nodded in recognition. Mrs Marjorie Higgins let loose another wave of anguish and tears.

The eulogy was brief and had little sentiment or humour. There was no mention of him being a *"top bloke"*, or *"a great laugh"*. Nothing about a kind, generous, loving personality. But that was because he didn't have one.

Brenda briefly searched inside herself for any fond memories she had of their time together. Something she could focus on, just for a moment. But there were no such memories. All her recollections of their time together had been tarnished by the images and memories of the violence and the rapes. The mockery and the verbal abuse he had given her constantly through the years. She could think of nothing nice, because there *was* nothing nice.

She could conjure up no sadness or remorse. No emotion or sense of loss. Over the years, she had shed so many tears *because* of Jeremy, she had none left to shed *for* him.

The Epilogue
(One year later)

Derek Donnelly never drove a number 63 bus, or any other bus for that matter, again after that fateful, rainy night in Peckham. It had been an amazingly short career. The nightmare of the man, he now knew as "Barry Saunders", collapsing under the front wheel of the giant, red, double decker and the rather surreal memory of watching his severed arm float away, would cause him to sit bolt upright in bed most nights. He could still feel the weight of the dismembered limb in his hands and clearly see the tattoos and the gold half sovereign ring on the index finger, caked in blood. Normally, the cold sweat was accompanied by a solitary shriek, which would invariably wake his wife beside him. The imagery and the sense of guilt would stay with him for the rest of his life.

Derek eventually found peace working in one of the local supermarkets. Standing just inside the main doors, with a big, golden badge that read,

"I'm Derek. I'm happy to help" on the front of his shirt, he welcomed the shoppers with a cheery smile. The chances of anyone being crushed to a pulp, or having their brains splattered everywhere were remote. But sadly, the night sweats and the legacy of Barry Saunders would haunt him forever more.

Since moving back to his hometown club, George Miller had experienced some great highs as well as some desperate lows. During his first five months in charge, he'd managed to guide the club into fourth place, ensuring qualification to the highly lucrative Champions League. In his first full season, he took the club to unknown heights when he clinched The Premier League title with two games to spare. His stock was once again on the rise and rumours began to circulate about his ability to take over the national side when the job became available.

His success, however, had been tempered by two equally distressing episodes that had shaken his way of life to the very core.

Signing the young Jayden Saunders had proved to be one of the most calamitous and potentially destructive undertakings he had ever been involved with. The boy was arrogant and disrespectful to all around him. He seemed intent on undermining not only George's position, but that of all the staff and players. After the unexpected death of his father, George saw an opportunity to move the lad on. It would probably be best for all parties. Originally, Jayden went out on loan, but eventually George sold him to a German Bundesliga team. He did very well and after only a year was being lauded as a future superstar. George made a healthy profit for the club and was overjoyed to see the back of him. He hoped he would never encounter the odious little shit again. He knew they would never "work" together again. That was for sure.

The other great sadness for George was having to part company with Brenda. They had been close ever since they first met all those years ago. They had both considered the idea of a romance, (one more than the other!) but things just didn't turn out that way. They had flirted and had fun when they were younger and had bared all in front of each other more recently. What Brenda had endured at the hands of her husband and her mother-in-law beggared belief. After what they had been through together they both knew it was the right time to go their separate ways.

Jayden Saunders became one of the most talked about talents in the game. His ability on the pitch was outstanding. His capacity to not only fall out but enrage anyone and everyone around him was equally impressive. He quickly gained the reputation as the bad boy of European Football.

But he didn't give a shit. He had never worried or taken any notice of other peoples' feelings, opinions, or advice.

Exactly a year after her son Jeremy Higgins had been laid to rest, in a ceremony that lacked emotion or feeling, Marjorie Higgins passed away too, quietly in her bed, in what doctors described as a peaceful departure. Her heart had, apparently, just stopped beating. At the relatively young age of sixty-six, this prompted a post-mortem. An investigation into what had led to the premature death of an otherwise healthy and active woman. Although the autopsy didn't say in so many words, it appeared that Marjorie Higgins had died of a broken heart, unable to cope with the grief of losing her only son. A son to whom she had been utterly devoted. Her body had been discovered by the police after they had been alerted by neighbours that she hadn't been seen for a few days. She was, rather dramatically, found clutching a framed photograph of her son to her bosom.

Marjorie Higgins was not a nice woman. She would be missed by few. Her lifelong obsession was her son Jeremy and he had died a year earlier. He was her God, her reason for living. He had chosen, very much against her wishes, to marry a woman whom she considered unsuitable and unworthy of him. A woman who was never going to be his, or her equal, either in intelligence or culture. Marjorie reluctantly satisfied herself that, if Brenda was the sort of woman her son desired, then she would tolerate her. She knew her son had high expectations and certain requirements of a wife. Brenda would just have to *knuckle down* and do her upmost to ensure her son's happiness. If she could cater to all Jeremy's needs and desires, she would gladly let them get on with their lives. Except, she didn't. She made Brenda's life a misery and she wallowed in the enjoyment of seeing her daughter-in-law's torment. Between them, she and Jeremy had made Brenda's existence a living hell. Marjorie loved the fact that Jeremy took her side in every argument and allowed her to belittle his wife. Championing his mother above her at all times. She was the Queen, the Matriarch and no wife of her precious boy would ever usurp her. She was a warped and evil person, very much like her son and there would be few people at her funeral who would mourn her loss.

For reasons Brenda found hard to explain to herself, she attended Marjorie's funeral. She was one of only seven mourners present. Marjorie disappeared from the human race without much of a fanfare.

Not only was she a bitter and jealous woman, she was also careless and forgetful. Since the death of her beloved son Jeremy, she had withdrawn from society. She spent most of her days drifting through the countless photograph albums that had recorded every moment of her son's existence. From a newborn baby, all the way to what proved to be his final week. She stroked the pictures and looked lovingly at them, whilst showering them in her tears. She was completely consumed by his death and the gaping hole it had left in her life. Her fastidious attention to detail, regarding everything and anything to do with the running of the house and her life in general, evaporated into the fog of her despair. Amongst many other lapses in her memory, she had failed to change her Will. Everything she owned had been left to her son. The house, her money, jewellery, savings, life insurance, the lot and through Marjorie's lack of forethought, as his widow, Brenda inherited all of it. Brenda considered it *'part payment'*, for all the misery and unhappiness Marjorie had been responsible for during her marriage.

From what Brenda had inherited after Jeremy's death, added to Marjorie's estate, she was sitting rather pretty. Financially, she was set for life and could spend her time doing exactly what she wanted. Having recovered from the injuries sustained at the hands of her deceased husband, she had reluctantly decided to leave her job at the football club. Having worked there for over seventeen years, it was a tough decision to make, but she knew in her heart that it was the right thing to do. After the time she had spent living with

George at his flat, it would be difficult to go back and carry on as if nothing had happened. She knew that, although Debbie was both trusting and understanding, her continued presence, working in close proximity to the man she had openly admitted to loving in her letter, would put an unbearable and unnecessary strain on all involved. Although George was disappointed to see her go, he knew, as did Debbie, that it was for the best.

It had been an emotional goodbye, but Brenda promised to stay in touch with as many of her old friends as she could.

Shortly after her departure from the football club Brenda had been introduced to an organisation called 'Refuge'. A group of people dedicated to caring for women who had experienced similar, traumatic relationships as she had. It had been a real eye opener for her. While she had been suffering at the hands of Jeremy, she felt completely alone and isolated. She had felt there was no one she could turn to, talk to or confide in. Since meeting the people at 'Refuge', she realised she hadn't been alone. There were hundreds, thousands of poor souls, suffering the same daily abuse that had blighted her married life. She knew what these poor women had been through and understood that their scars were not only physical, but mental too. She was desperate to do anything she could to help and spent more and more of her time volunteering, giving as much comfort and advice as she could. There was a constant flow of traumatised and broken women seeking shelter, a shoulder to cry on and of course, understanding.

Although she had thoroughly enjoyed her years working at the football club, for the first time in her life she knew she was doing something that actually mattered.

THE END

Acknowledgments

The research I undertook to write this book was both harrowing and disturbing.

Domestic abuse is sadly a common occurrence on our TV screens as well as in our newspapers today. It is something of which we are all aware. However, listening to some of the victim's stories first hand was truly shocking.

The testimonies of the women I listened to were both heartbreaking and sickening. Any form of mental, physical or sexual abuse is abhorrent. But to have it inflicted on you by someone you thought you loved, and who you thought loved you is truly crushing.

The atrocities suffered by Brenda in this book tragically reflect what many women experience on a daily basis.

If you or someone you care about is experiencing any form of domestic abuse you can phone *The National Domestic Abuse Helpline,* on 0800 2000 247.

"REFUGE" is a registered charity, (No. 277424). It is the largest specialist domestic abuse organisation in the U.K. It helps thousands of women and children overcome the physical, emotional, financial and logistical impact of abuse and helps them rebuild their lives, free from fear.

To contact them, call 0207 395 7700 or go to, *refuge.org.uk*

About the Author

Neil Bradshaw was born in South London. He attended "Haberdashers Askes Boys School" in New Cross.

He spent most of his working life in the film industry as a freelance camera technician.

He now lives in Buckinghamshire with his wife Yvonne.

For more information please go to, *neilbradshawauthor.co.uk*

Printed in Dunstable, United Kingdom